Strange Addiction

Alexis Nicole

URBAN
Renaissance

www.urbanbooks.net

Urban Books, LLC
78 East Industry Court
Deer Park, NY 11729

ISBN 13: 978-1-60162-362-1
ISBN 10: 1-60162-362-3

First Trade Paperback Printing September 2012
Printed in the United States of America

10 9 8 7 6 5 4 3 2 1

This is a work of fiction. Any references or similarities to actual events, real people, living or dead, or to real locales are intended to give the novel a sense of reality. Any similarity in other names, characters, places, and incidents is entirely coincidental.

Distributed by Kensington Publishing Corp.
Submit Wholesale Orders to:
Kensington Publishing Corp.
C/O Penguin Group (USA) Inc.
Attention: Order Processing
405 Murray Hill Parkway
East Rutherford, NJ 07073-2316
Phone: 1-800-526-0275
Fax: 1-800-227-9604

Strange Addiction

A Novel By

Alexis Nicole

Chapter 1

This was the day I'd dreamed of for my entire life. And I was trembling.

I stood in front of the closed double doors of Mount Sinai Church, shaking in my custom-made Pnina Tornai wedding gown as beyond the doors "When I First Saw You" played softly on the keyboard. My breath was hard and heavy, making my veil sway back and forth, catching at times on my lipstick. But that was not what concerned me the most. It was my heart—I was afraid it was going to beat right out of my chest.

"You okay, baby girl?" My father rubbed my right hand as if he sensed my anxiety and wanted to give me some peace.

"Yeah, I'm okay, Daddy. Just nervous, that's all."

My father smiled and I could see the joy and love he had for me shining in his brown eyes. And all the love he had for me, I had for him. He had been the greatest man in my life. He had taught me about life and love and had never given me anything less than unconditional love.

Stepping right in front of me, my father lifted my veil and looked into my eyes. "Take a deep breath, sweetheart," he said softly. "Everything will be fine."

It was the love in his eyes and the smile on his lips that made me take a deep breath and gather myself.

He said, "You make the most gorgeous bride, and you're going to be a wonderful wife. This is your day, princess, and I'm so proud of you."

He kissed me on my cheek before he put my veil back in place, just that single act calmed me. Now I was ready.

As if on cue, the church doors swung open, and I heard the first four chords of the wedding march. All three hundred of our guests stood up, and the oohs and aahs echoed throughout. I stood at the edge of the doors, taking in the pews, which were packed with my family and friends. The sanctuary was filled with the white roses and calla lilies that I'd wanted, and the slight scent of vanilla filled the air from the dozens of oversize candles that lit the space.

As I stepped down the aisle with my father at my side, I heard the sighs and whispers of appreciation as I strolled past each row. I wasn't paying attention to any of it. My eyes were glued to one place, to the one man who filled my dreams every night, the man who waited for me at the altar.

He blinked over and over, and I knew that he was fighting to hold back his tears. That made my heart flutter and brought tears to my own eyes. All I wanted to do was run the rest of the way so that I could stand next to him, because I couldn't wait until I would officially be his wife.

Before I took the last step, I inhaled a deep breath. Then I was by his side. Standing in between my father and the man I loved, I waited for the preacher to begin the ceremony.

"We are gathered here today to join this man and this woman in holy matrimony," the preacher started. "Who gives this woman's hand in marriage?"

My father took a deep breath of his own. "Her mother and I do." Then he lifted my veil, just like he'd done a few minutes before, and kissed me on my cheek. "I love you, baby girl," he whispered in my ear.

"I love you too, Daddy," I said, once again fighting back tears. "Thank you for everything."

He wrapped my hand inside my husband-to-be's and then took his seat of honor next to my mother.

Now I stood next to him alone. Just the two of us doing the thing we'd been planning for over a year.

The preacher continued reading the formal words from the little black book he held, and I stood staring into my soon-to-be husband's eyes, still amazed at the fact that he'd chosen me to be his wife.

In his expression I saw our life, our future . . . but I also saw our past. That was when my heart started pounding again, hard. I shifted from one foot to the other before I turned and handed my bouquet to my maid of honor.

Just as I was turning around, someone screamed, "Oh my God! She's got a gun!" Before anyone could even blink, two shots rang out and my fiancé hit the floor. Blood gushed from his chest and quickly pooled around him.

More screams and loud cries filled the air, but for me, the world was silent. I stood there shaking, not understanding, not knowing what had happened.

And then . . .

I was tackled from behind. I couldn't see who'd thrown me to the floor, but I figured it was one of the security men that we'd hired for the ceremony.

I felt like I was bolted to the floor as he wrestled the gun from my hand. Around us, there was still nothing but bedlam as the guests ran over each other to escape. From the floor, I lifted my head, and right in front of my face was my fiancé's lifeless body and . . .

"Heiress!" Blair's voice rang out loudly in my ear. "Heiress!"

I popped up in the bed, blinking rapidly, my head whipping from side to side. My body was drenched in sweat as I tried to calm down. I breathed deeply, over and over, until I felt my heartbeat slowing down to normal.

It had happened again. For the third time this week, I'd had this dream.

I was still in a foggy haze when I glanced around our bedroom and finally focused on Blair, standing in the doorway.

"I hate to tell you," my roommate began, "but it's almost eight o'clock, and if you don't get your butt out of that bed, you might miss the most important interview of your career."

"Oh my God!" I said as I glanced at the clock on my nightstand. I jumped from my bed and made a beeline to my bathroom. It was 7:43. That meant that I had to be dressed and fight Los Angeles traffic to get across town in less than an hour. It was a good thing I'd taken my shower last night.

With my toothbrush in my mouth, I figured I could multitask, so I dashed into my closet to pick out what I was going to wear. From the corner of my eye, I saw Blair sitting on the edge of my bed.

"So how excited are you to be interviewing all those fine men this morning?" she asked with such enthusiasm you would've thought I was going to a party.

I laughed. "For the hundredth time," I began, with the toothbrush still in my mouth, "I'm not the one interviewing them. I just have to be there to set up and be on call if anyone needs anything."

Hearing my words spoken out loud was kind of depressing. All my life I had wanted to be a journalist and had done everything I could to make that happen. I graduated top of my class at USC, was the senior editor of the college's newspaper, the *Daily Trojan,* and now I'd been working at one of the hottest new entertainment magazines in the country for almost a year. Yet with all of that, I still had not written a single article. If it had not been for my daddy telling me to keep at it, I probably would've quit by now.

"Okay. Well, then, walk me through exactly what's going on today."

As I rinsed out my mouth and then brushed my hair, I swore that Blair was tap-dancing on my last nerve. Not that I didn't appreciate her excitement for my job, but I was running late and really didn't have time to go over all of this again. Especially since I'd already told Blair what today was all about. I'd told her last week, when I first found out about it.

"Must we really go through this again right now?" I asked as I pulled the purple wrap dress from my closet. I knew I probably sounded a bit impatient, and I was.

"I promise I won't bug you anymore after this, but please," she begged in her baby voice, which was her trick to get her way.

She was lying, and I knew it. Blair would definitely bug me again, as soon as I got back to our apartment tonight. She'd want to know everything. Still, I decided to entertain my friend. It was always just easier to give Blair whatever she wanted, or else she would make sure that I never had any peace. So I took a deep breath and said, "*BME* magazine is having an all-male edition of who to watch this year in all aspects of entertainment, and there will be eight men who will be interviewed." I tried to say it all in one breath while I wiggled into my dress.

When I glanced at my nightstand, the clock blinked 8:03. Dang it! Lord, why did I pick today of all days to oversleep?

Blair sighed. "Girl! What I wouldn't give to be in a room surrounded by a bunch of hot black millionaires." She leaned back on my bed and stared at the ceiling as if she were in deep thought. "Maybe I should skip work and come kick it at your job. I need to start shopping for a husband." Blair held her left hand up and wiggled her ring finger. "It would be great to be Mrs. Millionaire."

"And on that note, I'm gonna get out of here." I paused for a moment and pointed my finger at her. "Keep your tail away from my job." I grabbed my bags from my desk and bolted toward the door.

"Heiress."

I didn't turn back as Blair called out to me. I tuned out whatever she was saying, just letting the door close on her words.

Taking a quick glance at my watch, I saw that I didn't have much time to get all the way across town. My stomach fluttered with anxiety, and that was when I knew that today was going to be a very interesting day.

Chapter 2

"I need water in rooms two and four, because both King Stevens and Devonte Reese are arriving in thirty minutes. We are wrapping up Alec Mitchell's photo shoot, so make sure he's taken care of before he leaves. Our singer is at a radio interview, so he'll be running late, which will put us behind schedule. Make sure everything is set up for his shoot so that we can get him in and out and try to catch up."

Carmen was in rare form. I walked three paces behind her as I jotted down notes the whole time, trying to catch all the orders she'd just barked at me. I was focused, making sure that I caught everything she was saying and that I didn't miss a beat. I'd never worked on an article of this caliber, and I wanted to make sure that every single part of this was right.

Carmen Joelle had been working here at *Black Media Elite* for about five years. She was best known for being able to pull in the big-name interviews before anyone else could get close. She was like a networking God, working all kinds of parties and various events over the years. She'd met people, made connections, developed friendships, and now her BlackBerry was as coveted as President Obama's.

I'd known Carmen for a while, ever since I'd tutored her brother during our junior and senior years in college. That was the reason I'd gotten this job in the first place. This whole cover article was her idea, and she had picked me to assist her. This was my shot, my chance to really be noticed by the higher-ups at *BME*. I was going to do everything to make sure that things ran smoothly.

"You can start with that, and then come report back to me." Carmen didn't even check to see if I had gotten it all before she darted down the hall to check on the photo shoot of the Heisman Trophy winner and number one draft pick in the NFL.

Looking at the long list, I decided the best way to tackle this was to work on the easiest tasks first. That meant that I needed to get the rooms set up for the next two interviews.

I was in and out of Devonte's room in less than ten minutes. He was low maintenance and didn't have a lot of demands. All he wanted were six bottles of Voss water and a bowl of fresh fruit. For a seventeen-year-old stylist who seemed to be wanted by every hotshot in the business, his requests were quite surprising.

King Stevens, on the other hand, was a pain in my side. Mr. Hollywood was definitely taking his acting fame to the max. This man wanted fresh espresso, two dozen pastries, four bananas, three apples, two bunches of grapes, a dozen bottles of water—Voss too—and some weird humidifier, which had to be on at least thirty-five minutes before he entered the room.

I hadn't met the man, and I already didn't like him. It took me almost thirty minutes to get everything organized in his room—and get that humidifier working—which threw me at least ten minutes behind schedule. But I had to make everything right. One of the reasons why Carmen could call anyone on the phone was that she always took care of them. So I had to make sure I didn't mess Mr. Stevens's room up. After taking a quick look around to make sure that everything was in place and presentable, I swung the door open and came face-to-face with the chest of a god.

I stood there, dumbfounded, just staring.

"Well, hello, gorgeous. Do you come with the room?" King Stevens flashed his gorgeous smile at me, as if flirting with the help was routine for him.

King Stevens hadn't come alone; there were three people behind him. Two men and a woman all had cell phones pressed to their ears, and each one was talking faster than the other, all sounding like auctioneers.

But my eyes never really left King. I stayed focused on him, shocked at the fact that he was even more handsome in person than he was on the big screen. How was that possible? Gathering myself, I took a few steps back and opened the door wider to let him and his entourage into the room.

"So are you going to answer me?"

I guess my question was written all over my face.

"I asked if you came with the room," he said as he moved past me.

"No, sir, I don't," I said, sounding and staying professional. I looked at him as if his words meant nothing, even though just the thought that he'd noticed me made my heart flutter. I said, "I was just setting up your room. Take a look around, make sure everything is to your liking, and if you need anything else, my name is Heiress Montgomery. I'll be more than happy to get it for you, sir."

He held his hand against his chest. "Damn, girl. You just hurt my heart. Please, please, please don't call me sir! It makes me feel like my father. King is just fine."

"I apologize, si . . . King," I said, catching myself before I said "sir" again.

He gave me that smile, and now I had firsthand knowledge of why women were always falling at the feet of this man.

"Just let me know if you need anything."

"All right," King said as he moved around, scanning the room for everything that he'd ordered. Just as I was about to step into the hall, he said, "So, Heiress . . ."

I spun around.

He continued, "Will you be the one interviewing me?" He seductively popped a grape in his mouth as his eyes roamed over me from my head to my toes, then slowly, slowly back up until he was staring into my eyes.

I stood at the door, because there was nothing else that I could do. This man was breathtaking, every bit of him. He couldn't have been taller than six feet, with his smooth caramel skin, bright brown eyes, and a goatee that surrounded his luscious lips and pearly whites.

"Um, no. That would be Carmen Joelle," I said. "She's going to do the interview."

"And why aren't you?" Never breaking eye contact with me, he lifted another grape and slipped it between his lips.

I sighed. I needed to be rescued, but as I glanced around the room, there was no help from his entourage. All three were still on their phones, apparently handling King's business and seemingly oblivious to our conversation. "Well, this is Carmen's assignment," I said, finally answering him. "I'm just an assistant."

"Are you a journalist?"

"I consider myself to be, but I haven't written an article here at *BME*."

He nodded slowly and gave me a sideways glance, like he had other thoughts.

"Heiress, what are you doing?"

I heard Carmen's angry voice before I saw her. I spun around.

She said, "There still so many things that haven't been done, and you're here fraternizing with our guest." She rolled her eyes at me before she extended her hand to King. "Hello," she said.

Before she could introduce herself, King said, "You must be Carmen."

"Yes, I am, Mr. Stevens. I'll be doing your interview. Just give me a moment to get my team all squared away, and then we can get started." Carmen turned to shoo me out of the room.

"Actually, Ms. Joelle," King began, "there's been a change of plans. I want this young lady to do my interview."

"What?" Carmen and I said together.

Carmen added, "Mr. Stevens, I'm sorry, but it doesn't work like that. I have everything set up for your interview. Plus, Heiress is not an experienced journalist."

What I wanted to do was interject and run down all my credentials. Of course, I was capable of doing this interview, but I kept my thoughts to myself and the words I wanted to say. I wasn't crazy. I needed this job to pay my bills, and this man, as fine as he was, and this interview, as tempting as it was, weren't worth me being jobless and, soon after that, homeless.

"I understand there is protocol and rules and all those other things"—he waved his hand in the air, as if none of that mattered—"but the bottom line is this. I only want to talk to *her*." He looked past Carmen and flashed that immaculate smile at me.

"Can I just ask why?" Carmen turned her stare from King to me. She was trying to remain professional, but I could see the look of disgust in her eyes.

The way King's lips spread into an even wider smile sent a chill up my spine. Once again, his glance roved over me, from my feet to my face. He said, "I like her smile."

That was it. Both Carmen and I stood there in amazement, and I did my best to wipe my smile off my face, but no matter how hard I tried, I couldn't.

The only woman in King's entourage clicked off her phone, then motioned to King for his attention. When he turned away, Carmen grabbed my arm, dragged me into the hall, and closed the door behind us. She was so pissed that she didn't even speak right away. She just paced back and forth, as if she was trying to keep her temper in check. I just stood there, shifting from one foot to the other, wishing I could just disappear. Being one of the stars of *BME,* Carmen was known for her temper. But in the year that I'd worked here, I'd never gotten on anyone's bad side. In fact, I was the one that everyone wanted to work with.

I guessed that was all going to change.

I stayed silent until Carmen stopped moving. She took two steps toward me, stared me dead in my eyes, and snarled. My heart was pounding with fear. The last time I felt like this, I was in high school . . . facing my parents. I'd just missed curfew because I'd stayed at Johnny Fletcher's house party an hour later than I should have.

I knew I was in major trouble then, and I knew I was in major trouble now.

"What did you do, Heiress?"

"Nothing!"

"What did you say to him?"

"Nothing. I promise, Carmen. All I was doing was what you asked. I was making sure that the room was right, and then he came in and asked if I came with the room."

Her eyes got thin, like she was trying to look through me or something. "I have no idea what you said or did to make this man throw me a curveball like this," she hissed. Carmen held up her hand, stopping me from protesting again. She continued, "But if you mess this up, I'll make sure you won't be able to sell a newspaper on a street corner, let alone write another article."

"I swear, Carmen," I said, shaking my head, "I didn't do anything."

She remained silent for a moment, studying me as if she was trying to figure out whether or not I was telling the truth. "Well, it doesn't matter now, does it?" She glared at me before she tossed a notepad into my hand. "Here're the questions. Stick to only these questions. And when you're done, escort him to his photo shoot."

Really? She was going to let me do this? Really?

"And you better not mess this up!" she said again.

I was going to tell her that I wouldn't, but she had already turned away, storming down the hall, mumbling underneath her breath. I could imagine the things that she was saying about me, but I didn't want to think about that right now.

All I wanted to think about was that I was going to interview King Stevens!

As I stood alone in the hallway, a mixture of emotions swirled through me. There I was, ready to do what I'd always wanted to do. And it had all happened in five minutes. No matter what, I wasn't going to pass this opportunity up. By the time this interview was over, everyone would know my name.

I scanned Carmen's questions, took a deep breath, and then opened the door.

Chapter 3

My heart was beating so hard, I was sure that everyone in the room could hear it through my dress. I wasn't sure why I was so nervous. I mean, yeah, this was my first interview for *BME,* and King Stevens was just the biggest movie star right now. But it wasn't like I was a total novice. Between my high school and college newspapers, I'd done hundreds of articles. Plus, I'd served as the editor of both.

Wait! Who was I kidding? There was no way that I could compare my high school and college experiences with writing the cover article for a major national magazine on one of Hollywood's hottest new stars. King Stevens was entertainment royalty. His mother was Terez, the four-time Grammy Award–winning jazz singer, and his father was Mann Stevens, who was a top-billing actor and was once even considered for the role of the first African American James Bond. Now his father and his uncle were Emmy–winning television series creators.

King had hit the scene a few years ago with small roles, first on television commercials and then on a couple of sitcoms. But last year he landed his breakout role when he starred in the dramatic war movie *Sons of Dawn*. The *New York Post* had dubbed him the "2012 Denzel."

I scooted my chair a bit closer to the round table where King sat across from me. "Okay, Mr. Stevens.

Let's get started." I was surprised at how calm my voice sounded, as if I did this kind of thing all the time. I had pushed my nervousness aside and had pulled out my professionalism.

As I clicked on the recorder, King reached across the table for my hand and rubbed it gently. His touch was strong and soft at the same time. And it sent chills all through my body. For a moment, I held my breath.

"I thought I told you this already," he said softly. "Call me King." He held on to me for a second longer, before he finally sat back.

I tried to relax at the round table that had been set in the center of this interview room. It was small, cozy, intimate, and filled with the interviewee's favorite things so that he or she would be comfortable and would feel more at ease.

Right now, though, I was the one who needed to be put at ease. I lifted the notepad once again and glanced at the questions. Hoping that my voice wasn't shaking, I asked, "So . . . King . . . have you always wanted to be an actor? To follow in your father's footsteps?"

He glanced slightly upward, as if he was thinking. Then he said, "Listen. Heiress, I'm sure you're a great journalist and you have some thought-provoking questions for me, but"—he leaned forward—"I don't want to talk about me right now. Let's talk about you."

I guess it was the surprised look on my face that was his cue to continue.

"Are you dating anyone?"

"Excuse me?" I made sure I threw him much attitude. Did he really just ask me that?

He shrugged, as if his question was no big deal. "I'm interested in finding out if a woman as fine as you is up for grabs."

Up for grabs? Was he serious? I knew he was playing with me. King Stevens could have anyone in Hollywood that he wanted, so I didn't understand this game.
But whatever it was, I wasn't with it. Right now all I
wanted to do was this interview. This was serious, this
was my chance, and I was going to get this interview
done one way or another.

"Mr. Stevens, I don't—"

"King," he interrupted before I could even get my
angry rant started.

"King . . . " I said his name slowly, purposefully. "I
appreciate the compliment, but I am not interested in
being *grabbed*. What I'm interested in is doing your
interview."

He grinned as if I'd just told a joke, or as if he was
impressed. "There's a little feistiness under that pretty
exterior. I like that in a woman."

The smile that he flashed was no longer intrigu-
ing, inviting. Now it was just downright annoying. He
was wasting my time, the magazine's money, and was
about to blow my opportunity. It was funny in a way.
King Stevens was responsible for me sitting here at this
moment. He was responsible for making my dream
come true. But at the same time, he was standing in the
way of it.

Dang! I should've known this man was going to be
a problem when he requested that stupid humidifier.
Well, I didn't care what I had to do, but this wasn't going to go down this way. Not on my watch. I was just
going to have to figure out a way to get King Stevens
focused back on this interview.

"You know the one thing I hate about my career,
Heiress?"

"What's that?" I asked, hoping that this was going to
be the start of the interview, since this was the first time
I'd heard any kind of sincerity in his voice.

"Talking to the press. That's what I hate the most." He paused, as if he was waiting for me to say something. When I stayed quiet, he added, "I was hoping you could change my attitude on that."

It was the way he grinned that made me think, *There goes his sincerity!* I was two seconds from getting up and saying "Forget it" to this whole interview. I would just go to Carmen, tell her I couldn't handle it, and turn the whole thing over to her, because I was tired of this man and his passes. This was so unprofessional, and I wasn't going to belittle myself just to get a shot. I'd heard lots of stories of women who did all kinds of things for their big break. That wasn't going to be me.

I pushed my chair back just a little. "Maybe I should let Carmen do the interview."

His smile went away. "Okay, okay, I apologize." He held up his hand, as if he were surrendering. "I know this is important to you, so"—he waved his hand—"go and ask away. I'll make sure this will be the best interview of your career."

I couldn't help it. I laughed, especially since this was the first article of my career. "You promise?" I asked, hoping that my tone would keep the mood light.

"I do. I promise."

"Great," I said, looking down at my notes, so ready to finally get started.

He said, "As long as you promise to go to dinner with me."

I sighed.

"Look, Heiress, this is not just a come-on. I really am interested in getting to know you."

I sat there for a moment, feeling like I was in the middle of some kind of standoff, or maybe *sit-off* was the better word for it. And I weighed my options. If he was going to give me a serious interview, I guess the least I could give him was dinner. Inside, I laughed to myself. Who was I kidding, acting like I was doing King Stevens a favor? It wasn't like there was a long line of movie stars waiting to ask me out on a date. Heck, there wasn't even a line of regular guys.

"Okay," I said, nodding. "It's a deal. But"—I held up my pencil—"only if I get the best interview of my career."

He grinned. "Well, let's get started."

I asked, again, "So, King, did you always want to be an actor?"

And I began the first interview of my career.

Chapter 4

I must've been living in a dream, because things like this didn't happen in real life, especially not in my life. I couldn't remember another time when I'd been this happy.

In just a matter of two days, I'd gone from assistant to journalist. King had kept his promise; he'd given me the best interview. We'd talked for over an hour; he was open and, I felt, honest as he answered my questions. I even improvised on a few extra questions myself. By the time another assistant came to escort King to his photo shoot, I knew I had enough to write an article that was going to impress.

Of course, Carmen was still pissed, but she hid her anger because our boss was impressed when I turned in the article this morning. And when Carmen made it seem like my doing the interview was her idea, our boss was even more impressed with her.

"It takes a good leader to let others lead sometimes, Carmen. Good job."

And with those words, all was forgiven.

Since I made Carmen look so good, she decided to give me a shot with another assignment. "Why don't you take a shot at doing some of the interviews for the Hurricane Katrina victims?"

"Really?" I asked. Next month *BME* was doing a humanitarian issue that was going to look at the effects of Hurricane Katrina all these years later.

"Yeah," Carmen said. "You can interview some of the people who moved here and never returned to New Orleans. Give me a list of your questions tomorrow. I'll review them, and you can get started."

To say that I was thrilled was an understatement. I couldn't believe that I was finally starting to be where I wanted to be. I was beginning my career, and it had all begun with King Stevens.

I smiled at my image in the full-length mirror, looking at myself from all angles. Tonight was the night. I was going to dinner with King Stevens, just as I'd promised.

"Blair!" I yelled out.

"Why are you screaming like that? I'm right here."

I turned around, and there was my roommate, standing in the doorway to my bedroom. "How long have you been standing there?"

"Long enough to wish I was you."

I laughed. "Can you help me with this?" I held up my necklace, and Blair nodded.

"I still cannot believe you are going out with *the* King Stevens!" Blair exclaimed as she fastened the silver chain around my neck.

As Blair stood behind me, I stared at myself in the mirror. I'd decided to go conservative with this classic black cocktail dress that hugged my five-foot-two, petite frame in all the right places. My hair lay on my shoulders in spiral curls, compliments of Blair. I wanted to look as natural as possible, so I had only powdered my face and put on a light berry lip gloss.

"I can't believe it, either," I finally said to Blair. "Who would've ever believed that my life could change so much in two days?" I fluffed out my hair. "But not so much has changed that I don't recognize this for what it is. This is just a dinner."

Blair rolled her eyes. "Girl, please. Just dinner. There is no such thing as just dinner when it comes to King Stevens." She fanned her face as if she was really hot. "This man could be your future husband."

I smirked at her.

Blair said, "Well, if you don't like him, you can pass him to me, 'cause he's definitely husband material and he could be mine."

While Blair spent her time fantasizing about King Stevens, I slipped into my pumps. It had been over a year since I'd been out on a date, so for me this was really more than just dinner. But I wasn't going to tell Blair that. And I certainly wasn't going to let my own mind take me there. I had to stay cool, calm, and collected, realizing that this was just a little more than a fantasy. Because, after all, this date was with King Stevens. There were girls swooning all over him all the time. And I was sure that he could have his pick of anyone he wanted. Truly, he was just being nice to me.

So I was going to call this date exactly what it was: a one-night fairy tale that would end at midnight. I wasn't about to act like or go out like a groupie, knowing that the carriage was going to turn back into a pumpkin.

"Have I told you how jealous I am of you right now?"

Before I could tell Blair to get over it, a knock at the door interrupted us, and right away the butterflies inside began to flutter. For a moment, Blair and I just stood there, staring at each other, until the knock came again. Then Blair dashed from my bedroom into the living room.

"Hey, I'm looking for Heiress," I heard King say.

Checking myself out in the mirror one final time, I took a deep breath, then moved toward my bedroom door. But Blair stopped me in the hallway before I stepped into the living room.

"Girl, he is finer in person," Blair whispered as she pushed me back into the bedroom. "If you're having second thoughts, I would be more than happy to take him off your hands."

I shook my head. My girl was taking this over the top. "I think I'm okay," I said as I moved past her.

But when I got into the living room, I knew why my best friend was losing it. King was standing by the door, as if he hadn't moved an inch. And he was wearing one of those expensive signature suits that he was known for: so tailored that it looked like it was sewn right onto him. For a couple of seconds, I just stood there, taking him in. And he did the same to me. I guess he was pleased, because his lips slowly began to spread into the cutest smile.

"Humph, humph, humph. I must say that you're working that dress, Ms. Montgomery."

"Thank you. You don't look so bad yourself."

He reached for my hand, and goose bumps filled my arms before he even touched me. He pulled me into an embrace, and I closed my eyes, inhaling his scent. Dolce & Gabbana, I knew that cologne from the magazine. D&G was one of our biggest advertisers, and the company's product managers were in our offices all the time with new samples.

"Uh . . ."

Blair's voice made my eyes pop open, and I stepped back from King. I guess I'd forgotten where I was for a moment.

"Well," my friend continued, "you kids have fun."

"We will," he said. "Nice to meet you."

"Nice to meet you too," Blair squealed.

I gave her a look and a smile, trying to tell her to stop getting all worked up. This was just King Stevens. But as we walked down the steps, I had to tell myself the same thing over and over—this was just King Stevens.

"Oh my God!" I said aloud what I'd been thinking.

"Sorry about that." He grinned. "I guess I should've warned you."

"No, no warning needed. I guess I kinda knew we might run into some photographers but . . ." I shook my head. "Is it like that for you all the time?"

He shrugged. "Yeah, kind of. But I got used to it a long time ago with my parents. It's part of the price of all of this." He stepped behind me and helped me slip my sweater from my shoulders. Then he held out the chair for me to sit at the single round table, which was covered with a black tablecloth and had a single candle in the middle.

I kept wanting to turn around and peek out the door to check out any other famous people in this place. But I didn't, because King's attention was completely on me.

"So do you have any questions for me?"

I cocked my head, not sure what he meant.

"I'm sure you heard them ask me about my ex."

Ah, Marlaina Douglas, the gorgeous young starlet who had been hot and heavy with King forever. For the last five years, they'd been known as the king and queen of young Hollywood. Their on-again, off-again relationship was tabloid fodder, and I'd read that they'd broken up, once again. But I had not heard that she'd gotten married, which was weird, since I thought everything passed through *BME*.

"I heard the question." I shrugged. "But I don't think it's any of my business."

"Oh, really?" he asked as he raised an eyebrow. "So are you telling me that you always date men who are attached?"

"This isn't a date."

He grinned when I said that. "It's not?"

"Nooo," I said, smiling back at him. "This is just a dinner between two business colleagues."

"Okay." He chuckled.

"So I don't think I have any right, or any need, to know about your personal life . . . in that way."

He tilted his head a bit, as if he was thinking about my words. "You're a very special lady," he finally said.

"Thank you."

"And just so you know . . . Marlaina and I broke up, and a month after that, she got married."

"I hadn't heard that part." I paused, planning to leave the conversation there. But I was curious, so I just had to ask, "Did that bother you?" And because I was a journalist, I added, "Off the record, of course."

"Of course." He shook his head. "No, I'm not upset at all. We were done, and I wish her nothing but happiness."

I wondered if he really meant what he was saying, but then I asked myself, why did I care? This was just a dinner, right?

He said, "Now that that's out of the way, let's talk about you."

"What do you want to know?"

"I want to know . . ." He paused. "How you're going to like this." He pulled out a long black velvet box and rested it on the table in front of me.

What was this? A gift? For a long moment, I stared at the box, before I said, "King, I can't."

"Just open it," he said, motioning with his hands.

I sat there thinking for another moment, before I slowly opened the cover and was immediately blinded by the diamond tennis bracelet inside. I couldn't help it; I gasped. All I could do was stare down at it in amazement.

"I was having a hard time finding something that could compliment your beauty, but there was nothing. I just hope that this will come close."

When I sat there, still saying nothing, King asked, "Do you like it?"

I kind of shook my head a little. I was completely speechless. I had never seen anything so beautiful, so magnificent before, let alone been given something like this as a gift.

Finally, I lifted my eyes, glanced at King, then looked back at the bracelet. I kept doing that again and again.

I managed to get out, "It's beautiful."

King nodded as if he was pleased. "I'm glad you like it."

"But still . . ." I shook my head. There was no way I could take this gift. Not only was this supposed to be just a dinner, not a date, but what about the professional implications? "King, I can't. I just interviewed you."

"So?"

"Professionally . . ."

"This is a *personal* gift."

"That could be the problem."

"Well, this is a personal date, right?"

"This is a personal dinner."

He laughed. "You're quick, and I like that." After a pause, he continued, "Look, the thing is, Heiress, I like you. And this is just my way of saying thank you."

I frowned a little. "For the interview?"

"No. For taking the time out of your busy personal life and having dinner with me."

I glanced down at the bracelet once again. It really was beautiful, but still.

King reached over and touched my hand. "Please, take it. It's just a little present."

I chuckled. "This is not little."

"To me it is," he said.

"It's too expensive. And you said that all you wanted to do tonight was take me to dinner to say thank you."

"And this, young lady," King began as he lifted the bracelet from the box, "is my way of saying thank you." He leaned across the table and clasped the bracelet onto my wrist. "And don't say anything about it being too expensive. Don't you know it's not polite to discuss money in mixed company?"

I laughed, because what King said was funny and because I was just thrilled with the way the bracelet sparkled against my skin. I wanted to protest again, at least one more time, but when King put his forefinger against my lips, I didn't say a thing.

King leaned back in his seat and smiled when I finally nodded, my sign that I was graciously accepting his gift. "Thank you," I said. "Thank you so much."

"You're welcome. Now, let's get this dinner started."

Just as King said that, a waiter appeared with two bowls of miso soup. I wasn't sure if King had chosen what we would eat or if the restaurant had done it, since no one had ever given me a menu.

As our dinner went from soup to sashimi and then to sukiyaki, I became even more comfortable with King. As we chatted about where we'd grown up—I in a small Ohio town, and he in the lap of luxury, commuting between New York and L.A.—and shared embarrassing college stories, I began to feel like I was just sitting with a friend. King, the famous actor, disappeared, and in his place was King, the fine man, the interesting man, the man who was a complete gentleman the whole night long.

When it was time for us to leave, I wanted to look for reasons to stay. But King glanced at his watch and said,

"I wish we could keep this going all night, but I have an early call in the morning."

"Of course," I said, as if I was in a hurry to leave too.

King had such manners: he helped me out of my chair and then held my hand as he led me once again through the restaurant.

King's car was waiting for him at the curb the moment we stepped out of the restaurant. That surprised me a bit. I hadn't seen him make the call to the valet, but I guessed it was just like that when you were famous. Having the car there, though, didn't stop the flashing camera lights. Once again, I kept my head down as King and I were accosted the moment we went through the door. He helped me into the passenger seat and then trotted around to the front, ignoring the lights and the questions.

When he jumped into the car, he put the pedal to the metal and we sped out of there like someone was chasing us. Looking over my shoulder, I wondered if any of the paparazzi would follow us.

King said, "Don't worry. We're alone now," as if he'd read my mind.

"So they don't come after you?"

"Nope."

"Not ever."

"Not anymore."

I knew what that meant. Now that he wasn't with Marlaina.

"I guess that's good," I said, turning back around. "They're not hunting you. Just stalking you when you're out living your life."

He chuckled. "Don't hate. They're just making a living."

I twisted to the side to get a better look at him. "So it doesn't bother you the way they impose on you while you're out?"

He shook his head. "Not at all. They're just journal-ists."

I sucked my teeth. "Please don't compare those peo-ple to me. They are hardly journalists."

He laughed. "I just said that to tease you, but really, I do believe that everyone has their job to do. I just let folks do what they have to do."

I smiled. I liked King's attitude about this and every-thing else. He was so easygoing, not a famous, uptight celebrity at all. That was just another reason for me to really like this dude. For the rest of the car ride home, King and I rode silently. But it wasn't an awkward si-lence. It was one of those quiet times that two friends shared when they'd just spent hours together having a great time.

When King stopped the car and then, once again, like a gentleman came to my side and opened the door, I wasn't sure what I was supposed to do. It had been such a long time since I'd been on a date. Yes, it felt like a date now. Was I supposed to ask if he wanted to come up? Was I supposed to ask if he wanted a drink or a nightcap, or say something corny, like all those lines that I'd heard in movies? I didn't say any of the above, and King followed me inside like he knew exactly what to do.

In front of my apartment door, he said, "Let me have your key." He opened the door, then kissed my cheek. "Good night, pretty lady. I'll call you."

I wanted to ask him when, but I had too much class for that. So I just told him good night, then stepped into my apartment. I didn't hear him walk away until I clicked the lock.

Leaning against the door, I listened to his footsteps as he went back to the elevator. I sighed. I wasn't one of those girls who met a guy and then started writing his last name in her notebook, but I had to admit that I really liked this man. Like I said, the dinner had turned into a date, and as I glanced down at the bracelet that graced my wrist, I felt like it had been more than a dinner for him too.

I didn't want to get ahead of myself, but I had to admit, I couldn't wait to see what the future would hold for me . . . and King. I couldn't wait for him to call; I just hoped he'd call tomorrow.

Chapter 5

Was it possible to be madly in love with someone after only three months? King was everything that I had never known I even wanted.

After our first date, he called me the next morning, waking me up to a song that he'd made up. He must've inherited his talent from his father, because his acting was far better than his singing, but the words were so sweet, who cared about the lack of melody?

We went out again the next night. By the third date, I had to admit that one dinner had become a date, and now we were an item. And I was one happy girl.

King was such a man. He showered me with gifts, took me to just about all the hot events that he attended—from red-carpet movie premieres to CD release parties—and introduced me to all his rich and famous friends.

"This is my lady, Heiress Montgomery."

The first time he said that, I almost fainted. But thank God I didn't, since I was standing in front of Idris Elba and a group of other actors.

What was so amazing was that behind closed doors King was just as sweet. His kisses were soft, his caresses were gentle, and the first time we made love, I felt like he'd taken me to heaven.

But it was more than all of that. King and I were just meant for one another. We liked to do all the same things. Mostly, that was stay close to home. All these years I'd seen King out on the L.A. town. Just about every night there was something about him on *Access Hollywood* or *Entertainment Tonight.* But what I discovered was that while he did enjoy hanging with his friends and being seen, what he loved most was just being with that special person. Being out was the life that people expected him to lead, not the one he wanted to live.

So we often stayed home, at his condo mostly, because when he came by my apartment, Blair still treated him like a celebrity. At his place we'd watch one of the millions of DVDs he had, especially the old movies, like *Gone with the Wind,* with Hattie McDaniel; *Lilies of the Field,* with Sidney Poitier; and *Carmen Jones,* with Dorothy Dandridge.

"I love watching the first African American actors," he said all the time. "Those cats could really act, especially with everything that they had to go through."

We would watch DVDs and eat microwave popcorn for hours. Or we would read. I loved magazines, but King loved to read history and political books, so much so that I wondered if he would run for office one day.

Almost every Sunday we would stretch out in his living room, with me lying on the couch with my head in his lap. We would stay that way for hours, silently reading our own things. Someone had once told me that when you could spend quiet time with another person, that was a sure sign that you could be together.

Well, King and I were made to be together.

It had all happened quickly, but King definitely was a part of me. He invaded my thoughts every moment that I wasn't with him, and when I wasn't with him, I wanted to be. I had never had dreams of being a wife and a mother, but after a month of being with King Stevens, that was all that I could dream about—being his wife, being the mother to his children. That man had definitely made me change my priorities in life. He was at the top of my list, and nothing was a close second.

The best thing was I knew I was at the top of his list too.

Life at *BME* was going just as well. I'd written only three articles in the three months since King's interview, but I still felt like I was on a good track. I went back and forth between being one of the writers and being an assistant, and today I was back on assistant duty.

It was even better since Carmen had called in sick, so there wasn't much for me to do but file papers and answer her office phone, which left me with lots of free time. And lots of idle time had my mind wandering toward King.

Sitting at my desk, I tried to last as long as I could, but before the first hour of work had passed, I pulled out my cell phone to dial his number. Just as I was about to press the CALL button, my phone rang. Looking at the screen, I rolled my eyes. I knew I was in big trouble.

Pressing the ACCEPT button, I put a smile in my voice, even though there wasn't one on my face.

"Hey, Mommy."

"Oh, so you're alive?" my mother asked, as if she really had some doubt about that. "Do you remember that you have a mother?"

Okay, it was a bit over the top, very dramatic, and filled with the tone of guilt that only my mother could muster. Still, I knew I had that coming. I had been so wrapped up in everything King that I hadn't talked to my parents in almost two weeks.

"Mommy, I am so sorry, but I've been very busy." I didn't feel too bad for saying that, because it wasn't a lie. It was tough balancing my demanding job and my demanding man.

"Uh-huh. Busy with that boy who plays make-believe."

"He's an actor, Mom. You know that. You've seen him in movies before."

My mother was just giving me a hard time because I'd broken our routine of talking at least once a week. Now she was lucky if she got two calls a month.

"I'm really sorry, Mommy, and I promise I'll do better."

"Uh-huh."

"No matter what I have going on," I said, ignoring the sarcasm I heard in her tone. "I promise."

I meant every word I said. My parents were hundreds of miles away, and I really did miss them dearly. I was their only child, so we'd been close all these years—especially me and my mother. It really was my responsibility to stay close to them, even though I was in L.A. and they were back in Ohio.

"Do you accept my apology, Mommy?"

This time I was the one putting guilt into my voice.

And it worked.

"All right, baby, I'm not going to give you too much of a hard time. You're a grown woman, and you have your own life. Just tell me one thing. . . . Are you happy?"

In a flash, the past months I'd spent with King sped through my mind, and all I could do was grin.

"I can honestly say that I am extremely happy."

"And that makes me happy," my mother said, and I could hear the smile in her voice. "Well, I just wanted to check on you. Get back to what you were doing, and I'll talk to you later. Just when you get the chance, call me and your dad."

"I will."

"We worry about you."

"I know."

"And we love you so much."

"I know that too. Tell Dad I said hey."

"All right. Take care, baby."

"I will. Love you, and I'll call you and Dad next week."

I hung up the phone and tossed it onto my desk. It had been good talking to my mother, even if it was just for that little while. Hearing her voice made me miss her all the more, and I made a note in my mind to check out flights for when I'd get a chance to go home. I didn't want to wait until the holidays. Maybe I could do it one of the weekends when King was out of town.

And there it was again—another thought about King. I swear, I couldn't go two minutes without thinking about him, and I really didn't want to be in this office right now. Especially since he was leaving for Connecticut next week to film a new movie. I didn't know how I was going to make it with him gone for so long, and I wanted to spend as much time with him as possible.

That was it. I had to call him. Grabbing my cell once again, I pressed TALK, but before I could dial his number, I felt a hand on my shoulder.

I jumped, startled, but before I could turn around, a voice whispered, "What do you say we get out of here and go someplace special?"

I didn't even have to turn around, because the chills and the butterflies that I always got gave me every indication that it was my man.

His breath was hot against my ear, and I was so turned on, I wanted to scream.

But of course, I didn't, since I was at work. So without turning around, I said, "Well, I don't know. I'm sort of involved with someone at the moment, and I don't think it would be appropriate for me to be whisked away by some strange man."

King moved his hand down from my shoulder to my waist, lifted me from my chair, and spun me around all in one motion.

"Whoever you're involved with is crazy."

"Uh-uh," I said, shaking my head and grinning at the same time.

"He has to be, because he should never let such a beautiful creature out of his sight."

King and I were standing so close to each other, I could feel the heat coming off of his body, and I wondered if he could feel my heat as well. This man made me melt, and I wanted to go wherever he wanted to take me.

"Sometimes I think you should write cards for Hallmark." I stepped back from him a little. Not because I wanted to, but because we were, after all, at my job.

He laughed. "I think I'll stick to acting." Then he added, "Listen, grab your stuff and let's go. I want to take you somewhere."

"You're serious?" I couldn't believe he was really about to have me leave work.

"Absolutely." He glanced over my desk, which was pretty bare. "Were you doing something more important?"

I took a beat to think. For the entire twenty-five years of my life, all I'd wanted to be was a journalist. Well, maybe not the entire twenty-five years, but my very first memory was telling my kindergarten teacher that I was going to be a newspaper reporter.

As I got older, I made a commitment that I was going to do whatever I had to do to be the best, to get to the top. As I gazed into the most beautiful pair of light brown, seductive eyes, it was like my old dreams meant nothing. Without saying a word, King was so persuasive. He confused my whole world, turned my dreams upside down, and I was falling deeper and deeper.

"What do you say?"

Now his deep baritone voice was added to the mix, and I was gone.

There were lots of things I had to do, but all I did was grab my coat and purse, and without saying a word to anyone, I followed my King right out of the building.

Chapter 6

"I want you to come to Connecticut with me," King said. He held my cheek in the palm of his hand as we sat on the rooftop of his condo.

All I could do was laugh, because of course this was a joke.

"Why are you laughing? I'm serious, Heiress."

Now my laughter stopped.

He said, "I need you with me because six months is too long for me to be without you."

Now my heart started beating so hard that I was sure King could feel it, even though he was inches away from me. Over the months that we'd been together, King had said some wonderful things to me, but I had never seen him in such a vulnerable state before. His emotions were written all over his face; he really wanted me by his side.

"Babe, what about my job? And what about my apartment? I can't have Blair pay the rent all by herself. And what about—"

Before I could say anything else, his lips were on top of mine, stopping me from speaking.

When King let me up for air, he said, "I'll take care of all of that."

"Really?"

He nodded. "Whatever you need, whatever you want, I can provide it for you."

"But what about my job?"

"I have a little bit of money." He chuckled. "You won't ever want for anything."

"But . . ."

He pressed his fingers against my lips. "Just say that you'll come with me."

In an instant, so many thoughts flew through me. Like did I really want to leave my job? Did I really want to leave L.A.? What would my parents think? They had paid for my education for me to have a great career, and now I was running off with some man.

Many other thoughts came to my mind, but there was only one that stood out above them all. And that was that I loved King Stevens.

I threw my arms around his neck and kissed him with all the passion I could muster from the depths of my soul.

With my kiss, I wanted this man to know how amazing he was to me. I wanted him to know that all I wanted to do was be with him, and if it meant I had to do that in Connecticut, and give up everything, then I was more than willing.

My lips were still on his when King mumbled, "I'll take that as a yes."

I didn't say a word as I leaned back on the plush sofa and pulled King with me. The sunset had turned the September sky pink and purple over the Los Angeles skyline, and I wanted to make love to my King underneath it all.

Hours later we stepped back into his condo, and I slept in his arms on his California king-sized bed.

I awakened to the magnificent smell of rich coffee, which came from King's Keurig machine, and when my eyes fluttered open, I knew why the smell was so strong. King was standing over me with a tray filled with two coffee mugs and two Danishes.

"Breakfast in bed, baby," he said.

I scooted up and pulled the sheets to cover my naked torso. "This is breakfast?"

"Yup," he said. "Breakfast King style, for my queen."

"Awww." I took the tray from him and held it until he had settled back in bed with me.

I was sure that he was going to turn on the flat-screen television that was on the wall, the way he did every morning so that he could check out the news. But he left the remote on the nightstand, and in the next moments I knew why.

"I just want to make sure I wasn't dreaming last night," he said.

I smiled. "It feels like a dream every time I'm with you."

"Yeah." He chuckled. "That too. But I'm talking about what you said. You're going with me to Connecticut, right?"

I nodded, and he hugged me.

"I just want you to know that I'm going to take care of you, Heiress. I love you. You're not like any other girl I've ever known."

He'd said that to me often, telling me that he loved me because I loved him—not the actor. Just him, the man. He loved me because he could be himself and didn't have to put on any airs or play any games, because I wasn't in the business. He knew that I didn't care about any of that. I just cared about him, and he just cared about me.

"I promise," he said, breaking through my thoughts. "I'm going to take care of you."

"I know," I said, excited and anxious at the same time about my new adventure.

This was going to be so different. I was going to be dependent on a man for the first time in my life. Not that I had lived all that long, but I had always imagined myself as an independent woman. And I was. But what was more important to me was being independent with King. I knew with him I would still be who I wanted to be. I was just going to be doing it in Connecticut for the next six months.

King wrapped his arm around me as we sipped our coffee and finished our Danishes. I wanted to stay cuddled under him all day, but he had a bunch of interviews to go to and I had to go home and tell Blair the news.

Like I expected, Blair was lounging on the couch when I walked in the door, doing her favorite thing— watching the Saturday morning cartoons. Yup, she might be twenty-five, but my best friend was still a kid in her heart.

"Welcome home, Mrs. King," she said. She'd been calling me that since my first dinner with King.

"His last name is Stevens."

"And you're telling me this, why? You think I don't know?"

We went back and forth like this every time, and for just a second, I knew I was going to miss my friend. I mean, yes, I was going to be away for just six months, but it felt like I was beginning a new phase of my life. And I wasn't sure what I would be doing when King and I returned.

"I have some news," I said, keeping my eyes on the TV.

Slowly, Blair sat up on the couch. "Oh my God! Oh my God! Oh my God!"

Now I faced her, and when I looked into her eyes, I knew what she was thinking.

"No, Blair, I'm not getting married," I said as fast as I could, because I was afraid she was going to become hysterical.

"You're not?"

"No!"

"Well, what?" Then she gasped and put her hand over her mouth. "You're pregnant!"

"No!" I said. Now I knew I needed to just get it out before my overdramatic best friend came up with every scenario—except for the right one. "I'm going with King to Connecticut. While he shoots his movie. I'm going there with him," I said as fast as I could.

Blair squinted, as if she didn't understand. "You're moving to Connecticut?" she asked in a tone that sounded like she wanted to strangle me. I knew her concern was financial, but I thought that she would be happy for me. I mean, it wasn't marriage, but it was still King and I being together.

"It's only for six months."

Blair was silent for a moment as she glared at me. Then, with her arms folded across her chest, she asked, "So what am I supposed to do here by myself while you gallivant all over the country with the black Fabio?"

"Whoa!" Just a moment ago she was asking if I was getting married, and now this? It was like her attitude had changed in just a second. All because I was going away? "Blair, you'll be fine. I promise. King said he would take care of my half of the rent and bills, and I'll be back before you know it. Six months is not that long."

She didn't change her pose. Her lips were still poked out; her arms were still crossed in front of her chest. She was still mad. But then she said, "Can you at least slide my number to an actor on set or something? I mean, dang, how selfish can you be?"

I knew my eyes were filled with both amusement and confusion.

She said, "What's the point of you dating someone rich and famous if you aren't hooking your girl up? I'm not trying to bartend forever."

Another second passed before we both fell out laughing. The thing was, I knew Blair was serious. My girl was always looking for a come up. When we first met in college, she was dating some football player, not because she liked him, and not even because he was fine. No, his only qualification was that he had promise. There was talk of him making it to the NFL, but as soon as he hurt his knee in the second game of his recruiting season, Blair was on to the next.

I was still buckled over with laughter, but once I caught my breath, I said, "I'll see what I can do."

"You better."

"I'll try for the director, because I know you'll only take a man who's high on the food chain."

"Awww, girl, you know me so well." Blair wrapped her arm around my shoulders and put her head close to mine.

This was one of those special best friend moments, and I hated that I was leaving my bestie like this. It had to be shocking, and it was such short notice. But I needed to be with King.

"Do your parents know you're going?" Blair ended our embrace and jumped up from the couch.

"Where're you going?"

"To your room."

I cracked up again, but I followed her. I knew what Blair was going to do. She was going to go through my closet to see what she could take before I started packing. As if I was really going to let her do that.

"My parents," I moaned.

From the moment that King had asked me last night, I'd thought about what my parents were going to say about this. It didn't take a genius to know that they weren't going to be happy. I didn't care how grown I was, they would never approve of me moving to another state . . . not for a man.

"I gotta figure out what I'm going to tell my parents."

"Well, whatever lie you come up with, you're going to have to do it soon since you're leaving next week."

"What do you mean, lie?" I protested. "I'm not going to lie."

Blair looked at me as if I was lying already.

I lay back on my bed and said, "Maybe I can tell them I'm doing an on-location assignment for the magazine."

"In Connecticut?"

Blair was right. They'd never buy Connecticut. After a moment, I had the perfect answer. "I'll say New York. They'll definitely believe that."

My best friend peeked her head out of my closet. "See? Lie." Then she went back to whatever she was doing.

Blair was right. This was a lie, and I couldn't believe that I was going to blatantly lie to my parents. I had always tried to be completely honest with them. This time there was no way that I could tell them the truth. I had to do what I had to do. My man needed me, and I needed him. I was going to Connecticut for both of us.

"I hope it's all worth it, Heiress," Blair said as she stood over my bed, staring down at me.

Her words cut deep. It sounded like she doubted what I was doing. As if she doubted my judgment.

But I pushed the feelings that were rising up inside of me back down. How could this not be the right thing? Here was a man who had given me so much in so little time. And I wasn't talking about financially and all the gifts. I was talking about how King completed me. How he made me feel like a whole woman. How he satisfied me emotionally, and in some ways even spiritually.

I was certain that he was worth it, and I was going to make sure that everyone else knew it too.

Chapter 7

Connecticut was boring and was getting colder by the day. King was on the set for twelve hours every day, sometimes even longer, and I was stuck at the condo we'd rented, cleaning, cooking, and watching the OWN network.

I had no friends, no family here, and even though King had rented me a car, I didn't know where to go to do anything. Of course, King gave me money and kept telling me to go shopping, but I'd never been a girl who just wasted money. My closet was filled with designer dresses, bags, and shoes. There wasn't anything else that I wanted to buy.

I couldn't believe how much I missed working. Without a job, I almost felt like I didn't even have a purpose. Two months had passed, and besides strolling through the malls, the only thing I'd done was go out to dinner a couple of times with King and his costars.

This was not how I had envisioned Connecticut. This wasn't what I'd imagined at all. I was supposed to come to Connecticut and spend wonderful days with King. I thought we would go around discovering the town of Greenwich together, but I guess I hadn't really thought it all the way through. King was working. How was he supposed to have time to socialize and hang out with me? Even though I understood that, it meant that I had no one and nothing.

And now the reruns on OWN were getting old to me, and I clicked off the television. I sat in the quiet of the living room, glancing slowly around the condo. This place was nice enough, with the cream micro-suede sectional and the fifty-inch flat-screen TV. But unless some of the plants started talking to me soon, I was going to go crazy.

I jumped up and slipped into the four-inch Gucci pumps that King had bought me last week, then took a quick glance in the mirror. This jean set I had on was cute enough, and so I grabbed my coat, purse, and keys.

Sitting around and waiting for King to come home was over. I wasn't going to sit at home anymore, and the only place I knew to go was the set. Watching King couldn't be any more boring than sitting at home. Plus, I'd never been to the set to watch King. I'd gone with him on the day we arrived in Connecticut, just so he could see where he had to show up for work in the morning.

As I backed out of the development in which we lived, I started getting excited. The good thing was that I knew where I was going. Although the set was about five miles away, the drive entailed just three turns, and in ten minutes I was pulling into the parking lot.

I was shocked that there was no one there to stop me. I'd expected security guards roping off the area, checking people's IDs, but I guess this wasn't Los Angeles. I was able to drive right up close.

The moment I stepped out of the car, I knew I'd made the right decision. This was far better than staying at home. The park where the shoot was taking place was loaded with people, cameras, other equipment and trailers. As people dashed back and forth in front of me, I slowly strolled through the madness, just enjoying the energy.

I wandered around for about five minutes without finding King, but I wasn't concerned. I had no idea where I was going, but I had to bump into King eventually.

"Ma'am, did you need help?" a voice behind me asked. "You look like you're quite lost."

I turned around to face this fine, tall chocolate brother. Without being obvious, I took in his outfit: he wore fitted jeans, a raggedy button-down, a fitted cap and a big cord wrapped around his right shoulder.

I smiled, because he looked so nice and because I did want to know which trailer belonged to King. "Yes. I'm looking for King Stevens. I'm his girlfriend, Heiress Montgomery."

"Really?" he said, as if he was surprised. He looked me up and down quickly, as if he needed to check out King's girlfriend, and I was glad that I looked good.

Not only was my outfit fly, but my hair was flat-ironed and laid, and my new fitted coat was tied around my waist, emphasizing my shape.

The guy nodded, as if he approved. "Okay," he said. "King's actually filming at the moment, but I can take you to his trailer and have you wait for him there." Without saying anything else, he turned and started walking away.

It took me a moment to realize that he wanted me to follow him, and I trotted behind in my four-inch heels. "Wait," I said, calling behind him. The brother turned to face me, and I asked, "Is it possible for me to see his scene? I mean, I've never seen an actual shooting, and I would love to see everything."

He paused, as if he was hesitant.

"I promise nobody will even notice me," I said.

"Okay, but you have to be invisible. When they say, 'Quiet on the set,' they mean it."

"Okay," I said and tried not to grin too hard. I didn't want him to think that I'd get over there and act up.

We walked around a couple of corners, and soon we faced a set that looked like the main street of a little town. I saw King first and smiled. Then I saw the actress that he was talking to.

It was Tonya Winters, the beautiful soap opera actress. This was my first time seeing her in person, though there had been a lot of publicity about her playing this part. This was her first major role away from television, and the tabloids were already speculating about what kind of chemistry King and Tonya would have.

I wanted to get closer, but the guy motioned for me to stop where we were. He held his finger to his lips, as if he felt he needed to remind me to stay quiet.

I nodded, then turned back to the set. I was too far back to hear what was being said, but I could tell this was a dramatic scene. Tonya was crying, and King was comforting her. Just watching the two of them made me shift from one foot to the other. I didn't really know what this movie was about. I think that was one of the things that King loved about me. I loved him, not what he did. So I didn't pay a lot of attention to his movies, or who he was acting with, or even to all the things that were said about him in the magazines. There was no one out there who knew my man better than I did.

But now, as I stood there, I wondered if I should've taken more of an interest. It was weird standing there, watching him be so passionate with another woman. But even with that, I had to admit that King Stevens was mesmerizing.

"So this is your first time?"

I turned just a little to see the brother who'd escorted me over here. Just that quick, I'd forgotten that he was there.

"On the set?" he added, clarifying matters. "This is your first time on the set, right?"

"It is," I whispered. "Is it always like this?" I glanced around at the people behind the set. While those who were in front of me were quiet and were not moving, behind us, the madness continued.

"Believe it or not, this is actually an easy day. It's usually ten times more hectic when we film bigger scenes." He paused and extended his hand. "I'm Travis, by the way."

"Heiress," I said as I shook his hand, surprised that he was talking to me. He was the one who'd made such a big deal about me being quiet.

"I remember that from earlier."

I was about to open my mouth to say something else but was interrupted by my arm being grabbed. I must've been all into talking to Travis, because I hadn't even realized that they'd stop shooting. And King had snuck up behind me. I turned and grinned at him, so happy to see him.

Travis said, "Well, I guess that's my cue." He laughed. "It was nice meeting you, Heiress." Then he nodded to King. "Nice job."

When he stepped away and we were alone, I swung around to face my man. I was still in bed when he'd left this morning, before the sun had even come up. Maybe that was why King looked so good to me in the khakis and button-down shirt that the wardrobe department had him in.

"Baby, that was so good. I really couldn't hear what you were saying, but the emotion was there. I could feel . . ."

That was when I noticed that King was still holding on to me. But not in the way I was used to. His fingers grasped my arm, and he was squeezing me to the point that he was hurting me. I couldn't even speak.

"What the hell are you doing here?" he snapped .

"What?" I frowned. "Why am I here?" I just knew that I had heard him wrong. I had to be reading this whole encounter wrong.

"You heard me," he said, pulling me over to the side and away from those around us. Even though he was whispering, I guess he wanted to make sure that no one heard him. "What are you doing here?"

"I . . . I got bored at home. I wanted to do something else, and I thought I'd come and see you." When he twisted my arm slightly, I winced. "King!" I said his name as softly as I could through the pain. "You're hurting me."

He stared at me for a second, and I wondered, *What is that that I see in his eyes? Anger? But why?*

Then he gripped me tighter and pulled me across the lot. People still hustled and bustled all around us, and even though he was King Stevens, no one seemed to notice this man dragging me toward his trailer.

By the time he pushed me inside his trailer and then slammed the door behind us, I was pissed.

I rubbed my arm where he had accosted me and glared at him. He stared back at me with the same fury. I had no idea why he was angry, but at this point, I didn't care.

"What in the hell just happened?" I asked. "What the hell is wrong with you?"

"If I don't ask you to come to my job, you don't come to my job."

I guess he wasn't worried about anyone hearing him, because now his voice was so loud, I was sure that the trailer vibrated.

"What?" I asked. Who did he think he was? As if he could tell me what to do.

But then he grabbed my arm again and flung me across the room. I felt like I was flying through the air before I landed on the couch, one shoe slipping off my foot as I hit the leather cushions.

I sat there for a moment, frozen and stunned. "King!" I said, looking up at him. "I . . . I wanted to see you." The tears were already stinging my eyes.

"Don't we see each other at home?" he asked. His anger was still so apparent. "This is my place of business. I don't need you here."

I was completely speechless, not having any kind of clue about what was going on with King. How many times had he shown up at my job? How many times had he taken me away when I was supposed to be at work?

When he came to me, I was always so glad to see him, and I'd expected his reaction to be the same for me.

But this was what I got instead, and I had no idea why. "King," I began.

Before I could say anything else, he said, "Just go home, and I'll be there when I'm done."

I studied King for a little longer as he stood over me, his fury almost coming in flames out of him. As he huffed and puffed, I gathered my composure. I smoothed out my pantsuit, slipped my foot back into my shoe, and fought like hell to keep the tears behind my eyes.

If there was one thing that I didn't want to do was let anyone outside this trailer see me break down. I walked past King with no words, not even a look, and stepped out into the bright sunshine of the day.

Like before, the people moved across the set as if everyone had something important to do. I walked out the same way I'd come in—with dignity. But by the time I got in the car, I let the tears flow. I tore out of the parking lot as if I was fleeing the scene of a crime. In a way, I was. . . . King had just stolen my innocence.

What had just happened? And why? Not that the answers to my questions mattered. There was no way I was going to let anyone treat me that way.

If it had taken me ten minutes to get to the set, it took me only five minutes to get home. I dashed up the stairs, rushed into the condo, and grabbed my suitcases. I wasn't thinking about folding clothes and packing neatly. All I wanted to do was get out of there.

I had never seen that side of King before in my life, and I wasn't about to stick around to see it again. If he didn't want to see me, I was going to make sure he didn't see me. Not that I wasn't hurt. I couldn't stop the tears from flowing, though I didn't try. I had thought King and I would be together forever. Well, I guess it was best that I found out about this side of that man now. It was better now than later.

In less than an hour I had all my things together, my clothes, my toiletries. I'd done so much shopping while I'd been here that not everything fit into my suitcases. But that was okay. Anything I was leaving behind, I didn't want anymore . . . including King.

The tears were still coming as I rolled my suitcases into the living room. I knew I'd be crying for many days, but I'd get over it. I just couldn't figure out why. Why?

Rushing back into the bedroom for my shoes, I decided that I'd take a cab to the airport, then worry about getting a ticket there. But just as I walked back into the living room, the front door opened.

My heart pounded as King walked in the door. What was he doing here? He hadn't been home before dark since we'd arrived in Connecticut.

He glanced at me, then down at the suitcases, then back up at me. "Heiress, baby. What's all this?"

My eyes opened so wide, I was sure that I was going to hurt myself. Was this man serious? How could he be surprised that I was leaving after what had just happened?

In the trailer my shock had left me stunned and silent. But after an hour of crying and thinking about this, I was going to speak my mind now.

"You're surprised?" I asked as I crossed my arms in front of me.

He frowned. "Yeah. What is this?"

I chuckled, though I didn't find anything funny. "I would've thought you would've been more surprised that I wasn't already gone." I stopped and looked at my watch. "It took me an hour. I should've been gone thirty minutes ago."

"I still don't know what's going on."

"You can't possibly think that I would stay here after the way you treated me." I took a step closer to him so that I could look into his eyes. I wanted to feel his answer as well as hear it. But his eyes were squinted, as if he was confused.

I kept on. "You humiliated, belittled, and physically hurt me." Without thinking, I touched the top of my arm, where I could still almost feel his fingers. "I'm not about to stick around here to see you do that to me again."

King held out his arms. "Baby, today was just a bad misunderstanding." I guess he thought I was supposed to just fall into his arms, but he was going to be waiting forever. He said, "I was having a bad day. I kept forgetting my lines. The director made us do a million takes. Believe me, it had nothing to do with you. I was just surprised that you were there, that's all."

I stood in place, not planning to move. There was a little part of me that felt better that at least it wasn't me. But still, wasn't that worse? I mean, that meant that whenever he had a bad day or something happened that he didn't like, King would take it out on me. And not only did I not deserve that treatment, but I also wasn't going to stand for it at all.

"I understand having a bad day, but that's no excuse."

"You're right." He bowed his head as if he was sorry and stepped closer to me. His cologne was already surrounding me, making me remember better times. He said, "But you can't leave me."

"Why? Because you need me here?" I said sarcastically, slowly releasing my anger.

"No, because there isn't a plane going back to L.A. tonight."

I couldn't help it. I laughed, and I was mad at myself for doing that. "There's always a flight going to Los Angeles," I said. "What about a red-eye?"

He shook his head. "Red-eyes operate only from the West Coast to the East, not the other way around. Trust me. I grew up in New York and L.A., remember? I know the flight schedules."

"Yeah, well, all right. I'll just sleep in the airport and take the first flight out in the morning."

This time King laughed. "You? Sleep on those hard chairs when you could be sleeping in our comfortable bed right next to me?" He wrapped his arms around my waist, and when he leaned his lips into mine and kissed me passionately, I almost forgot about what had happened just a few hours earlier.

There was no doubt I loved this man. And there was no doubt I knew he loved me. Truth be told, I didn't want to go home. I never wanted to leave King's side. So, if I had to stay in this boring condo for the next four months, then that was just what I was going to do.

Anything to be happy.

Chapter 8

If I wanted to be really country, I would have fallen to the ground and kissed it, but I had too much class to do that. That was the only way I could express how happy I was to be back in Los Angeles. I loved King Stevens, but I could truly say that I hated Connecticut. Since I came from a small town in Ohio, you would think I would have enjoyed living there, but it was utterly painful when I wasn't with King.

The sun was shining brightly, as if it was welcoming us home, as King and I pushed through the terminal doors at LAX. King's people were gathering our luggage, and all we had to do was jump into the car that was waiting at the curb.

"Welcome back, Mr. Stevens, Ms. Montgomery," King's driver, Al, said as he held the town car's door open for us.

I slid across the leather, then leaned back in the seat. I'd been up late last night, packing all of our stuff. We'd been there for only six months, but we had to buy four new suitcases to accommodate all the new clothes we'd acquired.

Right now all I wanted to do was get in my bed and roll around in it, even though the city was so inviting when we stepped out of the airport doors to head to the car.

I soaked up the scene as we sped from the airport and passed all the hotels on Century. It felt like I'd been away at college and now I was coming home for summer break. Only this time, if I could help it, I wasn't going to leave. I might not be a Los Angeles native, but Southern California was definitely my home.

For some reason everything felt so new, so exciting. And I felt giddy. Not giddy enough not to realize that we were going the wrong direction on the freeway. When we excited the 405 and got on the 10, I turned to King and asked, "Baby, where are we going?"

"You'll see." King didn't even bother to look at me. He just kept his eyes on his window. But I just figured that he was as glad to be home as I was.

When we got to the end of the 10 freeway in Malibu and drove along the coastline on Pacific Coast Highway, I could feel the temperature cool down. We continued on PCH, and about twenty minutes later Al turned left into the driveway to a home that sat right on the Pacific's edge.

Dang! I thought as I looked at the huge home. It wasn't quite a mansion, but that was only because it was right on the beach. I guessed King was taking me to visit one of his friends and he hadn't even told me. I wished he had; I would've worn something besides these jeans.

When Al turned off the ignition, I said, "Baby, who are we meeting here? Because I'm not appropriate."

"You look fine," King said, dismissing my words.

Taking his hand, I sighed. There was nothing I could do about the way I looked now. At the door I stood to the side, imagining who was on the other side of the door. Really, it could be anyone. . . . King knew everyone.

But King didn't ring the doorbell or knock on the door. He pulled a key from his pocket and opened the door.

I followed him inside and gasped. It was absolutely gorgeous. A winding staircase greeted us at the door, and our heels clicked against the shiny pure hardwood floors. A crystal chandelier hung in the center of the foyer. And on the other side of the staircase, there were massive windows that faced the ocean.

It was all so breathtaking, and I hadn't even moved from the front door.

"Welcome home, Ms. Montgomery."

I had almost forgotten that King was with me. I whipped around to face him when I heard his voice.

"I'm sorry," I said, then blinked fast, as if that would help me hear him better. "Say that again."

"Heiress, I enjoyed coming home to you every night and waking up with you every morning. I didn't want that to end now that we're back in L.A., so I had my Realtor find us this."

It was hard for me to turn away from King, but I did for a moment. I spun around slowly, taking everything in once again, this time in total disbelief.

"This is mine?" I whispered.

He nodded. "It's ours."

"Wow!" I said, still not able to find the right words. But then I looked at King. "Honey, I'm so . . . I don't even know the words . . . honored that you bought me a house."

"Us."

"Us." I laughed. "But this is a big step . . . and it's so sudden."

"Sudden? How can you say that? We've been living together for six months now. It's not really a step, honey. It's more like a slide." He grinned as he grabbed my hands and kissed them both softly. "There's not a problem, is there?"

"No, not a problem, per se. There are things I have to think about. What about Blair?"

He shook his head. "Already taken care of. I bought her a town house, and it's paid for, so she never has to worry about rent."

"Wow!" I said, thinking that was a bit overboard. "You bought my best friend a town house?"

"Only because of you. I knew that you were going to be concerned about her, and I was right. She was the first one you asked about, so see?"

Okay, that made sense, but there was still my other concern. "What about my work? I mean, I don't have my job at *BME*, but Carmen told me to check back with her when I got back, and even if I don't go back there, I'll probably be someplace else up in the Valley."

"Baby . . . I don't really want you to work."

Okay, put a halt on this dream. Because it was a dream up to this point. But if he was asking me to give up working, this dream had turned into a nightmare. After what I'd just been through in Connecticut, I needed to be doing something, serving a purpose. Plus, being a journalist had always been my dream, and I wanted to get back to pursuing my goals.

"What would I do if I didn't work?" I asked, trying to keep it light, not wanting this beautiful moment to turn into an argument.

"What would you do? Take care of me," he said, as if that answer was obvious.

I looked at him with all my black woman attitude. I didn't pull it out much, but if there was ever a time when he needed to "see" me say, "Negro, please," this was the time.

He chuckled, as if he read my expression perfectly. "Really, I want you to take care of me, and I want to take care of you." He brought my hands back to his lips and kissed them softly. "I can give you whatever you want or need. I need for you to give me you, all of you."

This time he kissed me, my knees and my will weakened, as usual. That was what happened whenever this man touched me. And that was the way he got whatever he wanted out of me.

Pulling away from King, I sighed for two reasons: from a little bit of frustration, and from a whole lot of love. I stood there for a moment, measuring everything, and then said, "Well, at least show me the rest of the house so I can see my trade up."

He grinned, he kissed me, and then he took me on our first walk-through of our new home.

Chapter 9

"Blair, this is Heiress, again." I tried not to sigh into the phone, but I was sure that my friend heard my frustration. "Come on. It's been almost a month since I've been back, and I haven't seen or heard from you. You won't return any of my calls. Are you okay?"

I had left her the same message over the past few weeks, so I was sure that she'd not only heard my messages, but also probably knew this one by heart.

"Well, anyway, King and I are having a dinner party tonight at the house, and I really would like for you to come. So please call me. Please." I waited, trying to think of some other words to say. "Okay, then. Bye."

I felt nothing but sadness when I hung up the phone. This was the fourth time I'd left this message just today.

After the first week when I couldn't get Blair on the phone, I just thought that she was busy with her move. I never got to see her, since I didn't even have to go back over to our apartment to pack up my stuff. King had that all taken care of since he wanted me to focus on our new home. I let a few days go by, but when she didn't call me back the second week, I wondered why she was mad at me.

Needing to see her, I asked King for the address of her new town house, but he kept forgetting to get it from his Realtor. So I went by the bar where she worked, but was told that she'd quit months ago. Now the only way I could reach her was on her cell.

What was going on?

I was just going to have to talk to King again. If he couldn't remember to get her address, he needed to let me call the Realtor myself.

There had never been a time when Blair and I had gone this long without talking. The longest stint of silence between us was a week during our junior year in college, when she lost my favorite sweater while trying to fool around with Craig Wyatt, the star point guard who now played for the New York Knicks. A tiny chuckle came through my lips when I thought back about how Blair and I had almost fought LaShawn Jenkins when we saw her wearing my sweater as she was strutting around campus. And when we found out that Craig had given it to her, we wanted to kill Craig too.

Man, I really missed my best friend.

The doorbell pulled me out of my thoughts and interrupted my walk down that memory lane. I scooted across the shiny foyer floor to let the caterers in.

"Hello, Ms. Montgomery," Sol, the owner of the catering company, greeted me. We'd done so many parties that I felt like Sol and I were friends.

"Come on in," I said to Sol and his team. "You know what to do."

I watched the people walk in behind Sol, about a dozen of them. I didn't even have to lead them to the kitchen anymore. They catered for us so much, Sol and his people really needed to move in.

I didn't know what had gotten into King lately. It was like he was obsessed with entertaining. We'd been in this house for only a few weeks, and already we'd had four parties. Every week we had some kind of gathering. A card party with just a couple of friends turned into full-blown affairs. I had to admit that I utterly enjoyed the first few functions. After spending the first two weeks working with an interior designer and getting the ten rooms of our home exactly the way we wanted them, I was excited to show off what we'd done. For the first two parties, our home was filled with actors, producers, directors, athletes, and musicians of all types, who came to celebrate with us and partied to the wee hours of the morning. I felt like I was living a Cinderella life, being surrounded by all those rich and powerful people. But after the first few parties, entertaining went from exciting to mundane, and now it was just plain tiring. Who partied like this all the time? Certainly not the King I knew . . . at least not the King I thought I knew. Our entertaining had gotten out of hand.

And when King told me on Monday that we were having another party this weekend, I thought I needed to calm him down a bit.

"Baby, I really think we should slow down on the parties. We haven't had one weekend to enjoy our home."

"What are you talking about?" he'd asked me. "We've been here every weekend."

"I'm talking about not being here alone." I had said and had wrapped my arms around him. "Remember how we used to just stay in and hang out with each other? Let's do that this weekend."

"You got a problem with parties?"

"Not parties, just parties every weekend. And it is getting out of hand. Remember the guy who passed out in our den and the couple having sex in our pool? You didn't even know them."

"So what?" he said, as if finding strangers all throughout your house wasn't a big deal. "It was no big deal. I asked them to leave, and they did."

I sighed. "I just think the parties are becoming a bit much."

"Man, go somewhere with that stupid mess."

His words were shocking, and my eyes opened as wide as my mouth.

He said, "I pay the bills around here, and if I want a party, we're going to have a party." He paused just long enough to glare at me. "All you have to do is make sure everything gets set up and looks pretty." Shaking his head, he added, "Damn, how hard is that?" And then he stomped out of the house, leaving me standing in our living room, once again frozen with shock.

His outbursts were few and far between, and even though this was only the second one, I was still hurt. *It's just the pressure of his job*. That was what I told myself. Especially when he came back home hours later, so remorseful.

"I love you, Heiress. You know that, right?" he'd said.

I'd nodded, because I did know that he loved me. He showed me in every way. From the way he took care of me physically, financially, and—most of the time—emotionally. Truly, I always felt loved. I just figured that King had to get settled in his fame. He was becoming a bigger and bigger star every day, and really, he was still young. He was just a year older than me. In a few years he'd be used to all of this and everything would be better.

I was on my way to check on how Sol was coming along when my cell phone rang. A big smile spread across my face and I breathed a sigh of relief when I saw the name flash across my screen.

"Heifer, where have you been? I've been trying to get in touch with you for weeks," I playfully scolded Blair upon answering the phone.

"I know. I'm sorry. I've just been extremely busy setting up house and taking care of some business," she said with a slight sound of exhaustion in her voice. I was relieved that she hadn't been just ignoring me, but I was curious as to what she had been up to.

"I went by the bar to see if you were there, and they said you quit." I knew Blair well enough to know that she wasn't giving up the money she was making bartending unless she had someone else paying her bills.

"Yeah, I outgrew that place. So how is life in Malibu?"

It was kind of odd that Blair didn't want to elaborate on why she quit. I thought she would have this big dramatic story about how she had escaped the grasp of her evil manager and had fallen into the arms of a knight in shining armor. I had been gone all this time, and she didn't even give me details.

"Malibu is nice. It's so far from everything, though, but the house is beautiful."

"Well, I'm sure being with Mr. Perfect makes it all worth it."

"It kinda does." I giggled. "Listen, we're having a party tonight, and I would really love for you to come."

Blair was silent for a few minutes before she spoke. "Will fine, famous men be there?" There was the Blair I knew.

"Of course." I laughed.

"Well, if you're finally sharing the life of luxury you have been living, then I'll make an appearance." I began to fix my mouth to respond with excitement, but she quickly cut me off. "Just text me all the info. I gotta go, girl."

Just like that, the phone clicked off. I didn't know what had Blair so preoccupied, but I was happy that she was coming to the party. I needed to see my best friend. I hoped we would get our connection back tonight and return to normal. I smiled with satisfaction and ran upstairs to get dressed.

***

Hours later I was dressed in an Oni original, a mini sheath that the up-and-coming designer had fashioned just for me. After checking my makeup, I went down to the dining room to make sure that it had been decorated exactly the way King had planned.

The huge space had been transformed into a lavish Mediterranean experience. Along the wall, Sol had prepared an amazing food spread that included a Mediterranean salad, Greek spaghetti, and falafel. Two of the waitstaff stood behind the bar, ready to serve the guests any kind of drink they wanted.

Satisfied with the downstairs, I headed back upstairs to pull King's suit from the closet. Since I wasn't working, this was what I did every day, so King never had to worry. Once he came home, all he'd have to do would be to jump into the shower and then get dressed.

I'd just laid his suit on the bed when King came stomping into the bedroom.

I frowned. Ever since his tantrum on Monday, he'd been in a good mood. What could possibly be wrong now?

"What's wrong?" I asked him without even saying hello.

"What is all that ridiculous food down there?"

"What food?"

"In the dining room. That stuff doesn't even look good."

"That's what you ordered, King. You're the one who wanted Mediterranean cuisine."

"Well, I didn't know it was going to look like that!"

I wanted to tell him that it didn't matter how it looked, that it was too late now, and that if he had listened to me, we wouldn't even be having this stupid party. But I knew that would not be a good look. I just needed to calm him down.

"Baby, the food is going to be fine. We had some of these dishes when we went to that event for the Lakers, remember?"

He squinted like he was trying to remember. "Really?"

"Yeah, that was where you got the idea."

He nodded, though I could tell that he was still unsure. But I knew what he was thinking. If it was good enough for the Busses, the owners of the Lakers, then it was good enough for King Stevens's party.

When King went into our master bath, I sighed, relieved. One situation avoided.

King dressed just in time to greet our first guests. I stood at the door with him, but tonight I didn't recognize too many of the faces. It was as if this was a whole new set of people that I'd never seen in the year that I'd known King.

The more people came in, the more I was sure that I didn't have any idea who any of them were. There were men in what I called Keith Sweat music video attire: their bare chests showing through shirts that were open all the way to their navels. They were arriving with two, three, four video vixens on their arms.

There were dozens of people already in our home, eating our food, drinking our drinks, dancing to our music, when I pulled King aside.

"Baby, who are all these people?" I whispered in King's ear as I held on to his arm.

He yanked his arm away from my grasp. "Friends," was all he said, without even looking at me.

But if he thought I was going to be deterred by that, he had another thing coming. "Whose friends? I've never seen these people before."

Finally, he turned to me. His irritation was etched all over his face. He leaned so close to me that his lips were on my ear. "Are we going to have a problem?"

It was the look in his eyes, the tone in his voice that formed a knot in my stomach.

I couldn't even respond with words. I just shook my head no and hoped that would assure him.

"Good," he said, though he still didn't sound happy. "Now, go be a good girl, and continue to be a good little hostess."

Now my eyes were the ones on fire, but I wasn't going to start anything now. I spun around to walk away. That was all I wanted to do—to get away from him.

But King grabbed my arm, stopping me. His grip was strong, but it wasn't threatening. When he leaned toward me, I leaned back for a moment, not sure what he was going to do. But then he rubbed his lips across my cheek.

"Thank you," he said as he kissed me softly. Then, just as quickly as his words came, King disappeared back into the crowd.

I had no idea what I was supposed to do other than smile. So I just wandered around my own house, making my way through the people who filled the rooms, drinking, eating, smoking, dancing. I walked up the spiral staircase and stood on the step that was exactly halfway up. From that vantage point, I could see most of the living room.

And I could see King in the center of the room, the center of everyone's attention. Women were all over him, hugging him, adoring him, and even from this far away, I could see that he was eating it all up.

I folded my arms across my chest, trying to warm my bare arms. Even though it was burning up in this house, I felt cold. As I watched King, for the first time I could say that I truly felt uncomfortable. Not quite jealous. King had never given me any reason to be jealous at all. Whenever he was with me, he let everyone know that I was his lady, and if a woman ever came up to him in some kind of crazy way, he always let her know that he wasn't interested. But tonight . . . I didn't know. There was something about King. Almost like he'd forgotten that I was there.

I began to think that maybe I needed to disappear. Maybe that was exactly what I needed to do. Why put myself through this? There was no one at this party for me, and I was totally convinced that King would not miss me.

I had turned to continue up the stairs when I heard the front door open. Looking back down, I stood frozen for a moment. And then I screamed out, "Blair!" as I dashed down the steps.

"Oh my God," I said to her as I hugged her. Then I stepped back and gave her the once-over. "Oh my God! You look fabulous. I love your haircut," I said, wanting to run my hands through the waves that fell softly onto her shoulders. "And that dress!" I stepped back some more and took in the red knit that hugged what looked like all her new curves. "Have you lost weight?" I didn't even give her a chance to answer before I asked, "Where have you been?" All the words rolled out of me. I was just so happy to see my friend. Not only because she was someone I knew, but also because I had missed her so much.

Blair looked stunning . . . and different. Like she was the one leading a glamorous life.

"How you doing, Heiress?"

"I'm good. But where have you been? Did you have any trouble finding the house?"

"No."

"That's great," I said as I hugged her again. "I'm so glad you came."

"Well, I wanted to see your new place, so here I am."

"I have so much to tell you," I said, taking her hand after one of the staff took her coat. "So much is going on, and so much has changed."

We had eight months' worth of gossip to catch up on, and though I didn't think I could tell her everything tonight, I was going to try.

Then, over my shoulder, I heard, "Blair, hey. Glad you made it." King swooped in beside me. He stepped right in front of me, like I wasn't even there, when he added, "Come with me. I have someone I know you want to meet."

And then they were both gone.

It had happened so fast, I wasn't even sure what had gone down. I watched King and Blair disappear into the living room crowd. I couldn't see them through all the people, but rather than try to follow them, I returned to my perch on the steps.

All kinds of thoughts were going through my mind as I searched the crowd for the twosome. Like how did King know that Blair was coming to the party? And when had they become so friendly? Plus, I wanted to know who King was introducing Blair to.

It was all so confusing to me; I had no idea what was going on.

Finally, I spotted the two of them, and I watched with eagle eyes as King led Blair through the party the same way he'd done me. He paraded her around like she was a trophy. His hand was around her waist as he took her from one guy to the next. I frowned the whole time, until I watched King settle in front of some guy that I had seen before—not at our house, but at some of the other Hollywood parties we'd attended.

The guy—I couldn't remember his name—was all over Blair. Now he was the one who was holding her and whispering in her ear. King stood back like he was the proud papa. Then I watched him chat until the guy pulled out something from inside his jacket pocket. I was too far away to see exactly what it was, but it didn't take a genius to figure it out.

It was a plastic bag, and I suspected there was some white powder or some pills inside.

I watched as King led Blair and the guy into the study off of the living room. When they disappeared, I started down the steps. But when I got to the bottom, I stopped. Why was I going to follow them? What was I going to do? It wasn't like I was going to do any drugs.

Truly, I wanted to know what was going on, especially with Blair. I hadn't seen her in eight months, and she came to my house and just left me?

It didn't make any sense.

But I just turned around and walked back up the stairs. Maybe King was just introducing Blair to someone in the industry. Before we went to Connecticut, she was always talking about King introducing her to someone. Maybe that was what this was all about.

Maybe, or maybe not. I didn't know. But I was so over this party, so over these people, so over Blair and even King. Honestly, I was tired and couldn't care less about what was going to happen for the rest of the night.

Inside our bedroom I locked the door, stripped, then went into the bathroom and took a Valium that King's doctor had given to me to help me calm down as we were moving into our house. This was only the second time I was taking one of these pills. I didn't want to start a bad habit, but with the music blasting and all the people talking and laughing, I was going to need something to help me sleep.

I slipped underneath the heavy satin duvet and closed my eyes. In no time, I was able to tune out the world. My last thought before I lost consciousness was that it would all be different in the morning.

Chapter 10

Breakfast in bed was a rare luxury. But that was what I woke up to this morning. When I finally opened my eyes, King was standing over me.

"Sleeping Beauty," he said.

It took several moments for my eyes to focus and fully see King, smiling down at me, holding a tray.

"What is this?" I asked, knowing that I sounded groggy. I was still a little out of it; I guess it was the Valium.

"Breakfast."

As I scooted up in the bed, pulling the sheet with me, King laid the tray across my lap.

"Good morning," he said as he kissed my cheek.

"This is wonderful," I said, looking down at the tray, which held a plate filled with eggs Benedict and salmon croquettes, and a glass of fresh squeezed orange juice.

Looking up at King, I couldn't help but smile. I knew he could see the love I had for him in my eyes. It was wonderful. This was the reason why I loved this man. He treated me like his queen when he wasn't so stressed out. "Baby, thank you so much for this," I said as I scooped a forkful of salmon into my mouth.

"I thought you deserved a little pampering after all you did to make sure that the party went off without a hitch. Did you have fun last night?"

I did everything I could to keep my smile in place and the words that I really wanted to say out of my mouth. I wanted to tell King, "Hell no!" That I hadn't had fun at all. And that I would be happy if we never, ever had another party in our house again. I didn't say any of that. I just nodded sweetly and kept on eating. At least I didn't lie out loud.

"Yeah, it was a great party," King said. I guess he was pleased that I seemed happy. "But you went to bed early, huh?"

"It wasn't that early," I said, betting on the fact that he hadn't missed me.

"When I came up, the door was locked."

"Sorry about that. It was just that there were a few people still here when I came up here."

"That's okay," he said, kissing me again. "I know where we keep the key. Finish up. I have another surprise for you when you're finished."

"What?" I said, clapping like I was a five-year-old.

"You'll just have to wait and see." Then he disappeared into our master bath.

I didn't have to wait too long to find out about my next surprise. As soon as I pushed aside the tray, King came back in, took my hand, and lifted me from the bed.

There was a bubble bath already prepared for me, and as I settled into the warmth of the Jacuzzi tub, King pampered me. He washed my back, my arms, my legs, and everywhere else. And then he carried me back to our bed, where he laid me underneath the covers and told me to relax.

"Just lay back and let your King take care of you."

As Kem sang all my favorite ballads, I closed my eyes and melted under the gentle massage from King's fingertips. I fell deeper, deeper, deeper into a state of relaxation. With the music still in my ears and King's hands still on my body, I dreamt about what my life would be like when King and I made our relationship official, when we became husband and wife. By then King would be more settled, more used to being a star, and I imagined that our life would be this wonderful all the time. Breakfast in bed, massages all the time.

As King made his way up to my shoulders, I knew that I never wanted this to end. Not any of it. He was too wonderful a man for me to give up just because he had a few bad moments. I just had to remember times like these. I just had to remember that through it all, he loved me.

My eyes were still closed when King leaned over and kissed my neck. Then his tongue made its way to my ears, my cheeks, until he turned me over and kissed my lips passionately.

I moaned, hardly able to wait for what was next.

But when King pulled away from me, my eyes snapped open.

"Babe, I gotta head out."

I frowned. Was he serious? He gave me this beautiful morning of pampering, and then, just like that, he was leaving me?

"What?" I asked, thinking that I had misheard his words.

"I have to make a run."

"But what about all of this? You planned such a beautiful morning." I put on the best pout that I could muster.

But that did nothing for King.

"Heiress, I can't," he said, not budging a bit. "I have to make a run, and then I have loads of meetings today." He kissed me softly on my forehead. "I'm sure you can find something to do. Right, baby? I mean, the people have to come clean the house and put everything back in order from last night. I'll see you later."

Two seconds after that, he was gone. I sat up in our bed for several minutes afterward, asking myself what had just happened. I couldn't believe it. Here I was, alone again. When I finally pushed myself out of bed, I wrapped myself inside my bathrobe, then wandered through the eight thousand square feet of our home. That was all I had to do, just wander. I moved from room to room, glancing in all the guest bedrooms and the two libraries and the gym, which I never used. I wandered until the phone rang. I sighed until I saw the number on the caller ID screen. I couldn't believe it.

"Blair!" I couldn't hold back the excitement in my voice.

"Hey, Heiress."

"What's going on, girl? How've you been?"

"I'm good. I'm sorry we didn't get to spend any time together last night. After King introduced me around, I was looking for you but couldn't find you."

"Girl," I said, "I went straight to bed. We've had so many of those parties, I was so over it."

"Well, I was wondering if you wanted to do lunch at my town house, since, like you said, we haven't had time together."

"I would love that!"

"Me too, because we really have to catch up."

"Definitely. Hold on. Let me get your address." I jotted it down on a notepad and told Blair that I would be on my way soon. "All I have to do is get dressed. Give me an hour."

It turned out that Blair wasn't really that far away. King had set her up in a town house in Venice Beach, so all I had to do was head down PCH, then make a right onto Lincoln. Within thirty minutes I pulled into the driveway of the address that Blair had given me, and peered through the car window. There were four matching town houses, all new. I parked, then trotted up the steps and rang the doorbell.

When Blair answered the door, just like last night, I had to pause to take in my best friend. My goodness, she had changed so much in just eight months. Not that Blair didn't always look good, but now she was so . . . Hollywood. Her hair and makeup were as flawless as they'd been last night, though today they were much simpler. Her hair was slicked back in a bun, and her makeup was light. Even though she was home, she was wearing a vintage Chanel suit and some killer Versace shoes. But the thing that looked most different about Blair was that she glowed. I knew what it was immediately. . . . Blair had a new man in her life.

Inside I chuckled. No wonder I hadn't been able to get in touch with her. She had been spending all of her time with some man. And now she wanted to tell me all about him.

"Come on in, girl," she said, sounding more cheery than she had last night. "Welcome to Blair's lair." She opened the door wider so that I could step in.

When I walked inside, right away I could see that this place was gorgeous. It was decked out with leather furniture, expensive rugs, and had mini chandeliers everywhere. Clearly, Blair hadn't decorated this place herself. Not that she didn't have good taste—she did. But having worked with an interior designer myself, I knew when a place had been professionally laid out.

"Oh, my God, bestie," I said as I moved slowly through the living room, "this place is gorgeous."

"Thanks," she said with a big grin on her face.

"Wow, King really felt bad for taking me away from you, huh? I guess he figured this would make up for that."

"Well, he did get this house for me, but I decorated everything myself," she said quickly.

"Really?"

She nodded, walked over to her coffee table, and picked up the remote for the sound system. In an instant, soft music flowed through the living room.

I smiled, impressed.

"Come on. I have lunch set up in the dining room."

I followed her, feeling like we had both changed so much in less than a year. I felt so grown up as I sat at her mahogany table, where she had two fish salads set out for us.

"I guess we're not struggling college graduates anymore," I said as I sat across from her at the table.

"I guess not."

"Just think, a year ago we were both struggling, trying to make it in the City of Angels. And now . . ."

"We're living the life that we talked about," she said, finishing my sentence and my thought the way she used to.

"Blair, everything here is so beautiful." I eyed the paintings on the dining room walls. But then I shook my head and turned back to my friend. "Okay, tell me what's up."

"What do you mean?"

"What's up with you? I mean, look at you. You're glowing."

"Well, you don't look so bad yourself."

I laughed. "Yes, and it's because of King." I put down my fork. "So tell me, who's the man in your life?"

Even though she was the color of rich peanut butter, I could tell that Blair was blushing. The blush of new love.

Bingo! I was right. Not that I had any doubt. I knew Blair, and all these changes . . . It was all about a man.

"So . . ."

Finally, she opened up . . . a little. "It's very new, and I don't want to ruin it by saying too much."

"You can tell me. I'm your best friend."

"Well, I will say this. He's really great." She began to smile harder.

That made me want to ask her all kinds of questions, but I figured that I wouldn't press it. There was enough to talk about with me, and so I told Blair all that had been going on: how I'd been so bored in Connecticut and how we'd come back and how King did not want me to work.

"How do you feel about that?"

I shrugged. "I don't know. I'd always wanted to be a journalist. You know that. And I miss it, but . . ."

"King wants you to stay home."

I nodded. "He says that he loves taking care of me."

"That's a good thing, right?"

"Yeah, but I'm just afraid that I might lose myself to King's life, and I don't want to do that."

"I'm sure that's not what King wants to do. I'm sure he's thinking that he's doing what's best."

"Yeah . . . maybe . . . yeah."

"Let's not talk about this anymore." She pushed her plate aside. "Come into my bedroom. I want to show you my photo albums. I've been taking lots of pictures."

"You're going back to that?"

"Uh-huh. The guy I'm dating thinks he might be able to get a book of my photographs published."

"Wow. Now, that would be great."

Inside her bedroom we kicked off our shoes, lay on her bed, and talked and laughed for hours. We reminisced about our college days, past relationships, and our families.

It was almost seven o'clock by the time I glanced at my watch.

"Girl, I need to be heading home. King will be there soon."

"It was so good seeing you," Blair said as she held my arm and walked me to the door. "We can't go for months again without talking."

"I agree. Just make sure that you answer your phone when I call."

Blair laughed. "Okay, I will." When I gave her a long look, she added, "I promise."

Just a few minutes after that, I was back in my car, heading toward Malibu. As I let the evening air into the car, I thought about the hours I'd spent with Blair. Days like today were what life was all about to me. I had started the morning with the man I loved and had spent most of the daytime hours with the friend I adored. Life was truly good now, and I had a feeling deep down that everything was only going to get better from here on in.

Chapter 11

King was working on a new film, which gave me time to do some of the things I'd been wanting to do since we'd returned to Los Angeles. Like some serious shopping.

I rarely made the trek from Malibu to Beverly Hills, but when I woke up this morning to find that King had already gone to the set, I decided that I was going to do some retail therapy.

As I dressed, I thought about King. It had been only two weeks since he'd started filming, but in that time he'd been so distant, that is, when he came home. Of course, he came home every night, but it was often after midnight, and he'd just drop into our bed, exhausted.

We hadn't talked all that much, and that meant we definitely weren't making love. It had been only two weeks, but still I was worried. I might have been young, but I knew how important romance was in any relationship. And I didn't want too many more days to pass without King and me connecting, especially since our one-year anniversary was approaching. I needed to come up with some ideas, and Rodeo Drive seemed to be the best place to brainstorm.

It was a forty-five-minute drive to Beverly Hills, and after I pulled into a parking lot, I strolled through the streets. It really did feel like the streets were paved with gold in this city.

I passed by all the famous stores and stopped in front of a china shop. The windows were filled with wineglasses and dinner sets, and for some reason, I wanted to go inside and get a better look.

Now, I wasn't the type to be excited about plates and glasses, but in this place I was in a trance. The beauty of these pieces was so apparent, and I walked from one chest to the next, studying them all. Every glass seemed to be unique, and I loved the way the crystal ones sparkled, some of them even brighter than diamonds.

"This one is called Heiress," a deep voice said from behind me. "I named it after a girl I once knew."

My smile was instant when I turned around. I recognized him right away, but it was only because of his smile. Because the scrawny, nerdy, goofy boy that I'd grown up with was now a handsome man.

"Donovan? That cannot be you."

His smile got bigger, and now I was sure.

"Oh my God, how are you?" I leapt into his arms and wrapped mine around him. I held on to him for as long as I could before I finally released him. Taking a step back, I took in the sight of him.

"I'm doing great." He laughed, and it warmed my heart, as well as brought back so many memories. The last time I saw Donovan back in Ohio, he had braces. But now he was a man with a model-beautiful smile.

"What are you doing here . . . in California?"

"You're standing in my shop."

I took another quick glance around and couldn't believe that all of this belonged to Donovan. I remembered that he used to work with blown glass and stuff like that, but it wasn't like I had spent a lot of time paying attention to Donovan or his hobbies.

"How did you . . ."

Before I could finish my thought, Donovan explained. "Remember Mrs. Patrick from church?"

I nodded.

"Well," he continued, "I made a vase for her niece's birthday, and she loved it. It turned out her husband was a venture capitalist, and the rest, as they say . . ."

"Is history," I said, finishing for him.

Donovan nodded. "He invested in me, helped me to expand, at first in Ohio, but then I really believed there was a market out here."

"And how are you doing out here?"

His smile was enough of an answer, but he said, "It's going pretty good."

"Donny, this is really great. I am so proud of you."

"And what about you? How does it feel to be a big Hollywood journalist?"

That statement was like a knife in my side.

"Yeah," he continued, "I heard that you were out here writing stories about the stars."

My explanation was stuck in my throat. How was I supposed to say that I hadn't written anything in months, and for no good reason? I didn't even realize how much I had missed being a journalist until this moment.

Finally, I found the words to tell the truth. "I'm actually not doing journalism anymore."

"You're kidding. As good a writer as you were?"

I shrugged. There was nothing to say.

Donovan rescued me. "That's too bad," he said. "I know that was always your dream."

"Yeah, well, sometimes dreams get deferred."

We stood in silence for what seemed like an eternity.

Donovan broke the awkwardness. "Listen, I would love to catch up. I was just headed out to lunch when I saw you come in. Can you join me?"

At first, I was going to politely decline and tell him I wasn't hungry, but then my stomach spoke up before my mouth could.

"I'll take that as a yes." Donovan chuckled.

He put his hand gently on the small of my back and led me out the door. The French bistro was only two blocks away, and not even ten minutes passed before I was sitting across from him.

I couldn't believe this was the short, shy guy that spoke only when someone spoke to him. Now he sat there confidently, giving me suggestions on what to order.

"Of course, the French onion soup is the best," he said.

"Then I'll have that and a side salad."

Once we'd given our orders to the waitress, we sat back and caught up. As Donovan spoke, I tried hard not to stare. But his smooth Hershey's-colored skin and bright brown eyes made it almost impossible. It was easy to see that he'd been working out, and he'd even lost that little Midwestern twang, which so many people said I still had.

"You look amazing, by the way," he said all of a sudden.

"What?" I thought I'd been the only one staring, but I guess he'd been checking me out too.

He said, "I guess dating a superstar has its perks, huh?"

His statement caught me off guard, and I dropped the piece of French bread I held in my hand. I took a sip of water to try to mask my discomfort and give myself time to compose myself.

"You okay?"

I nodded. "Fine. Just a little surprised that you heard about that."

"Well, news does get around."

"I guess."

"Especially when you're in magazines all the time."

Well, that was a good point. It was hard to stay out of the public eye when your man was the star of the stars in Hollywood.

"The first time I saw you in one of those tabloids, I tore out the picture, because I couldn't believe it. I wanted to hang it in my store and tell everyone, 'I know her.'" He laughed.

I just smiled and nodded. It wasn't that I was ashamed of my relationship. I simply wasn't up to talking about it in depth, especially to Donovan.

I guess it was my silence that made him ask, "Are you happy?" His voice was so soft, I barely heard him.

I nodded. "It's been interesting adjusting to the life-style, but we're happy." I didn't know if it was what I said or how I said it, but Donovan looked at me with uncertainty in his eyes.

I'd known Donovan just about my whole life. But even though we went that far back, I didn't want to get into my relationship with him. Not only because I hadn't seen him in a while and it just didn't seem right, but also because I wasn't sure what my relationship was with King. I mean, of course, I knew we were in love, but there were so many things that bothered me. There were so many things that we had to work out.

"So how're you liking California so far?" That was my best attempt to change the subject.

"It's expensive and fast and a little superficial. Really different from home, right?"

I nodded.

"But," he continued, "I'm enjoying myself. I can see why you never came back home after you graduated."

From there, we never went back to talk about me and King. We just chatted about the good old days and about how different California was from Ohio.

Having lunch with Donovan was like breathing fresh air. It was so easy. It was good to spend time with someone who knew me before, who wasn't part of my life with King.

"I would really like to do this again," he whispered in my ear as he hugged me good-bye as we stood in front of the restaurant.

I didn't know why, but I hesitated answering. Maybe, it was because ever since the moment that King and I became a couple, I hadn't had many male friends. When I stepped back and looked into Donovan's eyes, there was a sincerity there that I hadn't seen in a long time.

"Sure," I said. "Let's make that happen. Give me your number."

His smile let me know that I'd made the right decision.

"I promise I'll call you soon."

Before I stepped away, he took my hand and kissed it softly.

I headed off, going in the opposite direction of Donovan's shop. Now I strolled down the street with memories on my mind and a smile on my face. Seeing him and reminiscing had done a lot for me. I didn't need to shop as much as I thought, but I did want to get down to Chanel before the store closed.

I was just about to step into Chanel when my cell rang.

"Hey, baby," I answered with delight when I saw King's name pop up on the phone's screen.

"Where the hell are you?"

The sad thing about King's outburst was that it didn't shock me. Now I just rolled my eyes and wondered why he wasn't as delighted as I was.

"I came to Rodeo to do some shopping. Are you okay?"

"Naw, I'm not okay. What are you doing over there?"

"I came to do some shopping," I repeated.

"You need to quit spending my money and bring your ass home now," he yelled before he hung up.

"Oh my God," I whispered.

As fast as I could, I headed back to the car. My hands were shaking as I put the key into the ignition and then sped out of the parking lot.

I wanted to break all speed limits, but the last thing I needed was to bring home a ticket. King would have a fit, and it seemed like he was already upset.

About what? I had no idea. I had no clue what had happened today, but King was not happy and I needed to do whatever was necessary to diffuse the situation.

Chapter 12

I twisted the car into our driveway, turned off the ignition, then sat there for a moment. I hadn't spent a lot of time praying over the past few years, since I'd been out on my own. But I felt like a prayer could be a good thing right about now.

I slipped out of the car, then eased into the house as quietly as I could. King was obviously already upset, and I didn't need to do a single thing to add fuel to that fire. Dropping my bag by the front door, I listened for a moment, trying to hear a sound and get a clue about where King might be. But when I heard nothing, I began to make my way through the house to find him.

As I'd driven home, I tried to imagine all the reasons why King would be upset . . . again. It had to be the new movie—he was always stressed out about new projects. At least, that was what I'd told myself. The first time King had ever gone off on me was on that movie set in Connecticut, and he was just as high-strung now.

This movie was even tougher. King was playing the part of a patient in a mental institution, and he had to go into some really dark places for this role. The critics, who had gotten wind of the film, had said this might be King's Academy Award–winning role, and that alone had added a lot of pressure. At the age of twenty-seven his father had already had two Academy Award nominations, and people were asking if King Stevens would ever be as good as his father.

I had searched most of the first floor of the house when I heard the music. It was soft, but I knew that King was in the den. The music got louder as I stepped down the stairs, and the voice became clearer. King was playing one of his mother's CDs, and at the bottom of the steps, I saw him, slumped on the couch and wrapped in his bathrobe. His head was down, and he held a bottle in his hand. I wasn't sure what it was. A bottle of scotch, maybe.

It was hard for me to move. I was shocked; I'd never seen King like this before.

"Baby," I began softly, "is everything okay?"

I had both concern and caution in my tone, not wanting to do anything that would startle him or upset him further in any way.

He stayed the way he was, not moving, as if he hadn't heard me.

"King?" I kept my voice low as I slowly walked to the couch, then lowered myself to sit right next to him.

Minutes went by, and a new song came on. Now King lifted his head and began singing with his mother. This song, I recognized. It was called "Baby, Good Night," and it was a song about him that his mother had written and recorded before he was born. He told me that his mother would hold her belly and sing to him every night, before she went to bed.

I sat and listened as King sang along, not wanting to interrupt, but also not wanting to set him off. Obviously, something was wrong.

At the end of the song, the CD stopped playing and we sat in silence for a moment. Just as I was getting ready to ask King again what was wrong, he spoke to me for the first time.

"What's the one thing I ask of you when I get home?" He didn't bother to look at me.

I wanted to tell him that I was a grown woman. I wanted to tell him that since he didn't want me to work, I was bored and had to do something. I wanted to tell him that he didn't own me, that he didn't own my life. Instead, I didn't say any of that. I lowered my head and said, "To be here," knowing that was the answer he expected.

Really, I should have known that King wouldn't be happy to come home to an empty house. But how was I supposed to know what time he was getting off the set? Was I just supposed to sit here all day and all night and wait for him?

"To be here," King said. "And why is that so difficult for you to understand?"

With those words he looked up at me. He glared at me, and I became uncomfortable, unsettled.

"Baby, I'm sorry, but I needed to get out. I thought I would be back before you got home, but I ran into an old friend."

His expression seemed to darken with my explanation.

"Old friend, huh?" Suddenly he jumped up and grabbed my arm at the same time, pulling me up with him. His grip was strong and tight, and already I could feel my muscles pulsating beneath his grasp. I knew I'd have another bruise when he finally let me go.

"Are you cheating on me?" he yelled as he let go of my arm and grasped my shoulders. He shook me as if I were a child.

"What? No!" I said, as if his words were ridiculous. Once again, tears rolled from my eyes. "I'm not cheating on you. I wouldn't do that."

"You out gallivanting with some other dude?"

"No!"

"You forgot you got a man at home?" he screamed.

"No!"

He continued to shake me with each word he spoke, and my head started to hurt.

"You wanna leave me?" He tossed me back onto the couch, and my side hit the bottle of scotch, which he'd left lying there.

I winced in pain, grabbed my side, and now I sobbed even harder. My eyes were closed, but I could hear his breathing over me.

"You will never leave me," he growled. "I have given you everything."

Take it back! Take everything back! Those were the words I screamed in my head, but of course, I didn't dare say them aloud. The room was silent except for my sobs and his breathing, and after a few minutes I heard King stomp away.

I didn't move. I stayed there, still crying and wondering what had just happened. King and I had been together for just about a year, and I had never given him any reason not to trust me. I loved that man. I told him that, and I showed him that. But this—his temper, his grabbing me, these ridiculous accusations—it was all becoming too much.

Still, I couldn't imagine leaving him. Most of the time King was so sweet, so kind, so loving. He had shown me the finer things in life, and like he said, he'd given me so much. It was just at these moments when he made me question it all. It was at these moments that I felt sick . . . well, sick to my stomach.

Just as I had that thought, I jumped up and dashed to the bathroom, just in time to kneel before the toilet and throw up. I released my lunch into the porcelain bowl and gagged until my stomach was empty. I stayed kneeling there for a while because my stomach was still twisting, but there was nothing left. I meant that. There was nothing left inside of me. Nothing emotionally, nothing spiritually. I was in pain.

Eventually I tried to stand, but it felt as if the room was spinning. I flipped down the toilet cover, then sat, taking deep breaths at the same time. I had to find a way to compose myself, to stop my head from hurting, to stop my heart from aching. It took a long time, at least a half an hour, before I was able to push myself off the toilet and make my way upstairs to our bedroom. I didn't have any idea if King was at home or if he'd left, but by the time I got to our room, I figured that he had stomped away again.

I had no energy to do anything but lie in my bed and sleep today's catastrophe away. I slipped under the covers and cried until I felt all pain ease from my body and my mind.

"Do you take this woman to be your lawfully wedded wife? To have and to hold till death do you part?"

King turned to look at me, and the sweetest expression, filled with nothing but love, came across his face. He looked deep into my eyes and kissed the back of my hand softly before responding, "I do."

My smile was wide. I adored this man. He was everything I could ask for and more. And finally, here we were, committing to each other. We were going to be husband and wife.

The pastor turned to me. "Heiress, do you take this man to be your lawfully wedded husband? To have and to hold till death do you part?"

For a moment, I tore my eyes away from King and scanned the sanctuary. Three hundred of our friends and family were on the edge of their seats, grinning and waiting for me to say, "I do."

Turning back to King, I thought about how lucky I was. This man was wonderful, so handsome in his custom tuxedo.

And then . . . screams and gunshots!

I shot up straight in the bed, drenched in sweat but shivering. The room was dark; there wasn't even any light coming in from the window. I had slept into the night. Then my stomach rumbled. I tried to roll out of bed, but at first I couldn't move. It took me a moment to realize that King had slid into the bed, and now his arm was wrapped tightly around me. With the rumbling rising inside of me, I squirmed, trying to get away.

"Where are you going?" King whispered in a half-asleep voice.

"I have to use the bathroom," I squeaked.

He loosened his grip and rolled over, probably asleep before I even jumped from the bed. I ran to the bathroom and leaned over the toilet just in time. I couldn't believe there was anything else inside of me. I hadn't eaten since lunch. But still, I was gagging on whatever was still left in my stomach. Finally, I leaned my back against the bathroom wall. I was totally spent, feeling like I had just run a marathon or had been in a boxing match.

What was wrong with me? Was King stressing me out so much that now I was physically sick? That had to be it, and that meant that things had to change. We had to find a way to get back to the complete bliss that I'd known before we left for Connecticut, or else I didn't know what I was going to do.

Chapter 13

After being in the bathroom for about an hour, I finally crawled back into bed. Totally exhausted, I fell asleep right away, but when I woke up the next morning, I was alone in the bed. I sat up slowly, not wanting to disturb my stomach again, and once I was sure that I was fine, I slipped out of the bed, grabbed my bathrobe, and then went in search of King. I looked in every room of the house, but he was nowhere to be found. He must've had an early call on the set.

Making my way back to the bathroom, I gasped when I turned on the light. I had halfway scared myself when I looked in the mirror. My hair was all over my head, going in every direction, my eyes were puffy and swollen, and there was white stuff all around my mouth. I looked like something out of a horror movie. I tried to stretch my tired arms over my head, but my arms felt too heavy. I shrugged off my bathrobe, then the T-shirt that I wore, and the first thing I noticed were the bruises on my arms.

I shook my head, not at all surprised that they were there. Running my fingers over my left arm first and then my right arm, I wondered how long I was going to put up with this. This wasn't the first time I had a bruise from King, but this was the first time that I had two at once. Meaning things were getting worse. And I didn't even know what had really set him off yesterday. There had been plenty of other times when I wasn't here when he came home, and he'd never gone off about my absence before. Something had gotten to him. Clearly, he wasn't himself, and I desperately wanted to help him get back to the place where he was when I met him. The place where we were so happy together.

I didn't know exactly what I could do to keep him happy all the time, but I was going to work on it. I didn't want to be part of his problem; I wanted to be his solution. I didn't want to be the one to put stress on him.

Hopping into the shower, I let the warm water wash over me, soothe me. I took a deep breath and tried to relax, to ease my mind and my body, but my mind and my thoughts were on King. It was surprising to me that he was having this kind of stressful reaction to fame. I would've thought that it would've been easier for him since he'd grown up in this life. Maybe that was part of his pressure—trying to live up to what everyone else felt that he should be. Maybe having famous parents wasn't as easy as I thought.

I needed to talk this over, talk this out with someone, and before I was even out of the shower, I decided that I would call Blair. It was so good to have my friend back now that we had reconnected. I needed to talk to my bestie. After I got out of the shower, dried myself off, and wrapped myself up in the towel, I called Blair, but her cell went straight to voice mail.

"Where could she be?" I asked myself, glancing at the clock. It was barely seven o' clock. Where could Blair be this early in the morning?

Flopping down onto the bed, I fought to keep the tears back in my eyes. I needed to talk to someone about what was going on, and without Blair, I didn't have anyone.

Once I became involved with King, he became my life. There was no time for me to develop my own friendships, and I certainly wasn't going to call any of his friends.

Maybe I could call my mom, but what would I tell her? She and my dad would go crazy if they knew how King had been treating me. I could call and leave out the details. Just tell her that things were getting tense.

My mother wasn't my first choice, but she was my only choice. I lay on the bed for minutes that turned into an hour, and then another, until I finally pushed myself up. I was going to do it. I was going to call my mother. Just as I reached for the phone, it rang and UNKNOWN flashed across the screen. I never answered unidentified calls, because I wanted to know who I was talking to first. But at this point, I needed to talk to anyone. Just hearing a friendly voice was going to do me good.

"Hello," I said cautiously when I answered.

"Do you know how long it takes to blow out a wineglass?"

It was a simple question, but the masculine voice sounded so sexy and he made me smile.

"I have no clue, Donovan. How long?"

He paused. "You know, I really don't remember myself. I was just trying to make conversation."

We both laughed, and I felt 1000 percent better already.

"How did you get my number?" I asked him, remembering that I had only taken his. I had to admit, I was glad that he'd called, but I was leery about it at the same time. Especially after what had gone down with King yesterday.

"I have a confession to make. I spoke with your mom about a week before I moved here, and she gave me your number then."

I couldn't believe my mother. She never told me she had even spoken to Donovan, let alone given him my number.

"She never told me that. And why haven't you used it before now?"

"Well, the move and setting up the store were hectic. I never stopped saying that I was going to call, though. But seeing you yesterday was so good, so I decided today was better than tomorrow. I hope I'm not calling too early."

"No, you're not."

"I wanted to catch you before you got into your busy day."

Busy day? Donovan had no idea.

"Listen, I was actually calling for a reason. I don't know if you have plans for today, but I have to make a run out to Malibu. You live out there, right?"

I frowned. "Yeah, how did you know that?"

He chuckled. "You're King Stevens's girl. The world knows everything about the two of you."

I guess I still hadn't gotten used to that fact. Donovan was right. King was a star and was considered a public figure. And I guess that meant that I was too.

"So," Donovan continued, "I was just wondering if I could stop by your place, swoop you up, and you could go with me. Maybe you could give me a tour of Malibu at the same time."

"Well, I don't know Malibu all that well," I said, purely as a stall tactic. There was no way I could go out with him. Especially not after yesterday.

"That's okay. Maybe we can explore it together."

I didn't respond.

Not until he added, "Please, Heiress."

It was the way he said my name. So softly, so full of adoration, and friendly, of course, that made me say yes.

Plus, I needed to get out. Even if I didn't talk to Donovan about what I'd been going through, I'd get out and get some air. Maybe that would help to clear my thinking.

"Sure," I finally agreed. "How long will it take for you to get out here? I can meet you wherever you're going."

"I'm actually on my way now, so I'll be in Malibu in about thirty minutes." He gave me the address where he was going, and then I hung up.

Thirty minutes. I didn't have much time. I dashed into my closet and spun around, looking at all the choices I had. Why was I making such a big deal about this? I just needed to put on a pair of jeans. That was all. This was just Donovan, and it was not a date.

I jumped into a pair of jeans but chose one of my favorite white blouses, grateful for the long sleeves. I didn't need Donovan seeing my bruises.

When I slipped into my first pair of Louboutins, the red-bottom pumps completed the outfit.

I checked out all the angles as I looked in the mirror. I didn't know why I was so concerned about my appearance. Maybe it was the prospect of some male attention . . . from someone besides King. Maybe it was the fact that I was going to hang out with an old friend . . . someone who really knew me. Or maybe it was just that I was getting out of the house when I really needed to. Whatever it was, I was so excited when I grabbed my purse and jacket and slipped into the car.

I wasn't far away from where I had to meet Donovan, but when I got there fifteen minutes later, he was standing outside, waiting for me. I smiled when I saw him, pulling my car to a stop right in front of him.

"You made it," he said when I turned off the ignition and he opened my car door.

"You seem surprised." I chuckled and gave him a hug. His embrace was comforting, and I held on to him probably a little longer than I should have. But I needed the affection.

Sure, King held me. He'd held me early this morning, when I first got up. But at times after his hugs came his grabs. I needed this genuine affection, which had nothing to do with love, just friendship.

I followed Donovan inside a gigantic warehouse that was filled with glass, all kinds of glass.

"I'm glad you agreed to come out with me today."

His heart was so sweet, and my heart warmed.

"Thank you for inviting me. I needed to get out." I sighed.

I didn't know if it was my tone or the way I'd sighed that made Donovan sigh. He looked at me sideways. "A little trouble in paradise?" His tone was filled with concern and not a hint of sarcasm.

I paused. I needed to talk. I needed to talk. I needed to talk. But to Donovan? How could I talk to him about King?

Still, I needed someone, needed to do something. So I said, "Well, relationships are a roller coaster. And this one has . . . let's just say, a lot of loops."

"Loops? That's an interesting way to put it."

I nodded. "That's how I see it, because there are a lot of ups and a lot of downs." I sighed. "I guess I'm still getting adjusted to this life."

Suddenly we stopped moving, and Donovan put his hand on my shoulder. Looking me straight in the eye, he said, "Heiress, are you having problems?"

I didn't say anything, but I didn't have to, because Donovan watched me blink back tears.

He held me, but his touch was gentle, nothing like King's. "If you're having problems, you need to tell someone." He paused, as if he was waiting for me to say something. I didn't. He said, "It doesn't have to be me, but you need to talk to someone. Someone who can help you fix it."

I heard his words and let them digest, but then something inside of me got defensive. There was nothing to fix. Nothing was wrong. Didn't every couple have their problems? Wasn't this normal?

I blinked my eyes faster, keeping the tears away, and pasted a smile on my face. I needed to stop this conversation right now, before it got too deep.

"Thank you, but I'll be okay."

"Are you sure?"

I paused for a moment before I said, "Definitely. King and I are fine. Wonderful, actually."

Donovan stared at me a little longer; then he nodded slowly. "Okay."

We began to walk again in silence. At least a couple of minutes passed before Donovan said, "You remember that time in the fourth grade when we went on that field trip to the museum?"

It was a brilliant move to change the subject to something that he knew I would remember. Something that he knew would make me laugh.

"I remember that. You kissed me on the cheek in the IMAX theater, and we both thought that was such a big thing."

We laughed together.

"Yeah, I thought we were a couple after that, but you started hanging out with Charlie Thomas more than me."

"Oh, yeah. Charlie," I said, feeling a rush of new memories.

Charlie Thomas was the weirdest kid in our grade. He ate glue when we were in elementary school, and he was still doing that craziness in junior high. I could not remember how or why I started hanging out with him.

"I'm sorry about that, but you were my best friend, and even at that young age, I knew that I didn't want to ruin that."

"You should've ruined it, 'cause you were the love of my life," Donovan confessed.

"Love of your life?" I said, surprised. "That's a little over the top." I laughed. It wasn't like Donovan and I were ever an item. We had never dated; we'd been too young for all of that.

"I'm serious," Donovan said. "It's not over the top. You were the love of my life." And then he added, "Back then," I guess to soften what he'd said.

This time I didn't want to make fun of him. So I said, "I never knew that."

He nodded and looked straight ahead. "I think I've always been in love with you, but we were friends, so, like you said, there was no need to ruin that."

Now I was speechless. Donovan was serious, really serious. How did I not know this? We had spent our whole lives together, going to the same schools, the same church, and our parents were friends. We'd gone to the prom together, but that was because neither one of us had a date, and that was what friends were for, right?

Never once did I think he liked me for real. I wondered why he had never told me. Even more, I wondered why he was telling me this now.

"So, anyway, is there a lucky lady in your life?" I asked, glad that we were heading to the checkout section.

"No lady, yet. These Los Angeles women are too superficial for me."

"Oh, come on. They aren't that bad. You can find some really good women here."

As he began putting his items on the checkout belt, I reached into the basket to help him. At that moment, our hands touched as we both reached for a lighting fixture. I felt a spark. It was a spark that I'd felt only with King. A spark I thought I could feel only with him.

"I think I'll stick with my Midwest women," he said as our eyes locked together.

It took me a moment to break the spell, to let go of the fixture and turn my eyes away from him at the same time.

Okay, this was crazy. This wasn't like when we were kids. This wasn't even like it was when I was with him yesterday. This was chemistry, real chemistry. The kind of chemistry that was making me feel guilty.

"Listen, thank you for getting me out of the house, but I better get going," I told him.

"But—"

"No, really, I have to get home," I said, thinking about last night with King and this . . . chemistry I now felt with Donovan.

"But there is another stop I have to make, and I was thinking that we could grab lunch again."

"I'm sorry," I said, shaking my head, "but I have some things to do at the house before King gets home."

"Well, at least wait so that I can walk you to your car."

"No, that's okay," I said, truly wanting, needing to get away from him. "I'm fine. It's right out front, and . . . I'll be fine."

He frowned as I gave him a quick hug, then high-tailed it out of there like my hair was on fire.

My life was already complicated enough. I was trying to make things simple again. Take my life back to where it used to be. So I certainly didn't need Donovan. Especially not with all this newfound chemistry.

I jumped into my car and sped out of that parking lot, never once looking back in my rearview mirror.

Chapter 14

It had been a good week, and I wanted to keep it that way. That was why I hadn't argued with King when he said we were having dinner at his parents' house.

"That's what we're going to do for our first anniversary?" I'd asked.

"Yup!" He'd grinned, as if he'd just told me that he was taking me to the Taj Mahal. So if going to his parents was what he wanted to do, and if it was going to keep the peace, then I was all for it. It wasn't my idea of a romantic night, but it was fun enough, at least the way it was starting out as we drove to Beverly Hills.

"Do you know what it's like to show up on the set with one black shoe on and one brown shoe on?" he asked.

I laughed as I glanced at him behind the steering wheel. He always looked so good to me when he smiled, when he was this happy. "That's what I tell you about getting dressed in the dark."

"Well, I never want to wake you like that in the morning."

"I keep telling you that I love when you wake me in the morning. I hate to wake up and see that you're already gone."

He squeezed my hand. "See, this is why I love you."

I held his hand as we drove up La Cienega, thinking that this was how it was always supposed to be with us. When the Commodores came on the radio, King turned up the volume to the highest level and we sang along with Lionel Richie.

"Thirty-six, twenty-four, thirty-six, oh, what a winning hand!"

We laughed as we sang, both of us so far off-key. But it didn't matter, did it? We were in love. That was what we told each other when the next song came on. It was another oldie, another Lionel Richie song. Only this time he sang with Diana Ross. And King and I howled along.

"My endless love!"

I never wanted this car ride to end, because to me this was how it was supposed to be.

When we arrived, the Stevenses' housekeeper, Anna, met us at the door. "Mr. King, it's so nice to see you," she said through her thick Guatemalan accent. She wrapped her five-foot-two frame around his waist and attempted to pick him up, as if this six-foot guy was still a child.

"Anna, I'm a little bigger than I used to be."

"Well, you should have stopped growing."

I laughed at the two of them, deciding at that moment that this had really been a good move. Anna, who had worked for the Stevenses even before King was born, had already put King in a good mood. I knew that he loved this woman, who had spent as much time raising him as his parents had. He'd often said that she was like his second mom.

Anna turned her attention to me, gave me a hug, then took my shawl and purse.

"You two go on in there." She pointed toward the living room. "Your mother is waiting in there for you. I don't know where your father is," Anna said, shaking her head as she took my shawl and purse and King's coat away.

On cue, Mrs. Stevens appeared at the living room doors, looking like old Hollywood. She was so glamorous. She was a fifty-something-year-old woman who could have easily passed for King's sister. She reminded me of a younger version of Nancy Wilson.

"Look at the two of you," she said, holding out her arms. "Aren't you the picture of perfection?"

She was the one who was perfection, with her shoulder-length hair swinging casually in a bob. She was dressed in a peach pantsuit that made her cinnamon complexion glow.

Mrs. Stevens and I were just about the same height, so when she hugged me, we were eye to eye. Next, she turned and hugged her son before she stepped back and smiled at us like she was so pleased. Holding both of our hands, she said, "Heiress, you get more beautiful every time I see you. I hope my son is treating you right."

Every argument, every time King had grabbed me and tossed me around, flashed through my mind in an instant, and instinctively, I rubbed my arm where my bruise was just beginning to fade away.

I imagined myself opening my mouth and telling Mrs. Stevens everything. But I knew her statement was rhetorical. She didn't really want to know, and I didn't really want to tell her, especially not with King standing right here.

So all I did was nod and smile.

But King answered for both of us. "Mom, you know I try to treat my girl the best and to the best." King put his arm around me. "In fact, today's our anniversary."

"Really?" His mother frowned a little, but she had too much class to ask her son what he meant exactly.

"Yeah. We had our first date one year ago today." He grabbed me around my waist and kissed me on the cheek.

Again, all I could do was smile.

"Oh," Mrs. Stevens said. "That's so nice. Well, let's go
into the dining room. Dinner is waiting." She glanced
over King's shoulder. "Anna dear, can you fetch Mr.
Stevens and let him know our son and Heiress are
here?"

King grabbed my hand as we followed his mother to
their grand dining room. Everything was decorated so
beautifully. The twelve-person table was set like Mrs.
Stevens was about to entertain a dozen people for a
holiday dinner. Pewter candlesticks and fresh roses
adorned the center of the table, and the buffet against
the wall was covered with a feast that would make any
Southern black family proud. We might have been in
Beverly Hills, but the dishes that were spread across
the buffet top—macaroni and cheese, collard greens,
candied yams, rice and gravy, and, of course, chicken—
were straight out of the Carolinas.

My mouth started watering right away. King and
I didn't eat like this too often, since both of us were
always trying to be healthy. But tonight was a celebration—even if Mrs. Stevens didn't know it until a few
minutes ago—and I planned on having a good time.

"Mrs. Stevens, this all looks . . . and smells so wonderful."

"Thank you. It's just a little dinner," she said, waving
her hand as if this wasn't a big deal.

"Well, thank you for having us," I said as King pulled
out my chair for me. The perfect gentleman, making all
the right moves. My prayer was that this would put a
spark once again in our relationship. All I wanted was
for King to not be so stressed and for us to get back to
where we used to be.

"Well, look who's here." Mr. Stevens's voice boomed
throughout the room.

King stood up to greet his father, and after they hugged, Mr. Stevens leaned over and kissed me. "Welcome to our home, Heiress. It's so good to have you here." He pulled out the chair at the head of the table, then sat down.

"Where were you, Dad?"

Before Mr. Stevens could answer, Mrs. Stevens waved her hand. "You know where he was. In his man cave." She pouted a bit, and I couldn't tell whether she was playing with her husband or not.

Mr. Stevens laughed heartily. "Yes, my man cave, son."

King had told me all about the man cave, his father's studio, which was a large room behind the garage.

"Well, at least you joined us," said Mrs. Stevens. "I thought I was going to have to send a search party out for you."

"Don't mind my wife, Heiress," Mr. Stevens said as he laid his napkin on his lap. "She hasn't come to grips with the fact that I still have a career and hers died ten years ago."

An uncomfortable silence hung in the air for a moment, and I could tell that Mrs. Stevens was about to say something, but she held back.

"So what were you up to in there?" King asked his father.

I pretended that my focus was on Mr. Stevens, but really, I was watching King's mother from the corner of my eye. She sat across from me with her lips pressed together, as if she was fighting to keep her words, or maybe a scream, inside.

This was so interesting. In the year that I'd been with King, we hadn't been around his parents enough for me to have their family dynamics figured out. It was clear that they certainly weren't like my parents, who were always so loving with each other. At first, I'd attributed that to the fact that the Stevenses had a lot of money and my parents were working class. But there was more to this. I could see that now.

After we all filled our plates and returned to the table, Mr. Stevens asked, "So, son, how's that new project coming along? Feeling the heat yet?"

I'd heard this discussion between King and his father before. Almost every time we'd gotten together, his father said something that I knew made King feel just a bit insecure. If there was ever a time when King was not the confident actor, it was when his father started playing "whose career is bigger."

This made me wonder even more what kind of family this was. There were times when it felt like Mr. Stevens did want his son to surpass his accomplishments. At the same time, it seemed he loved pointing out that King had not yet achieved that level.

"Let the boy eat before you start pulling out the measuring stick," Mrs. Stevens interjected before King could respond.

If I were keeping score, I would've given that one to Mrs. Stevens. If I were cheering, I would've stood on my feet right now.

Instead, all I did was cut through my chicken breast and put a forkful of it in my mouth so that no one could ask me anything.

For the rest of the time, either we sat there in silence or the Stevenses exchanged sarcastic retorts. The battle was between Mr. and Mrs. Stevens; King and I were just caught in the cross fire.

While his parents bantered, King paid most of his attention to me. As his parents exchanged verbal jabs, King was being so sweet. He gazed into my eyes, kept whispering about how much he loved me, and kissed my cheek in between bites.

It was weird. In the middle of this hostile environment, I felt like King and I were on our first date. I relished every minute of it, not only because I enjoyed this attention, but because I had missed it too.

I had completely missed this man I'd fallen in love with a year ago, and I wanted to get on my knees and thank God for bringing him back to me. Maybe it was because he saw his parents and he didn't want to be like them. Whatever it was, I was thrilled to have King back.

After dinner, when his father asked him to go to the studio, I hated to see King go.

"You gonna be all right, baby?" King asked me.

But Mrs. Stevens answered for me. "Of course she'll be fine. She'll be with me." With her hands, she scooted King away and then led me to her music room, where Anna served us tea.

I had never been alone with Mrs. Stevens, and I didn't know what to expect. For a moment, I wondered if this was a setup. Had King set this up so that I could spend time with his mother?

As soon as Anna left us alone, Mrs. Stevens said, "The two of you seem happy."

There it was again. The chance to tell Mrs. Stevens what was going on. But after this dinner, was there really anything to tell?

I carefully calculated my answer. "I love your son. We've had quite a year." I took a sip of my tea, hoping that was enough for her.

"Dating King must be very different."

I frowned. "What do you mean?"

"Well, he's certainly not your average guy."

I nodded. "That's true. It does take time to get used to it. I'm still trying to get adjusted to the attention from the media and the fans when we go out. And then there's all the demands that come with the territory. Plus, I know it's stressful for him, so I just want to make his life as easy as I can."

Mrs. Stevens slowly lowered her cup onto the table. When she sat up and stared at me, I could tell that this conversation was about to get real deep.

She was silent for a while, as if she was contemplating exactly what she wanted to say. "You know, besides Marlaina, you're the only girl that King's ever introduced to me and his father."

I didn't know what I was supposed to say to that, so I just smiled.

She continued, "So, because of that and because I really like you, I'm going to let you in on a little secret."

That made me smile. As close as I was with my parents, I'd always hoped that the parents of the man I married would love me like a daughter. King and I weren't anywhere near ready to get married, and Mrs. Stevens had said she liked me, not loved me. Nevertheless, this was a good start.

"To be a Stevens woman takes patience, understanding, and sacrifice. The men of this family can be passionate, to say the least. I guess that's why most of them became actors. They need women like you and me in their lives to keep them grounded." She paused, and the way she searched my face, I could tell that she was trying to figure out if I understood her point. "I'm guessing you already know, since you have been with King for a year, that this isn't a cakewalk."

This felt like my chance to say something, even if it was only something small. So I tested the waters with, "Yes, ma'am. King and I have had . . . our moments."

With those words, the challenges of the past few months once again flashed through my mind, and again, I rubbed my arms. Then I took a deep breath.

King had been so different tonight, and I felt like this was a real change.

Mrs. Stevens said, "Well, sometimes as women we have to put up with a lot to receive a lot."

I didn't respond, since I wasn't sure if I believed it or not. So I just took another sip of tea.

"So does King know?"

I squinted. "Know about what?" I had no idea what she was talking about.

"About the baby," she responded nonchalantly, like she had just asked about a puppy or something.

Now I was even more confused. "I'm sorry, Mrs. Stevens, but what baby?"

It was her turn to look like she was confused. Then she leaned back and laughed as if I'd just told a joke. "Oh dear, you must know that you're pregnant. It's written all over you."

Pregnant? Me? I had no kind of vibe I was giving off. What was she talking about when she said it was written all over me? But one thing was for sure. . . . I was not pregnant. I didn't want to be pregnant. I wasn't ready for kids. . . . Heck, I didn't even know if I wanted to have babies. Right now all I wanted was for me and King to get back on even ground.

"I guess you really didn't know," she said.

I shook my head. "No, Mrs. Stevens, I'm sorry. But I'm not pregnant. King and I aren't even trying to have a baby."

She nodded. "Yes, you are. I have a sixth sense about these things."

I wasn't going to sit here and argue with her. I wasn't going to tell her that there was no way . . . except . . . I began to think of the feelings I'd been having. And the throwing up. When was the last time I had my period? I tried to recall.

"If I were you," Mrs. Stevens began, "I'd make an appointment with a doctor just to be sure before I said anything to King. Because if my son is anything like his father, he'll want proof . . . that you're pregnant and that it's his."

"That it's his?" I said, almost insulted. *Who else's would it be?*

Before I could say anything more, I heard King's voice right before he and his father came into the music room.

"Hey, babe." King kissed my cheek. "Are you ready to go?"

I was more than ready, and I nodded. After that little chat with his mother, I couldn't leave fast enough.

"I have an early call in the morning," he said to his mother.

I jumped out of my chair and went into the hall in search of Anna so that I could retrieve my shawl and purse and King's coat without having to wait. I wanted to get out of that house as fast as I could.

King and his parents met me at the door, and we said our good-byes before King and I both made a dash toward the car. I didn't know what had gone on with King and his father, but if it was anything like the talk I'd had with his mother, then I understood why he was running as fast as I was to escape.

Once we were in the car, King turned on the music. And though he held my hand when he could, most of the ride home was silent. I was fine with that; his mother had given me a lot to think about, a lot to figure out.

I took a sideways glance at King. What if I was pregnant? What would King say? What would we do? I closed my eyes and leaned my head back. I didn't want to think about that. But, really, that was all that was on my mind.

Chapter 15

I felt as I was sitting on death row, ready to be executed. This was just the doctor's office, but I swear, I felt like I was going to die.

I had never been a fan of doctors' offices, but today was especially horrid. From the way the waiting room was packed with women, a couple with crying kids, to the way I'd had to wait for more than thirty minutes past my appointment time before I was called in. Then there was all the explaining, the prodding and the blood tests, which always came with long needles, which I hated.

Yup, this was death row for real.

I'd done everything I could to postpone this visit for as long as I could. But by week three of spending most of my time hugging the toilet, I figured it was time to face whatever had my stomach so upset.

Maybe this was nothing. Maybe this was just a stomach virus, and all I would need was some kind of antibiotic. At least that was my prayer.

I'd prayed to God all night for a stomach virus. That would certainly be way better than what Mrs. Stevens had told me.

I swung my legs over the edge of the examining table as I waited for the doctor to return.

"Please, God . . ."

Just as I started that prayer, Dr. Robertson and a nurse finally returned. He held an electronic tablet in his

hand, and my first thought was that this was so cool. . . .
The medical field was going digital.

For a moment, I focused on the doctor's hands, wondering what kind of tablet he had. But I couldn't keep
my eyes away from the doctor's gaze forever, and when
I finally looked up, he spoke to me.

"All right, Ms. Montgomery. Your results are back."

I held my breath and counted silently, *One, two,
three . . .*

"It looks like you are indeed pregnant."

Four, five, six . . .

"Congratulations," the doctor said, with happiness
just dripping in his tone.

Seven, eight, nine . . . I didn't know why I was counting. Maybe it was to keep my mind from accepting this
truth. Because once I accepted it, I'd have to face the
fact of how horrible it would be to be pregnant.

Ten!

I was going to stop counting there because no matter
what, now I had to face this.

I asked, "Can you tell how far along?" I was surprised
that question even came out of me. This was impres-
sive; I was able to think when all I wanted to do was
die.

"I can't tell you that. Not until we do an ultrasound,
but you're at least eight weeks." With a stylus, he began
making notes on the tablet, and now my mind overwhelmed me with questions.

How was I going to tell King? Was he going to be
happy about this? Would he ask me for proof, like his
mother said? What about my parents? How was I going
to tell them? Did I want to tell them? I didn't even want
this child, did I?

I felt like I was drowning in this uncertainty, and
tears filled my eyes. It was clear. . . . I was in no way

mentally or emotionally ready for a child. I was still learning how to be a woman and learning how to have a relationship with a man. There was no way to bring a child into this mix.

As soon as the first tear spilled from my eye, I lost it. I began to cry uncontrollably.

"Wait, Ms. Montgomery," the doctor said as the nurse handed me a tissue. "I know it's overwhelming, but everything will be okay."

The nurse moved from behind him and came to the side of the examining table to comfort me. She rubbed my back, while the doctor sat on a small round stool and rolled right up to me.

He said, "So I take it that you're not happy with this."

I shook my head.

He paused. "Well, you're very early in your first trimester. You have lots of options."

Those words made me cry louder.

"No, no," he said, as if he was upset that he'd made me more upset. "You don't need to talk or think about any of that today. You have time. I just wanted you to know."

I tried to gather myself. There was no need for me to be acting like this in front of this white man. This was a personal situation that I needed to handle myself. With King. Maybe.

The doctor said, "Go home, get some rest, talk it all over with your partner, and then you can decide what you want to do. All right?"

I nodded.

"The nurse is going to give you some things to read over," he said as he scooted away from me before he stood. He nodded at her before he said, "Just give us a call when you make your decision, okay?"

I was able to squeak out an "Okay." I took a deep breath, then added, "Thank you, Doctor Robertson."

I waited until I was alone before I jumped down and put my jeans back on. I could have done this before. There was no need for me to stay undressed. But as I waited for this news, I just couldn't move.

Well, there was no need to sit and pray now. The facts were the facts—I was pregnant.

As I walked out of the examination room, the nurse met me with three pamphlets.

"Read over these," she said as she stuffed the pamphlets into my hands. "And then call us when you decide either way."

"Should I make an appointment?"

"No, not yet, because we'll need to know what you want to do." She put her hand on my shoulder. "Just take your time, think it through, and then let us know." She paused and looked me in my eyes. "Make sure you do what you have to do for yourself, okay? This is your decision," she said, sounding so motherly. "No one else's. Just yours."

By the time I made my way to the parking lot and slid into the car, I expected a flood of tears to come. But nothing came.

Still, I sat there, not really wanting to go home. Not until I had thought this all the way through. I thought about calling Blair, but this was one thing that I couldn't share with my best friend. Not until I talked to King. He deserved to know first.

As I sat and thought, my thoughts became clearer. Maybe this was a good thing. Maybe my being pregnant could bring King and me closer together. We hadn't ever talked about having a family; we hadn't even talked about getting married. But we could figure it out together, right?

King had just finished shooting, so at least the timing of this was good. He didn't have the stress of the movie, and tonight we planned to celebrate our anniversary again, which was three weeks ago.

So that was what we were supposed to be doing tonight. And we would celebrate two things, I guess. At least we'd be able to sit down together and talk about what we wanted to do.

This was going to be about my approach . . . how I decided to break this news to King. So I started the car and sped over to the Santa Monica mall. As I got closer, I began to feel better and better about this. Why shouldn't King and I have a baby? We were going to be together forever, right?

At the mall I was glad that at least one thing worked in my favor. It was a Tuesday afternoon, and so the mall was relatively empty. I was thankful for that, especially since I looked a mess. I didn't usually go out of the house this way, but I'd been feeling so bad, and this morning it was all I could do to put on enough clothes to make it to the doctor. So my loose T-shirt and my Levi jeans were the very best that I could do. And the bun that I'd wrapped my hair in was totally a mess.

My mood changed when I came upon a baby store and walked inside. The feeling of motherhood hit me, and I was overwhelmed with the love that could be entering my life.

Maybe I can do this. Maybe I can be a mommy. Those were my thoughts as I wandered through the store, checking out the clothes, which looked like they could fit a doll. I strolled by the onesies and the bibs and the shoes and the pacifiers, the cribs and the strollers. This place was like a baby heaven.

I stopped in front of a display of unique baby rattles. This was it! This was what I wanted. This was what

I needed to tell King that I was pregnant. I smiled as I held one of the rattles in my hand. I could see King and myself tonight as I presented him with this gift, wrapped, of course. And from there, we would decide what to do.

"Does shopping for babies give you anxiety too?"

I turned to face the woman next to me. She was tall and slender, with a short, asymmetrical bob. With her smooth, flawless skin and perfect smile, I was sure she was some kind of model.

"I've actually never done this before," I said and turned my attention back to the rattle.

She picked up a chrome rattle and began inspecting it. "I actually hate shopping for babies, and my little sister keeps having them just to spite me."

I couldn't help but chuckle, even though her comment seemed rather cruel to me.

"I'm Leslie, by the way." She stuck out her hand.

"Heiress Montgomery." I shook her hand firmly; then I turned away again. Really, I was not in the mood to hold a conversation, but that wasn't going to stop Leslie.

"So who are you buying a gift for?" she asked.

Dang, that seemed like kind of a nosy question to me, but I decided to tell her. "I just found out I was pregnant."

"Really?"

I nodded. "So I'm trying to find something to give to my boyfriend, a little gift to break the news." My words were interesting, even to me. I wasn't one who usually told my business to anyone, let alone a stranger. But, for some reason, I wanted to hear myself saying this out loud.

"Oh, wow. Well, congratulations. Are you excited?"

I shrugged. "Actually, I'm still in shock, so the excitement hasn't quite kicked in yet." What was wrong with me? It was like I was word vomiting. My personal business wouldn't stop coming out.

Maybe it was the look on my face that made Leslie say, "I'm sorry. I know I'm asking a lot of questions. I guess that's the therapist in me. I'm always in somebody's business."

Ah! So that was it. I knew there had to be something that made me open up to her so easily. Well, she was definitely in the right profession.

"That's okay," I said. "You don't have to apologize. I guess it's just easier sometimes to talk to strangers than to people you actually know."

She chuckled. "Well, that's a good thing. I guess that's why I stay employed." She returned the rattle to its shelf. "Look, I won't keep bothering you, but I do want to give you my card. Not saying you need a therapist or anything. Just in case you ever want to talk easily."

She handed me her business card, and I read the embossed words: LESLIE HUNTER, RELATIONSHIP THERAPIST. I stuck her card in my pants pocket and thanked her.

"Congratulations once again on your baby. I hope the excitement sets in soon."

Just as fast as she appeared, she was gone. For a moment, I thought about how strange it was to meet her here, but I put Leslie out of my mind and settled on the rattle that I was going to give King tonight.

The sales clerk wrapped it for me, and no more than thirty minutes later, I was pulling into our driveway.

Inside our kitchen our chef was already making dinner, but I stopped him.

"I want to cook tonight," I said.

He looked at me as if I'd lost my mind, and I couldn't blame him. There weren't many days when I took over in the kitchen, but I wanted to cook for King tonight.

"I want to make a romantic dinner."

"I know. It's your anniversary. Mr. Stevens told me." He smiled. "I'm going to cook something really good for you."

"Thanks, but I want to do it tonight," I said.

"Or I can do it, and we can say that you did it."

I laughed. "You really don't trust me, do you?"

He shrugged, but I convinced him to go home. I mean, I was no Paula Dean or anything, but I could handle myself in the kitchen. With the few skills that my mama had passed on to me, and the right cookbook, I was sure that I could make something happen. I decided on my mother's favorite: barbecued salmon. When I found the salmon fillets the chef had planned to cook in the refrigerator, it was on.

The sun was setting by the time I had everything ready: the dinner, the dining room, me. The food was cooked, I had the candles lit on the table, and I was wearing the red dress that King had just bought me.

King's favorite Sade CD was playing in surround sound, and I was ready. When I heard the key in the door, I said a quick prayer that tonight would be the beginning of a new adventure for me and King. There would be no more stress. He would be my king, I would be his queen, and we would get ready to have a little prince or princess.

I stood at the base of the stairs and waited for King to step through the door. As usual, I had only one word for that man—handsome. And he looked even better because of the two dozen white roses he held.

Before he could say, "Hey," I was in his arms, kissing him passionately.

"Happy anniversary, babe," I said when I finally had pulled away.

"Wow! We should celebrate like this every night."

"That's what I'm saying." I took his hand and led him into the dining room.

"Something sure smells good. Chef did his thing, huh?"

"Nope," I said as I presented the dining room table to him. "I cooked."

His eyes got wide. "You?"

I grinned and nodded. "I wanted to. Because this is our celebration."

He smiled as if he was very impressed and wrapped his arms around my waist. "This looks wonderful, baby. Thank you for doing all of this for me."

"For us."

I took the roses, which he still held, and stuffed them into a vase. I didn't want to take the time to cut them right now; I'd do that part later.

I led King to the head of the table, then served him before I sat down in the chair next to him. As we ate and chatted, the night felt magical. Like this was a fairy tale life. A fairy tale that I had a feeling would always last.

When his plate was empty, King reached for my hand. "Heiress, this was really nice. Just wonderful." He kissed my palm, and I got a tingle in my spine. "I have something for you." He leaned back in his chair, and from his jacket pocket, he pulled out the famous blue box.

I started to clap before he even gave me the box.

"This is for you . . . because I love you so much."

I took a deep breath before I opened the top of the Tiffany box, and it took a moment for my eyes to adjust to the twenty-four-karat canary-yellow diamond necklace.

"Oh my God!" I exclaimed. "Baby . . ." There were tears in my eyes when I looked up at him. "This is gorgeous."

"I thought you'd like it."

"I'm scared to put it on," I said. "This is just so beautiful."

"It's no more beautiful than you are," he said as he pushed back his chair and came around to where I sat. He lifted the necklace from the box and hung it around my neck. "You deserve it." He kissed my cheek before he returned to his chair.

I fingered the necklace for a moment as I thought about the fact that now it was my turn to give him a present. From the moment I'd found out about the pregnancy today, I'd talked myself down from being scared. But I felt the flutters in my stomach now, not having any idea how all of this was going to turn out.

My hands were trembling when I pulled the box from under my chair and slid it over to him.

"I, uh, got you something too."

His smile was wide and bright, as if he was delighted that he had a gift. He opened the box, and it seemed like we both held our breath at the same time. Slowly, he lifted the rattle.

"What's this?" he asked, frowning as he twisted the small microphone shape in his hand.

I took a deep breath, hoping that I took in enough air, because I didn't know when I'd breathe again. "Well . . . ," I began and then kept going. "I went to the doctor today because I've been feeling a little funny lately, and he told me that I was . . . I was . . . I was . . ." I couldn't get the rest of the statement out. But I guess I'd said enough, because his face registered that he'd received the message.

As his lips spread into a slow smile, I said, "Congratulations. You're going to be a daddy."

The silence that followed felt like it lasted a lifetime, and as I waited for him to respond, the flutters returned. Maybe I had read his reaction wrong. Maybe that wasn't a smile. Maybe that was a grimace of disgust. Finally, King looked up at me and his face was as bright as a Christmas tree and then I breathed.

"I'm going to have a son?" he whispered.

Even though his voice was low, I could hear his excitement, his joy.

"Well, it's way too early to know what we're having, but I guess having a son is a fifty-fifty possibility."

Another second, and then he jumped up and hugged me.

"Oh my God," he said, pulling me up from my chair. "Oh my God," he repeated. Then he kissed me as if it was our first time. So gently, so lovingly, so full of love.

I have to admit, his reaction was overwhelming . . . in a positive way. I was beyond happy.

"Baby, this is the best gift you could ever give me."

I squealed when he lifted me up and carried me from the dining room to the stairs, and then up the stairs to our bedroom. The entire time we kissed, and he broke away only long enough to say, "Thank you."

All through the night we made love. All through the night he said, "Thank you." And all through the night he told me how much he loved me.

By the time I laid my head on his chest, I was exhausted . . . exhausted from happiness and joy.

King's reaction was better than anything I could have ever imagined. As I closed my eyes, I tried to see into our future. We were going to be parents, and that meant a wedding was very near in our future too.

Chapter 16

I never understood what people were talking about when they said that a pregnant woman had a glow, that is, not until now. It was hard to explain the way I was feeling. All I could say was that I was loving every minute of every day.

It was like our baby had created a whole new King. The man treated me like a porcelain baby doll that he made sure would never break. He met my every need—things I asked him for, and things I didn't. Like the parties . . . he wasn't interested in having any more at our house. He was home much more, doing fewer interviews and having fewer meetings. And when he was gone, he checked in on me every minute that he could.

"How are you doing, baby?" he asked me over and over again.

I could hardly believe that this was the same man. If I had known this baby was going to change him in this way, I would've gotten pregnant long ago.

As much as I loved the attention, it was nice when I had a break. Just to bask in the truth of this pregnancy myself. So when King told me that he had to go back to the set to reshoot a scene for the movie that had just wrapped, I was thrilled. He'd be gone for the whole day, and I'd be able to do something that I'd wanted to do for a few weeks now.

Talk to his mother.

I hadn't spoken to Mrs. Stevens since the night she predicted my pregnancy, and I felt like I owed her this announcement in person. So as soon as King left, I called his mother and invited her for lunch.

"You've just been over here that one time," I said to her. "It would be nice if it was just you and me this time."

"I'd love that, Heiress," she said.

She agreed to be at our home at noon, and I had our chef set up lunch by the pool. As I sat and waited for King's mother, I let my eyes wander through the backyard. I'd always loved this spacious backyard with the pool. This was my favorite part of the property.

I smiled; this was going to be the perfect place for our child or children to play. My smile widened as I thought about children in the plural. Resting my hand on my belly, I whispered, "You're the first, baby."

I heard the doorbell and rushed to the front of the house. When I opened the door, we both smiled at the same time. Mrs. Stevens had arrived, looking absolutely flawless, as usual. Today she wore a black-and-white dress that flattered her petite frame, and like always, her hair and her makeup were perfect, natural.

Right then, I said a quick prayer that I would look half as good at her age.

"Heiress dear, you are glowing."

She kissed me on both cheeks, and I thought, *See? There's that glowing remark again.*

"Thank you. You look beautiful too, as always."

"This old thing? It's just something I threw on."

As we walked through the house, I informed her that since it was such a beautiful day, we'd be eating outside. We sat down at the patio table, and the chef brought us our salads. Mrs. Stevens looked around as if she was impressed with the way I was keeping her son's house. That was good. I wanted her to like me. Like I said before, I wanted her to think of me as a daughter, especially since I was carrying her first grandchild.

"So tell me, dear," she began without looking up from her plate, "how're you feeling?"

I really didn't know where to begin with that question. I was feeling so many different things, all of which were hard to describe. "I'm doing well," I began, knowing this was the perfect way to tell her the news. "I'm in . . . my morning sickness stage."

Now she looked up with a smile. "So I was right."

I nodded.

"Well," she said as she wiped the corner of her lips with her napkin, "how do you and King feel about that?"

"We're happy. We're really happy about this."

"That's good." She nodded.

"King has been really wonderful. When I told him, he was so excited."

Her smile widened, as if she was proud of her son. "I'd hoped that he would be. I'm glad to hear that."

She lowered her head once again, but even without her eyes on me, I could tell that there was a lot on her mind. I wasn't sure if her thoughts were about me or herself or what I'd just told her. Whatever it was, I could tell that she was thinking hard. It was like she was watching a movie and reacting to scenes in her head.

In that instant, I wanted to know everything about King's mother. I wanted to hear all that she had to teach me. She had to have an interesting story given her own success, and then being married to King's father. Whatever she had to tell, I wanted to know it all.

"Mrs. Stevens, can I ask you something?"

She glanced up. "Sure, dear."

"What exactly did you mean when you told me it takes a lot to be with a Stevens man?" I'd thought about those words quite a bit over the past few weeks, and now that I had her here, I was glad to have the chance to have her clarify.

Slowly, Mrs. Stevens let her fork fall to her plate. Again, she wiped her mouth with the napkin and then finished chewing her food before she spoke. "My husband used to say, 'Nothing else matters but the arts.'" She paused for a second, while she pondered the hurtful nature of that statement. "My husband has been acting since he was three years old. That's all he knows and all that he knew when he met me. Making your family a priority was not an easy concept for him."

Already I could hear her pain, and I began to wonder how deep I really wanted this conversation to go. Maybe it was best to change the subject. To keep this conversation and this visit as light as I could. But I didn't have a chance to make that decision.

Mrs. Stevens continued, "When you love a man who immerses himself so deeply in his craft, you begin to live with some interesting characters. Your life becomes very dramatic."

Who was she telling? I knew exactly where she was coming from. Every time King took on a project, his mood changed. It was as if he was living the role, even at home, even with me. So did that mean it was always going to be that way? No, it couldn't be. Because if Mr. Stevens had been like that all these years, I was sure Mrs. Stevens would've been gone by now. I mean, she had been married for almost thirty years, so something had made her stay. My first thought was that maybe she stayed because of the money, but then she had her own success.

"I'm not sure if King is like that," I said, trying to re-assure myself that he was different. I mean, really, he was. He never put his career in front of me. That wasn't our problem.

"King is a good man, but as his career grows, I see more and more of his father in him."

My heart felt like it didn't know whether to stop beating or to beat faster. For some reason, that state-ment seemed so eerie to me.

"Just be strong, Heiress."

It was time to change the subject. Mrs. Stevens had taken me way past the answer I was looking for. She'd gone deeper than I'd wanted.

I turned the conversation to her. "So how did you get started as a singer? Did you always want to sing?"

The melancholy on her face fell away. Her smile went from stiff to bright, and after a few minutes, I knew why. Mrs. Stevens laughed as she told me about how she began at the age of two in church, singing "This Little Light of Mine." Then she reminisced about her European tour when she was just nineteen, and I saw the bliss on her face when she recalled an affair she'd had in France with a French record executive.

The way she talked so fondly about motherhood and all the precious moments she could remember with King made my heart warm. I was ready for this.

Then she turned the conversation to me. She asked me about my family and where I'd grown up. I told her all about my upbringing and how my father made sure he attended everything I ever did, all my dance recit-als, the school plays, and every reception in which I received an award at school.

By the time she left, I felt like I'd achieved my goal, to get closer to King's mother. In just one afternoon we'd done that. Hours after she was gone, I couldn't get some of her words out of my head. I replayed the beginning of our lunch over and over again in my head. Phrases like "interesting characters," and "be strong," stuck out in my mind. She had made it sound like the Stevens men never stopped acting, even when the cameras stopped rolling. I didn't want to dwell on that, though. King and I were in a different place, a blissful place. He completely put his family first; he was nothing like his father in that way.

I was lying in our movie den, watching King's first movie, when he came home. I glanced up and saw his smile, but no words were spoken. He just leaned over, kissed my cheek, then stretched out on the sofa next to me, resting his head in my lap. I stroked his head as he kissed my belly for what felt like hours. These were the kinds of moments that I lived for. And this was why I finally let Mrs. Stevens's words leave my mind. Like I said, King was nothing like his father.

Now that we were about to have a child, things were different. We would be happy forever, and I fell asleep with King kissing my belly and with those thoughts on my mind.

Chapter 17

"Mom, it isn't that big of a deal." I rolled my eyes as I held the phone in my hand. Trying to keep my mother calm after hearing this news was next to impossible. I should've known that I wouldn't be able to do it over the telephone.

"Not a big deal?" my mother shrieked. "Heiress Denise Montgomery, you are pregnant by a man we haven't even met. That is a very big deal."

My mother had a combination of hurt and disappointment in her voice, and I knew there were lots of things that made her feel this way. First, she had very traditional values. I was supposed to go to college, get my degree, thrive in my profession, meet a man that they approved of, date for a while, get married, and *then* have children. The fact that I no longer worked, had moved in with King after only a few months of dating, and now was pregnant by him without marriage, or even parental introductions, was far more than she could take.

"I know this isn't the traditional way of doing things," I told my mother, "but really, I'm happy." I really was hoping that statement would tug on her heartstrings. What parent didn't want their child to be happy?

There was a pause, and then I heard the voice of my father. "Are we at least going to have an opportunity to meet him?"

I'd almost forgotten that he was on the extension, with the way my mother had been going on. "I'll ask King about his schedule and see when we can come to Ohio," I said.

With that, I heard the phone click and knew that my mother had had enough and had gotten off the phone. It hurt my heart to know I had upset her so much, but I couldn't help it that my heart had taken me in a direction that my mother didn't agree with. I wanted this family that I was beginning to build.

"How long do you think she'll be mad at me, Daddy?"

I had always been a daddy's girl. He was the only one who really understood me and gave me room to be myself.

"Oh, your mother will be fine. I'll talk to her. This was just a shock, that's all." He paused for a second and took a deep breath. "Are you sure you're getting everything you want out of life, princess?"

His question took me aback and at the same time made me feel bad. While I was growing up, something my father always told me was to get everything I wanted out of life, because my life belonged to me and I'd have only this one. When he felt like I was slacking or didn't have my priorities straight, he would always ask me that question.

"Daddy," I finally said, "I'm happy." Those were the only words I had to tell him. Now that my mother was gone and I could hear my father's disappointment, I wanted to get off the phone. But I would never tell my father that. I would never disrespect him in that way.

"Well, in that case, your mother is right. We need to meet him . . . and soon." The way he said that, I knew he meant business. If I didn't get King on a plane to Ohio soon, my folks would end up on our doorstep.

"Yes, sir. Daddy." And then I rushed the next words. "I love you and Mom both, and I'll talk to you guys later."

"Where do you have to go all of a sudden?"

I had to think of a quick excuse, or else I'd be on the phone for another hour, and I didn't have the fortitude to do this anymore.

"I have to run to the grocery store and pick up some things," I lied. "My cravings are ridiculous, so I want to just stock up." I knew pulling the pregnancy card on my father would work. I wasn't even sure what a craving was since I hadn't had any. I was still at the try-eating-without-being-nauseous stage.

"All right, baby girl. We'll talk to you later."

"Love you, Daddy."

"Love you too, princess."

We hung up, and I sat on the bed for a little while after, thinking over all that my parents had said. I really was sorry that I'd disappointed them, but I figured that once they saw me and King together, once they saw how happy I was, all would be forgiven. And they'd be just as excited about their first grandchild as the Stevenses were.

Jumping up from the bed, I decided that I needed to head to the store, after all. We did need a few things for the house, and our chef was fighting the flu at the moment. I threw on some jeans and a fly T-shirt and headed out.

The grocery store was relatively empty, which was always a great thing. I didn't have to worry about the stares from people who were sure they'd seen me someplace but couldn't quite place it. That was what happened when you were the insignificant other of someone who was significant. After grabbing a gallon of ice cream, I headed to the magazine aisle to pick up the latest editions of all my favorite fashion magazines. As soon as I got to the aisle, I froze.

On the cover of one of the tabloids was a picture of me, King, and some woman I'd never seen before. The headline LOVE TRIANGLE was splashed across the cover. My eyes roamed to other magazines, and there was the same story, front and center. What was this?

Glancing to my right and then my left, I made sure that no one was watching me as I picked up one of the magazines and turned to the story, which was entitled "Has King's Queen Been Dethroned?" I kept reading the article, which reported that King Stevens had a secret lover, while his pregnant girlfriend sat home, crying. There were shots of King and this petite, trashy-looking woman leaving a club, a restaurant, and even a hotel.

Pushing that magazine back in place, I picked up another one. One article had a picture of what was supposed to be my sonogram, but it was of an almost fully developed baby and I wasn't even showing yet. So that was obviously a false story. Was the other story a lie too? I didn't know how to react to all of this, so all I did was gather the magazines that had King's picture splashed on the front and toss them into the cart I was pushing.

On the ride home, I could feel my anxiety building, but I did everything that I could to push it back down. There was no need for me to get upset. First of all, this kind of stress wasn't good for my baby. Secondly, it was all lies, anyway. So why would I get upset about a lie?

At home I was surprised to see King's car in the driveway. I thought he'd be at the gym a little longer. It still amazed me that he left home to work out when we had a fully equipped gym in our home, but King said that he needed to have other people around him. So he went out just about every day.

The moment I put the key in the door, it swung open and King grabbed the two bags from my hands. I held on tight to the magazines I purchased, hiding their covers from sight.

"Baby, let me help you with those." He kissed me on the cheek. "Why didn't you wait until I got home to go shopping? I would've done all of this, or I could've gone with you."

I walked behind him toward the kitchen. I sat in our breakfast nook as he unpacked the groceries, and as he moved, I tried to put him together with the man that the tabloids had written about. I just couldn't make the connection. The man they were talking about wasn't the man who was in front of me now. The man they were talking about wasn't the man who had made my life perfect since he'd found out that I was pregnant.

Still, I'd often heard that where there was smoke, there was fire. And the girlfriend was always the last to know. So I needed King to tell me that it was all untrue. I needed him to call those journalists liars. I formed the words in my mind so that they didn't come off as accusing him of anything. But the moment I opened my mouth, my heart started pounding.

"Babe," I began, "I saw these magazines at the store and wondered if you had seen any of them." I spread the magazines across the table so he could get a good look at each and every one.

He walked over, glanced down, and had no reaction. He didn't twitch, didn't flinch. But then, suddenly, he broke out in laughter. "Baby, I know you don't believe this stupid gossip trash."

His reaction completely caught me off guard. I expected him to be as shocked as I was.

"Well, it is a little shocking to see you and some woman creeping around. I mean, they have pictures."

I paused and softened my voice, because I didn't want to sound too aggressive. I asked, "Are you seeing her?"

He stopped laughing, and when he looked at me this time, his face was stiff with seriousness. "Heiress, listen. Those magazines make their money by printing lies." Then he walked away and went right back to the groceries.

I guess for him, the conversation was over. But not for me. I still wanted to know who the woman was. I mean, they had pictures!

I got up from the table and followed behind him. "Okay, so who is the girl?"

He whipped around, and now all seriousness was gone. Now he was just irritated. "Why are you questioning me like this?"

I shrugged, hoping that would diffuse the situation just a little. "Because I just want to know." I left out the part about needing to know if there was something going on.

He sighed as if this was all getting on his nerves, but he answered, "She's a friend I've known for years. We hung out when I was on location." He looked me dead in the eyes, raised his voice, and added, "Now drop it." He stomped away from me, back to the table. And with a single sweep of his arms, he grabbed the magazines and threw them in the trash.

A part of me wanted to apologize for not trusting him, but he walked out of the kitchen, leaving me standing there, wondering why I had pushed him like that. There was no reason—I knew they were lies. Just like the picture of the sonogram. If I couldn't believe one, I shouldn't believe any of them. Plus, I should just believe in my man. King would never cheat on me. Especially not now, now that we had a baby coming.

I just prayed that I hadn't messed everything up. For the rest of the day King stayed locked in the studio downstairs, and I stayed in the den. I wanted to go to him, tell him that I was sorry, but I decided that I'd give him space to cool down. I waited until I heard him go up to our bedroom before I got up, went upstairs, then crawled into bed next to him.

He kept his back to me, and I sighed. He needed to know that I was sorry and that I did trust him. Plus, I wanted to get back on this path of bliss that we'd been on. Wrapping my arms around him, I gently kissed his head. "I'm sorry," I whispered in his ear.

He didn't budge.

I could feel the tears forming in my eyes, but I didn't give up. I kissed him and apologized. Apologized and kissed him.

Still, there was nothing from him.

Finally, I rolled over, because I couldn't hold my tears back and I didn't want them falling on him. Then, a moment later, King rolled over and wrapped his arm around my waist.

My eyes were still filled with water, but at least my heart was smiling. I didn't have a thing to worry about. King was mine, I was his, and whatever those magazines said didn't matter. They didn't matter at all.

Chapter 18

I had been calling Blair for weeks, and I just kept on getting her voice mail. I didn't want to leave a message that I was pregnant. That was something I wanted to tell her in person, or at least live on the phone.

"Heiress," King called out. "If you're not down here in two minutes, I'm leaving without you."

King had been rushing me for the last five minutes. He was leaving for a promotional tour for the movie he filmed in Connecticut, and I had insisted that I ride with him to the airport. I hung up the phone without leaving another message on Blair's answering machine and ran downstairs.

"How is it you were the one who wanted to come with me, but you can't be ready on time?" King said once I made it to our foyer.

"I'm sorry, babe. I was trying to make a phone call, but I'm ready now."

Our driver, Al, carried King's bags to the car, and I locked up the house after we walked out.

This was the first promotional tour King was going on since we'd been together, so I really didn't know what to expect. I just knew that he was going to be gone for two, maybe three weeks, and I wasn't crazy about being alone all of that time.

In the back of the car I snuggled up to King, but he didn't seem to notice me. The phone was pressed to his ear. First, he talked to his agent, then his manager, and finally the studio's publicist. By the time he hung up, we were at the entry to LAX. While Al retrieved King's bags from the trunk, King and I had a private moment together.

"Don't look so sad, Heiress. I'll be back before you know it." With the tips of his fingers, he lifted my chin and kissed me softly.

"I still wish I could go with you."

"Come on now," he said gently. "We've been over this. All the ripping and running would just be too much for you and the baby."

"I know."

"You're going to be fine."

"I know. Promise that you'll call me whenever you get the chance."

"I promise. You'll be sick of hearing from me."

I chuckled a little, though I was not happy. "That will never happen."

He kissed me again, then without another word, he slipped out of the car.

I watched as he checked in with the skycap and then headed into the terminal. It took everything I had not to cry, but I made sure I didn't shed a tear. I was trying my best not to make a big deal of this. This was part of King's life, it came with the territory, and it was the life that I'd chosen.

When I couldn't see King anymore, Al pulled the car away from the curb. As he headed out of the airport, I pulled out my cell and tried Blair's phone once again. But just like before, my call went straight to voice mail. What was this about this time? Was something wrong, or was Blair avoiding me purposely? Either way, my feelings were hurt. When we'd gotten together last time, Blair promised that we would stay in touch. So why hadn't she kept that promise?

"It's probably that man," I whispered. That thought hurt my feelings even more. Even though King was the center of my life, I made time and room for Blair. Oh, well, there was nothing I could do about it. I settled back into the leather seat and closed my eyes, deciding to just enjoy the ride back to Malibu.

But then my eyes popped open. I was out, King was gone, and there was something I wanted to do. "Al, minor detour. Swing me by Rodeo Drive, please."

While I was in the city, I could at least stop by and apologize to Donovan for running out on him weeks ago at the warehouse. I hadn't talked to him since, and I knew that it was incredibly rude to just leave him hanging and confused. Maybe I could treat him to lunch.

I really wanted to do this, because my life was all about King. I didn't have my own friendships, which was clearly obvious with what was going on with Blair. So I wanted Donovan to know that I thought of him as a friend. As we got closer to Rodeo Drive, I gave Al the general vicinity of the store, since I didn't have the exact address, and we found it easily.

"Okay, I'll give you a call when I finish shopping," I told Al as I climbed out of the car.

Taking a deep breath, I proceeded into the shop, but then I stopped. It was complete madness in the store. Clerks, who were dressed in all black, wore headpieces and tried to service all the customers. I wasn't sure if a tour group had come in or what, but there were more customers than the store could hold. People were shoulder to shoulder, picking up items, asking for the prices. The space was so crowded that I imagined if someone turned around too quickly, they would hit a table and knock over one of Donovan's gorgeous pieces.

As a short blond clerk passed in front of me, I stopped her. "Excuse me. I'm looking for the owner," I said, figuring it would be much better for me to find Donovan that way rather than pushing through this crowd.

"He's busy at the moment, so he doesn't have time to talk to customers," she said sharply. "Is there something I can help you with?"

"No," I said slowly, trying to be patient. "I'm a close friend of his, and I wanted to speak with him."

"Well, like I said, ma'am, he's busy."

Now I had an attitude. "I'm sure if you tell him that I'm here, he'd want to see me."

"Why don't you try coming back later?" she said, as if she could dismiss me like that. "Or if you want to leave your name, I'll tell him you came by."

Okay, now I was about to go off. Who did this woman think she was? Matter of fact, who did this woman think I was? I refused to have a Julia Roberts in *Pretty Woman* moment. She was about to hear all of my mouth.

"Stephanie, thank you. I can take it from here."

Donovan appeared out of nowhere and saved Miss Stephanie from a serious black girl butt whupping. She gave me a final glance up and down, then turned to help another customer. I almost reached out to snatch that horrible bleach job out of her head, but then I felt a flutter in my stomach and remembered that my stress was my baby's stress. I had to calm down.

"I'm sorry about that," Donovan said. "My staff gets a little on edge when we have rushes like this."

Little did he know that no explanation was needed, especially not after the way he flashed that beautiful smile at me. He made me forget all that had taken place less than thirty seconds ago. "It's okay," I said, sudden-

ly feeling like it had been no big deal. "I understand."
Then, lowering my voice, I asked, "Is there somewhere
we can go and talk?"

"Sure. My office."

He led me out of the crowd to the back, passing his
stock area along the way. There were tons and tons
of wineglasses, vases, dishes, and other unique items
that he displayed throughout the store stocked up in
the back. Finally, we reached his office, and he tried
to quickly organize the papers on his desk before he
pulled a chair up for me to sit down. He sat in a smaller
chair right next to me.

"It's really great to see you," he began. "After you ran
out on me that way, I wasn't sure if I'd ever hear from
you again."

"I know. That's why I came. I wanted to apologize for
that and for not calling you after." I dropped my head,
thinking back to how I'd acted that day. Not calling
Donovan since then was really unforgivable.

Donovan chuckled. "Heiress, it's cool. We've known
each other way too long to have hard feelings about
things like that."

Relieved, I smiled. It wasn't that I thought that he
would hold that against me. Donovan had always been
so easygoing. He never took things to heart, never got
his feelings hurt too easily. I was just glad that he accepted my apology.

"Well, I still want to make it up to you. Can I take you
to lunch?"

"You don't have to make anything up to me, but I'm
not going to say no to free food."

I laughed as I got up quickly and grabbed my purse.

"Unfortunately," he began, stopping me in my tracks,
"I can't leave the store right now. I won't get out of here
until around six. So . . . can we make it dinner?"

I paused. The thought of heading all the way back to Malibu and then turning around to come back to Beverly Hills didn't really appeal to me. But I did owe Donovan at least that. Plus, if we had dinner together, I'd have company for the evening, rather than being in the house all by myself, doing nothing.

"Okay, but can we pick a restaurant in between here and Malibu?"

"Sure, that would be great. I'll call you before I leave here and we'll figure it out."

"Great! Let me just call my driver."

"A driver, huh?" he kidded me.

I waved him away, called Al, then followed Donovan as he led me out of his office, back through the crowd of people. When we finally reached the front door, he gave me a hug and a kiss on my forehead, which sent chills up my spine. That was the second time his touch had affected me like this. What was that all about?

I pushed that awkward feeling to the back of my head and walked across the street to where Al was parked. As I slipped into the car, I couldn't forget the way Donovan's hug made me feel. I hoped tonight wouldn't be uncomfortable. All I wanted was to have a little fun with an old friend.

Inhaling deeply, I settled back in the car. I needed to get some rest since I was going out tonight. Just then my cell phone rang. I looked down, hoping it was King to tell me he had made it safely, but an unknown number flashed across my screen. My first thought was that it was Donovan like before, but I had programmed his number in my phone.

"Hello?" I cautiously answered.

Blair's voice rang out. "No, I'm not dead, so you don't have to ask."

"Well, that's good to hear. Now I have the opportunity to kill you," I responded playfully. "How dare you go this long without talking to me? And what number are you calling me from?"

"My new cell. I lost my other one, and I'm just now getting a new one." That was understandable, and I was relieved to hear that she wasn't ignoring me.

"Blair, I have so much to tell you. I'm not sure I can do it all over the phone." I wanted to see Blair. I needed us to hang like the old days before I became someone's mommy.

"Okay. Why don't we meet sometime this week?"

We made plans to meet at her place and maybe hit Venice Beach. I hung up, feeling at ease. I was having dinner with Donovan tonight and hanging with Blair later on. Even though King was gone, I was thankful to have my friends around to keep me occupied.

Chapter 19

The time between seeing Donovan at his shop and meeting him for dinner flew by. His phone call jolted me out of my nap, and we settled on going to an Italian restaurant in Malibu. Of course that made me glad. Since I was driving, I was thrilled that I wouldn't have to make that trip all the way to Beverly Hills by myself.

I slipped on a black after-five pencil skirt dress that still made my figure look good even though my bump was starting to show. I made sure my makeup was soft and not overdone, then tussled with my hair to put all the curls in place. I scanned myself in the mirror one more time, and I had to admit, I looked good. Then I paused. Why did I care about how I looked? This was not a date. This was two friends going to an innocent dinner. I had a boyfriend and I was pregnant, for God's sake.

Surprisingly, the restaurant was less than twenty minutes away from my house, and when I arrived, of course, Donovan was standing outside, waiting for me. I took in his outfit as I pulled up to the valet. He had on black slacks and a blue button-down shirt that was slightly unbuttoned at the top. It suited him to a tee.

He opened my door before the valet could reach my car. After he gave my keys to the attendant, Donovan followed me into the restaurant. Once we were seated at a table in the back of the restaurant, he said, "Heiress, don't take this the wrong way, but you are wearing that dress."

I looked away from him and felt my cheeks grow warm. Why was I acting this way? Like I was a schoolgirl with my first crush? Dang! I was a grown woman in a committed relationship, and I was pregnant. I needed to get my mind right. As I glanced over the menu, I felt Donovan's eyes on me. Then I tried to take quick glances up at him, but every time I looked up, he was looking at me.

Finally, I just had to ask him, "Why do you keep staring at me?"

"I'm just honored that you got so dressed up for me. You look so good that if I'd known you were going to look this good, I would've worn a tux."

I laughed. It was crazy. Why did I get so dressed up? Most of the people around us were in casual pants or nice jeans.

"Oh, well. I can go home and change if you want." I moved, pretending that I was going to get up, but Donovan grabbed my hand and pulled me back into my seat.

"Don't you dare get up and leave me. Just sit and let me admire how beautiful you are."

This time the silence was comfortable for me as we both scanned the menu, trying to decide what we were going to eat. Not even ten minutes had passed, but already I was having a great time.

When I put my menu down, having made my selection, Donovan was once again looking at me. I had to admit, it felt good to have him look at me this way. With each passing day, I was becoming more self-conscious about my body, because soon, I knew, I would be as big as a house. But right now Donovan gazed at me as if I was a beautiful woman.

"So, Donny, how have you been since the last time I saw you?" I tried to take the attention off of me for a moment.

"Busy."

"I saw that. The store seems to be doing well." I was proud of the success he seemed to be having. And for a moment I felt a tinge of regret. Donovan was living his passion, and I'd tossed my passion aside.

"Yeah," he said, "we had an article in *Couture Home Living* magazine a few weeks ago, which really seemed to attract a lot of business." His eyes sparkled as he talked about the store. And as he told me more about the magazine's interview, I remembered how Donovan had always been fascinated by shapes and objects as we were growing up. Who would've ever known that his fascination would become his passion and then such a successful business?

As the night went on, we fell right back into our old vibe. We were a long way from the days when we used to hang out with each other and our other friends in each other's basements, but as we chatted, that was how it felt. Being here with Donovan was so easy and comfortable, and I cherished his company. We talked about everything from politics to all the fun times we had together.

And then he shocked me. He pulled out a picture of us at the prom and handed it to me.

"Oh my God, Donny. I can't believe you still have this." I laughed at the ridiculous photo, which was turned up at the corners and browned on the edges. We were only seventeen, thinking that we knew it all. I had thought I looked good with my big hair and my silver, sleeveless polyester dress. But Donovan wasn't much better. He had braids and wore flip-down glasses like Dwayne Wayne from *A Different World,* as if he was determined to bring back that style. He had on a cream suit with a silver tie and vest that matched my dress.

"Those were the days, huh?" he said, his voice filled with as much amusement as mine.

"We thought we were doing it back then." I couldn't stop laughing as tears fell from my eyes.

"I thought I was *GQ*," he said with such a serious, straight face that I laughed even harder. There was nothing about this picture that yelled *GQ* at all.

It took me a few more minutes to compose myself and catch my breath. I gave Donovan back the picture and told him never to pull it out again. I would have preferred he burned it, but he grinned and tucked it right back into his wallet.

"I needed that laugh, Donny." I wiped the tears from my eyes, trying not to smear whatever was left of my makeup.

"You know, you're the only person who still calls me Donny." He reached for my hand.

"You'll always be Donny to me."

Sitting there, with Donovan holding my hand, felt good, felt nice, felt natural.

After a couple of silent moments, he asked, "Heiress, are you happy?"

I sat back a little; his question had caught me off guard.

He added, "Are you happy with where you are in your life?"

Had this been anyone else, I would have immediately responded yes. And then I would have talked all about King and our baby. But sitting here with Donovan, looking into his eyes, I couldn't find the words to form the right answer. So instead of answering, I asked my own question. "Why do you ask that?"

"I just want to make sure. I've known you for a long time, and I know that sometimes on the surface you may seem happy, but I've always been able to see through your mask."

I took my hand back from his grasp. I should have opened my mouth and given him my soliloquy on my relationship, and on how being with King and having this baby were more than I ever thought I wanted. Then I should have thanked him for dinner, driven home, called King, and told that man how much I loved him. Instead, I didn't do any of that. I sat right there and looked into Donovan's eyes. Eyes that were filled with such genuine care . . . and desire.

A couple of minutes passed, but I felt like I needed to answer Donovan's question. "I'm living each day to find out. But I'm sure that I'm moving toward happiness."

He nodded, and then for the rest of our time together, we ate. We did chat a bit, but the dynamics between us had changed. By the time Donovan walked me out of the restaurant, I was back to feeling comfortable with him again, though his words still rang in my ears.

"I hope we can hang out more often than every blue moon," he said as he helped me into the car.

"Definitely."

He grinned, as if he'd just won a prize. "Then I'll call you tomorrow," he said excitedly.

A smile was on my face from the time I left that restaurant until I settled in bed. I didn't even notice that King had never called me to let me know that he'd made it to New York. All I could think about was how wonderful it was to be rebuilding my friendship with Donovan.

And I couldn't wait until tomorrow.

Chapter 20

I met Blair at Venice Beach, and as always, she was stunning. I had no idea what she had going on or who this new man was, which was unusual since we told each other everything, but it was doing her good. Her khaki shorts and cute tank top complimented her frame perfectly. I couldn't help but feel fat around her. We walked along the beach, trying to catch each other up on what had being going on.

"Every time I see you, I still can't get over how great you look," I declared, complimenting her.

She didn't respond. She just grinned, as if she was thinking about what was making her look so fabulous.

"I guess the mystery man has really got you going," I said, trying to pry some information from my bestie.

"Yeah, we're enjoying each other."

"So when can I meet him?"

"We're not at that stage yet," she said quickly. "I actually really like this guy, so I'm doing something different."

I could understand where she was coming from. There was something about love for a man that made you do things outside of your norm. I thought it was sweet that someone had Blair this open. As long as she was happy, I was happy.

"What about you? Still living the fairy tale?" She turned her attention on me.

"For the most part," I began. "I mean, he has been really great ever since we found out I was pregnant." I held my breath, waiting for her response.

"Pregnant? W-wow!"

I couldn't tell if she was happy for me or shocked or what. I had waited so long to tell her the news, I guess I expected a different reaction. I wanted her to be happy and excited for me. We walked in silence for what seemed like forever, trying to gather our thoughts.

"So?" I finally responded.

"So what?"

"Are you excited for me?"

"Oh, yes. Yes!" She grabbed me and wrapped her arms around me tightly. "You're going to make me an auntie."

I breathed a sigh of relief. "Oh, thank God," I said as we parted.

I told Blair how King and I had dinner at his parents' house and his mother was the one who told me I was pregnant. She seemed just as taken aback as I was when she heard that. I went on and on about everything that had happened in the past few weeks. It felt really good to talk to her openly and honestly. She seemed to be the only person I could do that with. When I got into King's mood swings, the energy of our conversation shifted.

"Well, what are you doing?"

"Excuse me?" I was extremely offended that she asked me that.

"I meant for you. What are you doing for you?"

I couldn't answer the question.

"Heiress, maybe you should get a hobby or something. Occupy some of your time. Join a charity or something. That's what a lot of athletes' wives do. I know I would definitely do it."

Blair was right. Maybe I needed to do something that I cherished so I could regain happiness within myself. Writing was the only thing other than King that I absolutely loved. It was my world once, and I thought it was time to return to it.

"I could do some freelance writing."

"See? There you go. Get back on that horse. King is out there doing his thing. Go do yours."

I knew there was a reason I wanted to talk to Blair so badly. She understood what it took to make me look at things differently. She wasn't negative about anything or discouraging. She was the one to tell me that I had the life that most women dreamed of, and I just had to make it work for me in all aspects. There was nothing like a woman who knew how to deal with a man who had fame and fortune to coach you through it.

We spent the rest of the day together, enjoying the city like two high school teenagers. I was able to get her to give me a little detail on her mystery man, but not much. She must've really wanted to keep this relationship in tact not to share the good stuff with me. Nevertheless, I was happy for her, and I was basking in my own happiness.

Chapter 21

It had been a little over a week since Donovan and I had dinner, and we had hung out almost every day since. He took me to the Los Angeles County Museum of Art, we had lunch on Redondo Beach, and we even headed up to Six Flags Magic Mountain, going on rides, eating cotton candy and funnel cakes like we were kids.

Hanging out with Donovan was refreshing. It was like I had a real friend, and I didn't have to be worried about swarms of women—and even men sometimes—attacking us as we walked around.

Today was the first time I was going to Donovan's warehouse, all the way up in Pasadena. I couldn't believe it wasn't closer to his store, but he said he creates better away from work.

"I want you to come to my place so that I can show you something," he'd said.

"What?" I had asked him.

He wouldn't tell me, and now, as I drove up the Pasadena freeway, the suspense was killing me. With my GPS system, it didn't take me long to find Donovan's place, an older building sitting high on a mountain.

The view from the street was absolutely breathtaking. I felt like I could see all of Los Angeles below me. But the building . . . wasn't so amazing. It was old—at least seventy-five years old—and looked worn down. Actually, it looked almost abandoned.

I stumbled along the dirt walkway in my three-inch heels and knocked on the metal door. After a moment Donovan slid the door back, wearing nothing but jeans and a white undershirt.

"You made it." He greeted me with a smile and a hug.

"What the heck are you doing way up here, in the middle of nowhere?"

He released his grip on me and slid the door open wider to reveal this huge warehouse with all kinds of machines.

"What is all of this?" I was confused and amazed at the same time.

"This is where I create all my pieces."

I was just stunned at the amount of machinery that he had. It looked like he had every piece of equipment any glassmaker could ever need to make whatever he or she wanted. They ranged from old machines that looked like they didn't even move, let alone work, all the way to top-of-the-line equipment.

"Do you operate all this by yourself?"

"No. I usually have a team of people here, but I shut production down today."

Until this moment, I had no idea how massive the process of making glass was. I could only imagine what this place looked like when people were here working.

"Do you still come here yourself and make some things?"

"Absolutely. I come here mostly at night, when everyone is at home. That's when I feel most creative. I think it's this view," he said, pointing to the massive window. "The city's skyline gives me a lot of inspiration. Sometimes I stay here till dawn, just to watch the sun rise."

He walked over to this big machine and turned it on. It took a little minute for it to crank up, and it hummed loudly. "This is Darcy. She's the first machine I bought when I was eighteen. She was made eighteen-ninety-two." He started turning some handle that made a part of the machine move in circles.

"Darcy? As in Darcy Phillips from high school." I laughed. Donovan had named his first machine after his first girlfriend. He and Darcy had dated in the tenth grade, for all of three months. He was so in love with that girl, but she broke his heart when she went off with Stevie Quimby.

"Let's not start with the jokes." He cranked the machine, and I sat down on a nearby stool.

I was fascinated as I watched him work, going back and forth, blowing out the glass into different shapes. It took thirty minutes to create one beautiful drinking glass. He set it aside to let it rest for a while, and then he took me to the roof of the building. There were chairs waiting for us, along with a wine and cheese basket.

"I loved watching you work. Wow, you really love what you do," I told him.

He nodded, and I looked toward the downtown skyline, trying to remember the passion I'd had for writing. It had been so long since I had written anything more than a thank-you card. And though I'd missed writing before, I didn't realize how much until I watched Donavan today.

"You know how it is when you love something," he said. "Your passion is who you are."

My spirits dropped even more when he said that. He was right; my passion for journalism was who I used to be. But I'd traded in my love for writing for my love for King.

"Donny," I said suddenly, "I'm pregnant." The words came out of me in a desperate attempt to change the subject. But as soon as I'd made that confession, I regretted it.

His eyes got big, then small, then big again. "Wow. Congratulations," he said with mixed emotions in his voice. Glancing down at my stomach, he asked, "How far along are you?"

"Almost seventeen weeks now."

We sat in an awkward silence for a moment. It was obvious neither one of us knew what to say next. Why in the world had I let that slip out?

He leaned forward, getting closer to me. "Are you happy?" he asked, looking deeply into my eyes.

There was that question again.

He said, "I mean, are you happy about this? Is this what you want?"

I stared back at him, and I could tell that he wanted me to say something, give him some kind of sign that said, "Rescue me." But I couldn't give him that.

"You've asked me that before, and I can honestly say that I am. I never thought I wanted children until now."

Donovan didn't look away. It was as if he felt that if he could stare me down, he could break me down. But finally, surprisingly, he gave me a smile. "Well, then, I'm happy for you. I think you'll make a wonderful mother." He hugged me like he never wanted to let me go.

It was comforting to know that I still had his support.

"Do you have anywhere you need to go?" he asked.

I shook my head.

"Do you want to stay up here and watch the sunset? I'm telling you, it's one of the most beautiful sights."

"I'd love to."

"Okay, let me go downstairs and get you something to drink," he said, "since you can't have this." He took the bottle of wine from the basket. "I'll be right back."

He returned with a bottle of sparkling cider. We didn't say much. Just sipped and snacked on the cheese and crackers. And then, just like he promised, I had a front row seat to one of the most beautiful sights as the sun bowed in the horizon, setting the sky ablaze with every color in the rainbow.

Finally, Donovan walked me down to my car, and just as I was getting in, he handed me the shopping bag he'd been carrying.

"What's this?"

"The glass I made earlier."

"Oh my God," I said, pulling it out of the bag. "This is beautiful." Looking up at him, I added, "You know that I'll cherish this forever."

It was another wonderful day with Donovan, and by the time I got home and went to bed, I didn't even want to call King. I didn't want to risk catching him in the wrong place or at the wrong time and upsetting him.

So I texted Donovan to let him know that I'd made it home and to thank him again for such a beautiful day. I shut off my phone before he could respond and closed my eyes.

I didn't shut off my phone often, but tonight I wanted uninterrupted sleep and dreams filled with the beauty of my day.

Chapter 22

The screams were ringing in my ears. I was pinned on the floor by the security guard who had tackled me from behind. It was all a blur to me, and all I could do was stare at King's lifeless body. The pool of blood that surrounded him grew bigger by the moment. His eyes were glazed over as they stared blankly back at me. I was emotionless as the chaos swirled around me.

Suddenly two men pulled me from the floor and . . .

My eyes popped open, and like always, I was shivering in my own sweat. What was up with this dream that just wouldn't go away?

I wiped my face with my hands and let my eyes get adjusted to the light. And then I screamed!

King was standing there, posing in the doorway.

"Baby, you scared me." I held my chest, wondering if I was going to have to push my heart back inside. "How long have you been here?"

Even though we had spoken, he'd never said that he was coming home.

"Only about five minutes," he said a little dryly, especially considering that he had been away for weeks. He gave me a peck on my forehead, then shrugged his jacket from his shoulders and headed toward the bathroom.

Wow! Weeks had passed, and that was the best he could do? I would've thought he would be happier to see me. Would ask how I was, how was the baby, would tell me about his trip.

But that was all I got, a little kiss on my forehead.

What was up with that?

It wasn't like we had talked all that much while he was away, and the few conversations we'd had were so short. He needed to do better than this.

I jumped out of bed and stepped out of my night-gown. Maybe he was tired. Maybe I needed to make the effort and go to him.

King was already in the shower when I stepped into the bathroom, and I opened the shower door and slipped in behind him. He jumped at first, as if I'd shocked him, even though we often took showers together.

But then he relaxed as I rinsed off the remaining soap he had on his back and kissed him on his shoulder. He turned around and looked me in my eyes. I smiled and prepped myself for a kiss. Instead, he opened the shower door and stepped out, leaving me just standing there, with my lips puckered, looking like a fool.

What was going on? Didn't he miss me? Or had he been away so long that we were back in that old place before I'd gotten pregnant?

I finished showering, and by the time I got back to the bedroom, King was already halfway dressed. I tip-toed around him and went into my closet. As I dressed, I tried to figure out what I was going to say to King.

"So how was everything?" I asked when I came out of my closet.

He shrugged. "Everything was cool." His answer was quick and emotionless.

I wanted more. I wanted to hear about what happened. Where he went, what he did, the interviews that he had, the people that he saw.

And I wanted to know what had happened to the sweet, caring, loving guy who had left home. I had imagined the day when he'd return. I saw him crawling into the bed with me, rubbing my belly while he talked to our unborn child.

"Well, maybe we can go have breakfast and you can tell me all about it." I sat on the bed and waited for his response as he buttoned up his shirt, then slipped into his shoes.

"Naw, I'm about to go."

"What?" I couldn't believe what I was hearing. He had just got home, and now he was leaving? What was this? Just a pit stop? "You just came in. Where are you going?"

"Out." With that simple answer, he walked out of our room and disappeared downstairs.

Was he kidding me? I wanted to run after him and stop him, but my legs wouldn't move. Actually, I couldn't get any part of me to move. I was in shock.

When the front door opened, then closed, I was still sitting in the middle of our bed, in disbelief. Slowly, I lay down and stared at the ceiling. I was there, in the same place, for over an hour after he left.

Finally I sat up. King owed me more than this. Grabbing my cell, I dialed his number but kept getting his voice mail.

Now, I was so hurt by this. What was wrong? I needed to talk this through with someone. I needed my friend. I called Blair, knowing that she would be a good supporting ear, but her cell phone number was disconnected.

I pulled the phone away from my ear when I heard that recording. Why was her phone disconnected? If she had changed her number, why didn't she call me to give me the new one?

Well, if Blair wasn't there, I needed someone else. And I dialed the number to my last choice—Donovan. If there was anyone who could cheer me up, it would be him. And I didn't have to tell him everything that was going on.

So I dialed his number, but the call went straight to voice mail too.

It felt like a conspiracy, and I was desperate to talk to someone. But there was no one else. I couldn't call my parents, not after I had tried so hard to convince them that I was in pure bliss. My momma would've said only one thing, "I told you so."

This was what being alone felt like. Alone and neglected. I curled up into a ball on the bed and closed my eyes. Hours later I woke to the sounds of laughter. At first I thought I'd accidentally hit the remote and turned on the television, but the bedroom was silent. Glancing at the clock, I was shocked to see that it was almost six o'clock. I had slept the day away, but I guess that was what you did when you were depressed.

Pushing myself from the bed, I rubbed my eyes, then grabbed my cell to call King. But then I heard laughter again, and this time the splash of water. I couldn't see the pool from our bedroom, so I was surprised that I could even hear that sound. The door to the backyard must've been opened.

As I dashed down the stairs, I wondered if I should grab a knife or something for protection, just in case it was a robber who had decided to take a swim in our pool. But when I got to the back door, I couldn't believe my eyes. King was finally home. But this time he had friends with him. Two women. Who wore bikini bottoms, but no tops. All three were splashing around as if they were kids. The women were hugging on King and kissing him like they were making a rap video.

My body grew hot with rage. This had to be a dream. No, a nightmare, because there was no way on this green earth that King would disrespect me, his pregnant girl, to this magnitude. I pinched myself, just for good measure, because I knew I was awake. And with each passing moment, I became angrier.

I stepped outside and stomped toward the pool. "What the hell is going on here?"

King looked up and so did the women, but not a one of them seemed surprised to see me. Nor did they seem to care that I was there. Not even King. He didn't get out of the water. He didn't push the women away. He did nothing but stare at me, as if he couldn't figure out why I was messing up his party.

"Maybe I wasn't clear!" I screamed. "This party's over. You two need to get your clothes on and get the hell out of my house." The only thing that kept me from jumping into that pool and snatching both of those heifers out of the water was this child inside of me. But now I wished that I had grabbed that knife.

The women began to move to the edge of the pool, but King motioned for them to stay. He hopped out, grabbed me by my arm, and dragged me toward our house.

"Your house, huh?" he whispered before he flung me inside. "What bills you pay around here?" Now that he was inside, he was screaming.

"What is wrong with you?" I screamed back, giving as good as I was getting. "You're gone for weeks, you come in today and barely say anything to me, and then you show up back here with those whores!" I was in his face, yelling, at this point. I had never jumped at him like this before, but this was ridiculous. This was major disrespect . . . and in my own house. After I'd given everything to this man.

Nothing prepared me for the sting of the back of his right hand on my cheek. I stumbled back and grabbed my face at the same time. My eyes were wide with disbelief. This man had hit me. And my tears were instant.

"Who do you think you are, huh?" he yelled. "All of this I gave you. If it wasn't for me, you would still be a know-nothing assistant at a second-rate magazine. I gave you this life, and I make the rules."

I took several steps back from him, not knowing who this man was.

"You better learn how to play the game, or you'll get cut from the team."

I stood frozen for a moment, still not believing any of this. Finally, I said, "I can't believe you would treat the mother of your unborn child like this." My voice was low; my tone, defeated.

He glared at me, looking me up and down, as I continued to cry in the middle of our kitchen. When I said nothing more, he turned away and walked back to the pool.

I watched as he jumped back into the pool. Once again, the girls were all over him, and I stood there, in the middle of the kitchen, in complete humiliation.

I ran upstairs, dashed into my closet, and started throwing clothes on the bed. I had no place to go, but there was no way I was going to stay in this house. I was dizzy from all the thoughts running through my head. *How could this be happening to me?* I wondered as I stomped back and forth from the closet to the bedroom.

The ringing of my cell phone startled me. Stopped me dead in my packing tracks.

"Heiress, hey. I'm sorry I missed your call earlier. It was ridiculous at the store today. I hope I'm not calling too late."

Donovan! The sound of his voice was so comforting, so calming. But I said nothing.

"Heiress? Are you there?"

"Yes," I finally said. I tried to keep my voice from quivering. I really didn't want Donovan to know that I'd been crying.

"Is everything okay? You sound upset."

I guess there was no way for me to hide it. He knew me all too well. Plus, I needed him now. He was my God-sent angel.

"Donny, is it okay if I come over to your place?"

I could hear the frown in his voice, but all he said was, "Sure. Definitely." A pause, and then he added, "It's not too much for you to make the drive tonight?"

"It's fine with me if it's fine with you." I needed some comfort, and Donovan was the perfect person to give it to me.

"You know you can come over anytime."

I blew out a sigh of relief and quickly grabbed something to write his address down. I packed up the rest of the clothes I had on the bed and headed out the door. I didn't even bother to see where King was or what he was doing. He clearly had no concern for me, so I drove to the only person in my life that I was sure, right now, did care.

Chapter 23

As I finished the story, I watched Donovan's facial expressions. In the twenty minutes that it had taken to tell him everything, I'd watch his face go through every emotion: surprise, then shock, then hurt, then anger. It was like seeing everything that I was going through play out on his face.

"Why have you put up with this fool for so long?" he said as he brought me a plate of hot wings, a biscuit, and a cup of tea.

My stomach growled. With everything that had happened today, it wasn't until I got to Donovan's house that I realized I hadn't eaten a thing all day. I was grateful for Donovan: for him, his place, and this food.

"So why have you stayed with him this long?" he asked.

"Because I know he isn't really this horrible person." I was very hurt, but I couldn't forget all that King had done for me. Even though his words were meant to cut my heart, they were true: he had given me a life that I had never dreamed of. I told myself, *Think about it. Without King, would I have any of it?* I was living in a beautiful house, driving luxury cars, going to celebrity parties, and traveling. I could buy anything that I wanted. I had a man and a life that other women envied.

"Heiress, no matter what, you don't deserve to be treated like this. No matter what he's given you."

Donovan sat next to me and wrapped his arm around my shoulders. I stopped eating and laid my head on his shoulder. A tear fell from my eye, and he held me tighter.

"I want to have this baby and be a family, Donny."

I wanted him to tell me that everything would be okay and that this was nothing more than one bad night. I needed that validation.

But I wasn't going to get those words out of him. He thought King was a fool, and I knew he was holding back other names for him. I was just glad that Donovan could hold me at this time. His arm tightened around me, and he rocked me, as if he was trying to give me comfort by just letting me know he was near.

After a few minutes of silence, he lifted my head up and looked deeply into my eyes.

"Heiress, you have to figure out what's best for you. Honestly, do you think this baby will make everything better?"

A month ago, a day ago, the answer to that question would have been yes. But then King had come home. Now I wasn't sure if we could ever get back to where we were, especially after what happened today.

"Honestly, I don't know, but is it crazy for me to want to try and see?"

The way Donovan sighed let me know that he was disappointed in my answer. I knew he was contemplating what he needed to say now.

"Well, you're welcome to stay here as long as you need to."

I gave him a hug, and he kissed me on my cheek. I couldn't have asked for a better friend. Even though I knew what he wanted me to do, he was still going to be supportive. He was still going to comfort me without judgment.

For the rest of the night he didn't mention another word about King. We lay on the couch and watched movies, and then, when it was time for us to sleep, he gave up his bed for me.

"Are you sure?" I asked him. "I don't mind sleeping on the couch."

Donovan simply shook his head, then closed the door to his bedroom, giving me privacy.

I lay under the covers, wondering what I was going to do. Did I have a plan in case it didn't work out with King? No, I couldn't think like that. I wanted to be happy, and I wanted to be happy with King. I closed my eyes, determined to figure out a way to make that happen.

The next morning I awakened to the wonderful smell of breakfast. I stepped into the dining room, wearing my bathrobe, and Donovan pulled out a chair for me.

"Madam," he joked, "your breakfast is ready."

Donovan had made me an omelet and some potatoes, and he had squeezed oranges for juice.

As we sat and ate, we didn't engage in much conversation. For some reason, the awkward silence had returned, and I didn't know if it was because he disagreed with my wanting to work it out with King.

"Thank you for letting me stay last night," I finally said, needing to break the silence.

"No need to thank me. You know I'm here for you. Whenever. Whatever."

When we finished eating, I lifted my plate, then reached for his. The least I could do was clean up as a way to show my appreciation. He quickly motioned me to stay in my seat and took my plate from my hands.

"I got this!"

There was nothing I could do but sit back and watch him. When he finished, I asked, "What time are you going to the store?"

He shook his head. "I decided to stay home today."

"Not because of me, I hope."

"Well, a little. I just really want to spend the day with you. We need to have some fun."

"But I don't want you to change your plans because of me." I already felt bad enough. I'd imposed, put him out of his bed, and now this.

"Heiress, I'm the owner. I can do what I want to when I want to do it."

I had to chuckle at that. What an awesome friend.

"So," he said, "are we gonna do this thing?"

I jumped up from the table. "Yes! I'll go get dressed." I rushed off to his bedroom and hit the shower to get ready for what the day would bring.

Within the hour we were in Donovan's car. "Where are we going?" I asked.

He turned and winked at me. "Just leave the driving and the fun to me."

And fun it was. When I realized that we were heading to Universal CityWalk, I clapped. "This is one of my favorite places," I told Donovan when we arrived.

"Really?"

I nodded. "But the last time I was here, I was a junior in college. This is where I celebrated my twenty-first birthday."

"Well, then, I guess I done good." He laughed.

"Yes, you did."

Just like when we'd gone to Magic Mountain, Donovan and I were like a couple of kids. We went in and out of the different shops and even visited a couple of the shows. We played games, bought souvenirs, and hung out like we were tourists. By the time the day was over, we were exhausted, and we ended up at the Hard Rock Cafe for dinner.

After we'd given our orders to the waitress, I said, "I had a really good time today, Donny. Thank you."

He reached across the table and grabbed my hand. "Both of us really needed this." When he squeezed my hand, I knew that was his signal to let me know that he was always going to support me. "So," Donovan added, "I was thinking about doing this again tomorrow. What do you think about a spa day?"

Oh, my goodness. Donovan thought that I'd changed my mind. That I was going to stay with him.

I let a second pass and then said, "Donny, I have to go back home."

He looked up at me, at first with surprise, then with confusion, and finally hurt settled into his eyes.

"Don't get me wrong," I told him. "You have been wonderful, and you were here when I needed you. But the thing is, I still have to deal with my relationship. Running isn't going to solve anything."

Donovan shook his head, as if he didn't understand my words or didn't want to hear them. He lowered his eyes, and I imagined that he was gathering his thoughts and emotions before he spoke.

"I'm worried for you, Heiress," he said softly. "These kinds of situations only get worse, and I don't want you to get hurt any more than you already have been."

He didn't know this, but I had the same concerns. Still, I had to face this situation and deal with it. I couldn't hide out at Donovan's house forever.

"I think I'll be fine, but you know I'll call you if I need you, right?"

He nodded. "Please."

"Of course I will. I know you're here for me."

"Always!"

The atmosphere had changed, and now we ate mostly in silence. When we finished our dinner, we got in his car, and that was when I told Donovan that I was going home tonight.

"Are you sure?"

All I did was nod.

At his house it took me only a few minutes to stuff the clothes I'd had on yesterday into my suitcase, and then Donovan rolled that small suitcase to my car.

When I was behind the wheel, Donavan leaned into the car and stared at me once again. I looked back at him, waiting for him to speak first. It was as if neither one of us wanted to make the first move to say good-bye.

"Are you sure you don't at least want me to go with you, in case there's a problem?" he asked as he brushed my hair out of my face.

"I got this. Don't worry about me." Reaching up, I grabbed him and hugged him tightly, wondering for a moment if I really wanted to leave.

He kissed my forehead, in exactly the same place King had kissed me when he came home from his promotional tour. But there was more love in Donovan's kiss, and I felt the difference. I took one final glance at him, and then I rolled off.

On the drive back to Malibu, all I could think about was what had happened yesterday. And what had happened when I left. What did King do with those women once I left? Did he even realize that I was gone? I glanced down at my cell phone, which was on the passenger seat. My phone had never once rung while I was with Donovan. Maybe King didn't even care that I'd left.

With each mile that I drove closer to home, I got angrier, and by the time I pulled into my driveway and parked next to King's car, I was ready for the fight. King was going to talk to me, and we were going to make some decisions tonight. But by the time I walked up to the door, my stomach was queasy, as the memories came back hard. I stood at the door for a moment, praying that the feeling would pass. I had to do this.

So I took a deep breath and walked through the door.

Chapter 24

I wasn't sure what I had expected when I walked back into the house, but I had no clue I was going to encounter a scene from a Quentin Tarantino movie.

As soon as I opened the door, King immediately rushed me, as if he'd been standing behind the door. His eyes looked crazed, and for a split second, I thought about turning around, running to my car, and heading back to Donovan's. But I stood my ground. This had to be done, whichever way it was going to go down.

King got right in my face. His pupils were dilated, he was sweating, and he smelled horrible—a mixture of funk and liquor.

"Where have you been?"

I was surprised. He didn't sound angry as much as frantic.

At this point, my anger outweighed my fear of losing him. I folded my arms and glared at him as if I wasn't afraid of anything. "I'm surprised you even noticed I was gone, since you were occupied with the double mint twins when I left."

I tried to move around him, but he put his arms up to block my path.

"Move out of my way, King," I said, trying to push him, but he was way stronger than me.

"Not until you tell me where you were."

The more I looked at him, the more I could tell he was high. Not like he had smoked some weed and had got a cool, calm, and funny high. It was on another level, like a hard-core high. I had never seen him like this, and I wondered what he had gotten into while I was gone. Since he wasn't going to let me move, I decided to just handle our business right there.

"Let's talk about you for a moment, King. What the hell was last night about?" I stared him down.

"What? What was wrong with last night? I just had some friends over."

I couldn't help but laugh. His words were so ridiculous. "Friends? Is that really the answer you have for me?" Maybe I *didn't* want to talk to him right now. I tried once again to maneuver around him, but he continued to block me.

"Move, King." I yelled so loud that he jumped back, as if I'd startled him. Good! I stomped past him and up the stairs.

"You still haven't answered my question," he yelled behind me. "Where the hell were you last night?"

I didn't say a word, and I heard him running up behind me.

"Did you hear me ask you a question?" he shouted as he followed me into the bedroom.

"Well, technically, you didn't answer my question." I whipped around and faced him. Looking him dead in his eyes, I asked, "Did you have sex with those girls?"

He kept his lips pressed together.

I glanced down at our bed and shook my head. Reaching for the duvet, I tossed it onto the floor. "Ugh! I don't even want to think about what happened in my bed." Next, I tore the sheets back. "I'm so tired of this."

"You know what I'm tired of? I'm tired of all of this questioning about my business."

I froze, turning only my head to look at him. I had to see if those words had really just come out of his mouth. He was questioning me and didn't expect the same treatment? Especially after he had given me something to question him about?

He said, "This is the lifestyle, Heiress. I'm famous, and my fame allows me to pay for everything around here. My fame allows me to pay for you."

Oh, no, he didn't. I wondered if he could feel the heat of my anger bursting from my body.

"Wrong, King. That may be the lifestyle for a famous person who's single, but you have a family." I placed my hands on my stomach to remind him that I was still pregnant with his child. "And furthermore, don't think that you've bought me."

It was as if he ignored my words. "Where were you?" he asked again.

I shook my head, ignored his question, and went right back to pulling the sheets off the bed. He hadn't answered me, so I wasn't about to answer him.

But then he stood there for so long, I finally said, "You know what I find amazing, King? How you could be gone for weeks, come home, and say almost nothing to me, leave, come back with women, and then have the audacity to ask me where I was. Are you serious?"

I took his silence as a sign that he was beginning to understand where I was coming from and I was waiting for him to apologize. Then the ringer on my phone broke the silence.

King rushed to my phone before I could get to it. I watched him read the text; then I watched his eyes grow wide with rage.

"Who the hell is Donovan?"

"A friend," I said in the same nonchalant tone that he'd given me when he told me those women were just friends. I tried to grab my phone from his grasp, but he pushed me back.

"Why does he want to know if you made it home safe and if you need him? Is this who you were with?"

I reached for my phone once again, but he grabbed my wrist and squeezed.

"So what? You having sex with this clown?" he yelled, his voice rising, and I finally broke free from his grip.

Stomping away from him, I marched toward the door.

"Answer me, Heiress," he shouted.

All I wanted to do was get away from him. I rushed to the stairs, but he was right behind me. And then my phone rang again.

"Argh!" he screamed as he threw the phone against the wall, and I watched it crumble into a million little pieces.

"Are you crazy?" I screamed.

"Yeah, I'm crazy!" He snatched my arms and shook me like I was a rag doll. "You want to see me get crazy, Heiress? Huh? That's what you want?"

Up to this point, I'd been more angry than scared, but now that switched around. Now I screamed out of fear. And the louder I screamed, the more he shook me.

I squirmed, trying to escape from his grasp, but he held me tight. Finally, I got one arm free and raised my hand, hitting him in his face.

My hope was that shock would make him let me go, but that blow only set him off. He shoved me down the stairs.

I felt as if I was moving in slow motion, hitting every step, feeling every bump. I was screaming, but it didn't sound as if anything was coming out of my mouth.

My whole body hit the marble floor in the foyer, and pain shot from my soles to the top of my head. My eyes were open, but I could hardly see. I definitely couldn't move. My ears were ringing, but still, I heard King's footsteps.

For a moment, I wondered if he was coming to finish the job.

I closed my eyes. Maybe this was the end of my life. Maybe I was supposed to live only until I was twenty-five.

"Heiress!" he yelled. "Are you okay?"

Now he was asking me that? He was the reason I was laid out like this.

"Oh my God! You're bleeding."

I screamed when he lifted me from the floor, and I screamed louder when he held me in his arms and dashed to his car. I didn't feel any relief until he laid me on the backseat, and as he climbed into the front of the car, I whimpered. It hurt too much to cry full out.

But then, as King sped down the street and hit a bump, a pain so sharp cut through me. I screamed, and then everything around me just faded to black.

I heard the sound of machines even before I heard the voices. Slowly, my eyes fluttered open, and it took only a moment for me to take in the situation and figure out where I was.

The hospital.

At the edge of my bed, King was speaking to a man in a white lab coat, a doctor, I supposed.

I moaned, and King rushed to my side.

"Heiress," he whispered as he reached for my hand. He kissed my cheek.

"I'm . . . thirsty. . . ."

"Can I give her some water, Doctor?" King asked.

The man in the lab coat nodded, and King held a cup of water to my lips.

When I finished drinking, I asked, "How . . . long . . . ?" It was hard for me to speak. "How long have I been here?" I finally got the words out.

The doctor and King looked at each other and then back at me, like they were harboring some big secret.

"You've been here three days, Heiress," the doctor revealed.

Three days!

The doctor continued, "You suffered a minor concussion and . . . " The doctor stopped and glanced at King. But King put his head down, as if he didn't plan on saying a word.

"I'm sorry to tell you this, Ms. Montgomery, but you suffered a miscarriage."

It took a moment for the words to register. *A miscarriage. The baby! My baby! Oh, no!*

There was no way I'd heard him right. With every bit of energy in me, I tossed off the light blanket that covered me and tried to see my stomach. But just as I did that, King tried to pull the blanket back on me. I slapped his hand away.

"Don't touch me!" I screamed.

Everyone in the room and right outside stopped at my scream. This was a bad dream. It just had to be.

King glanced at me for a long moment, then stepped out of the room. My heart was broken. My baby. I had never known true pain until this moment.

"I'm sorry, Ms. Montgomery," said the doctor.

I tried to nod. "Am I . . . am I going to be all right?"

He frowned. "Yes. You're going to have to rest for a few days, and we're going to want to do more tests, but you'll be fine."

I shook my head. "No. No, I mean, with my baby."

"You lost the baby," he repeated.

I knew that. I got that. But what I wanted to know was if King had ruined my life totally. Had he ruined my chances of ever having another child?

"I mean . . ." I looked up at the doctor and tried to convey my thoughts through my eyes.

The doctor nodded slowly. "We don't have to talk about this right now."

"No, I want to."

"I think you need to rest."

"Doctor!"

Maybe it was the way I screamed, or the fact that I wasn't going to stop, but the doctor pulled up a chair, and when he sat down, we were almost eye to eye. He said, "You had quite a bit of scarring on your uterus."

I felt tears behind my eyes.

"So the probability of having another child . . ." He paused. "It'll be slim."

My tears fell. There was no other emotion I had but pure sadness. I couldn't stop myself from crying. It was only at that moment that I realized how much I'd wanted my baby.

The doctor pushed back the chair and then put his hand over mine for a moment. "I'm sorry." Then he left me alone with my emotions.

I couldn't believe the turn my life had taken, and I was quickly realizing I wanted out. Finally, I was getting it. It was time for me to move on from this madness.

Chapter 25

I spent a week in the hospital before they finally discharged me. That was the longest week of my life. It felt like it moved in slow motion.

I was bombarded all week by people: nurses, who constantly picked and probed and took my vitals; the doctor, who checked on me every day; and even the police, who wanted details about my fall.

"Was it a domestic dispute?" the officer asked me.

But I spoke to no one. I was too distraught to open my mouth.

King came to my room and sat by my side every day, but the only reason he was there was that I didn't have the strength to stop him. But though he was there, we didn't interact. I never even looked at him. He was, after all, the reason that the life had been sucked out of me.

On the day of my release, I finally had to pay some attention to King, since he was the one taking me home. I didn't say a word to him, though. Not when I was being checked out, not on the ride home, and not when King finally pulled into our driveway.

The moment he stopped the car, I jumped out and didn't stop moving, even though he called behind me.

"Wait, Heiress. Let me help you."

Now he wanted to help me?

I ignored him and kept walking, stomped up the stairs, stripped, and curled up in the bed. It wasn't that

I was tired; it was just that I didn't have a reason to be awake. I just needed to shut out the world.

"Baby, did you need me to get you anything?" King asked from the door.

I curled up into a tighter ball and closed my eyes. All I needed was to have my baby back. Could he get that for me? If not, then all I needed was sleep. Because when I was asleep, I felt no pain. Sleep was my refuge, and I cherished it.

God granted my prayers, and I slept. But finally, He opened my eyes. The sun was going down, so at least I'd gotten through one more day. But my head was throbbing now, and I needed my pain medicine.

Slowly, I pushed up from the bed, then lifted my purse, and as I rummaged through it, I came across a business card. I frowned. What was this?

Leslie Hunter.

The memory of meeting her triggered thoughts of my baby. I was shopping for the rattle that day. The rattle that I'd given to King.

My tears were back. I would never have a chance to meet my baby.

To stop my tears, I went into the bathroom and took my medicine with water from the faucet. I splashed water on my face, hoping the coolness of it would help in some way. But then, right away, I went back to the bed.

I lay there, staring at the card that I'd just found. I knew for a fact that I didn't want to be bothered. I didn't want to have anyone in my presence, let alone to talk to them about my problems. Yet every time I put down the card, I picked it back up. There was something tugging at me to make this call. Finally, after thirty minutes of going back and forth, I picked up the phone. I decided to call her cell instead of the office. If I had any luck, she'd be in her office.

But after the first ring, she answered, "Leslie Hunter."

I froze and remained silent. Why had I made this call? What did I want? What did I want her to do?

"Hello?" she said, as if she knew there was someone on the line.

I cleared my throat. "Hi," I said, barely able to hear my own voice. "This is Heiress Montgomery. I met you at Babypalooza a little while ago."

There was a pause, and then she said, "Oh, yes, I remember. How are you?"

"You told me to call if I needed to talk, so . . ." I knew I hadn't answered her question, and I hadn't finished my sentence. I was just hoping that she could hear the distress in my voice.

"I have time today," she said quickly. "Where would you like to meet?"

Whoa. I hadn't expected that. I wasn't even sure why I'd called. What did I want from her? Since I wasn't sure, I remained silent, hoping that this would all go away.

"Listen, take down this address, and if you can, meet me there in an hour," she said, taking control.

I did what she told me. I wrote down the address, then hung up. It was a struggle getting out of bed, but I put on sweats and then called King's driver. I wasn't even sure if King was home, but when Al said he was available, I asked him to drive me to the address in Santa Monica, which wasn't too far away from where I'd met Leslie for the first time. Only an hour had passed since I'd hung up the phone when Al stopped in front of the town house.

"I'm not sure how long I'm going to be," I told Al.

"That's okay. I won't be too far away."

I smiled at him but couldn't look at him for too long. I hated to see the pity in his eyes.

I took my time walking up the steps, then took a deep breath, but before I could ring the bell, Leslie opened the door.

"Heiress, it's good seeing you again." She gave me a little hug, and even though she was gentle, I winced in pain. She quickly released me. "I'm sorry," she said and looked me up and down, then invited me in.

I followed her through the rooms to the back of the house and into an office. Her office looked exactly like a therapist's office that you'd see in a movie: black leather couch, a desk in the corner, and a big chair. I was sure Leslie occupied the big chair so that she could sit comfortably while hearing the problems of the distressed.

"Welcome to my home office, Heiress. Have a seat," she said, pointing to the couch exactly the way she would if *she* were in a movie.

I did as I was told, but I stayed silent.

"I'm glad you called me," Leslie said as she rolled her chair to her desk. "It's important for you to have a place to go . . . to talk."

To talk. Is that why I called her? Is that what I wanted to do? I thought.

"So . . ." she began and then stopped, waiting for me to say something.

I didn't.

"How have things been since I last saw you?"

I knew I had to say something soon. I didn't come all the way over here just to have her talk. But what could I say? I stared down at my hands, then lifted my eyes, but I didn't look at her. I turned my attention to the walls, then back to my hands.

"Is this your first time talking to a therapist?"

I nodded. At least that was a start.

She said, "Well, we can start slow. I can just ask you a few general questions, okay?"

I nodded once again.

"Okay," she said. "What do you do for a living?"

"I just lost my baby," I blurted out. And when I said it, I realized it was the first time I'd said it out loud. Just saying it hurt even more than just thinking it.

Leslie might have been a therapist, but she wasn't able to hide her shock. But then her expression quickly returned to neutral.

It wasn't until a sob passed through my lips that I realized that tears were falling from my eyes . . . again. Leslie handed me a box of tissues and let me cry. I was glad she did that. I didn't have enough energy to figure out how not to cry.

"I know that is a lot to handle at the moment," she observed.

I nodded.

"Besides grief, tell me what else you're feeling."

"What other emotion is there?" I said as I wiped my face with a tissue.

"There are several emotions that go along with grief."

I guess she was right. There was more than grief. There was anger. And grief. Fear. And grief. Heartache. And grief. Grief. And grief.

It was just too much for me. "I can't do this." I jumped up from the couch and grabbed my bag. "I'm sorry, Leslie, for wasting your time, but I'm not sure I'm ready for this right now." I turned toward the door.

"I understand, Heiress. Just know that you can come back anytime," she said as she followed me down the hall.

I was so glad that Al had kept his promise; he was right there at the curb where he'd dropped me off just ten minutes before, and I jumped into the car.

"Please get me out of here," I told Al.

"Okay," he said. Again, there was that pity in his eyes. And I just couldn't stand it.

"I'm not going home, though." I gave him Donovan's address. That was where I wanted to be. If there was one place I could get comfort without talking, it was with Donovan.

I just prayed that he was home.

Chapter 26

Donovan met me with open arms, even after I showed up at his door unannounced. I sent Al home; I was going to stay with my friend.

I went straight into Donovan's bedroom, closed my eyes, and had the most peaceful sleep that I'd had in weeks. Then, in the morning, he fixed breakfast, just like he'd done a little more than a week ago. Only this time when I burst into tears, he just held me. The thing that was so wonderful was, Donovan didn't ask me any questions. Not one question. He just let me breathe.

The next night I asked him to stay with me in his bed. I didn't even have to say anything else. I didn't have to explain that all I wanted was for him to hold me. He just did it. I cried through the night, and he held me and rocked me and rubbed my hair. I felt safe in his arms, as if he was protecting me from what I was running from. Again, I was so appreciative that he never asked what was wrong. He just let me live through my process of grieving.

On the second morning Donovan tried to get up to make me breakfast, but I wouldn't let him move. I needed to feel his arms. I needed that more than I needed food. If there was any way we could stay like this forever, I would make it happen. Donovan understood. He kissed me, and he stayed.

"Is this the plan for today? Because sooner or later someone is going to have to get up to use the bathroom," he joked.

My response was to hold him tighter and fight to keep new tears from falling. It was amazing to me that I had tears left. Didn't tear ducts dry up eventually?

"Have I ever told you the story about Sheila?" It was a rhetorical question, because he didn't wait for me to say yes or no before he continued. "Sheila was my dream girl. I met her when I went up to New York for a little while."

I had no idea why he was telling this story, but as long as he talked, I didn't have to. I could just listen.

He continued, "She was *fine*. I mean, she had it going on. She was tall, about five-seven, had long, black, curly hair, skin that didn't even need makeup. But I loved her beyond her looks. She was smart, really smart, and when she smiled . . ."

"I get the picture, Donny," I said, interrupting his trip down memory lane.

"Oh, okay." He chuckled. "Well, anyway, I really thought I was going to marry that girl, but it turned out that she was already married. Married with children." He shook his head. "Man, I wish I had never met her."

He tried to sound so sad, and I laughed. For the first time in a week.

"Why are you laughing at me? That was a sad, sad story." He chuckled, knowing that he'd just broken my grief.

"Yes, it was, and it was just as sad when Carl Thomas sang about it in his song."

It was hilarious that Donovan had taken that song and tried to make it into his personal story. But what was sweet was that he'd done that to cheer me up.

"A'ight, A'ight, you caught me, but at least I got a laugh out of you."

I fell silent again, my eyes focused on the wall.

He said, "I know breaking up is hard, but leaving King Stevens isn't the end of the world."

I smirked at his attempt to figure out what was wrong with me. He had no idea.

"What about losing a child?" I whispered. "Is that the end of the world?" Before he could say anything, I added, "Or what about probably never being able to have another one? Is that the end of the world?"

"Heiress," he said, whispering my name, and held me tighter. And then he said nothing more. We just lay there, wrapped in our embrace.

I wasn't sure how much time passed before Donovan finally spoke again. "I'm so sorry, Heiress. When did this happen?"

I rolled over to face him and smiled a little when I saw tears in his eyes.

"Last week."

His expression changed from sadness to anger.

"Last week? You were here with me. And you were pregnant then. So . . ."

I took a breath and gave him a moment to figure it out.

He jumped out of the bed, and his anger filled the room. "What happened, Heiress? Did he do this to you? Did he do this after you left here?"

"He pushed me and—"

Donovan didn't let me finish. "I'll kill him," he yelled, scrambling around, trying to find clothes to put on.

"No, you won't, Donny. Stop it." Then I raised my voice a little more. "Please, stop it and sit down."

It took him a moment before he sat down and grabbed my hands. "I knew I should have gone with you." He shook his head. "I should have never let you get hurt."

I raised his hands to my lips and kissed the inside of both of them. "Donny, it's not your fault. You have done more than enough for me."

"So what are you going to do?"

I shrugged. "I don't know yet. I haven't stopped crying long enough to figure it out."

He was pensive, as if he was trying to come up with a few ideas. "Maybe," he began slowly, "it's time for you to take a break from California. Maybe you should go home for a little while."

His suggestion shocked me. I hadn't thought about that at all. What would my mother say if she found out about this situation? What would my father do if he knew what King had done to me?

"I don't think I can go home right now."

"It's just that I want you to have someone to talk to. I mean, besides me. I'll always be here for you, but I'm a bit biased about the situation." He paused. "But you need someone to talk to."

I thought back on how I ran out on Leslie yesterday. It was clear that I wasn't totally ready to talk about how I was feeling. "I tried to see a therapist yesterday but couldn't go through with it."

This time he kissed the insides of my hands, then brushed my hair from my face and tucked it behind my ears. "You should go back," he said. "I know it's hard right now, but you should go back to the therapist."

"I will. As soon as I can, I will."

Then we lay back down, and he held me again, getting up only to order Chinese food. Inside his bedroom we watched reruns of *The Cosby Show,* then a marathon of *Law & Order.* It wasn't a normal day, but it was as normal as I had felt in quite a while.

By the time I rested my head on Donovan's pillow that night, I felt like things might just be okay. For the first time, I was heading back toward okay.

And right now okay was a beautiful feeling.

Chapter 27

I had been at Donovan's for three days now, and even though I tried to convince him not to, he stayed home with me the whole time. Of course, he called the store and was on the phone with his staff for a good part of the day. Even so, his attention was all on me.

I hadn't brought any clothes with me, so my wardrobe included Donovan's clothes: his basketball shorts, his T-shirts. And it didn't matter at all to me.

By the third day Donovan wanted me to go out of the house, and though I tried to fight it, Donovan won. Especially when he lifted me up and carried me out the door.

"Walking will get your endorphins going," he said, as if he was some kind of medical expert. "Plus, the sun will give you vitamin D, and all of that is good for your healing."

"When did you go to medical school?" I asked him as we began to walk around the block.

"Yesterday. While you were sleeping." I laughed, and he nodded. "Yup, didn't you know I was smart?"

We walked for about thirty minutes, then had lunch.

Right after lunch he said, "Get dressed and take a ride with me."

"Where are we going?" I really wasn't in the mood to go anywhere. Walking around the block was one thing, but actually going somewhere with people around . . . I wasn't feeling that.

"Just riding." He dried his hands on a dish towel and walked over to kiss me on my forehead. "Come on. I promise it'll be good for you."

He pulled me off the couch and pushed me lightly in the direction of his bathroom. As the water ran over my body in the shower, I had to keep thoughts of why I was even here out of my mind. But it was hard not to think about King, even though he couldn't be thinking about me. Just like the last time, he hadn't even tried to reach me. It was as if he didn't care.

How did it turn out this way? Life with King was supposed to be a fairy tale. Instead, it had turned into a horror movie.

By the time I made my way back into the living room, Donovan was already dressed. He looked me up and down and smiled sweetly before he walked over and wrapped me in his arms. No words were exchanged, but I felt everything he was trying to say to me in that embrace. We finally stepped away from each other and headed down to his car.

The entire ride Donovan was pretty quiet. He asked random questions from time to time, like what I thought I wanted to eat for dinner. Silence was an unusual tactic for Donovan when he was trying to cheer me up. He always talked so that I wouldn't get too deep in my head. Right now, though, I didn't mind the silence. I stared out the window as we raced down the freeway. When he exited, I noticed we were close to the mall. Was he going to take me shopping?

But then, after a few more turns, my heart began to pound. I knew exactly where Donovan was taking me.

I watched Donovan dart his eyes back and forth between me and the road, and by the time he stopped the car, I was raving mad.

"Donovan, what are we doing here?" My arms were folded. I felt so betrayed.

"Before you get mad"—he held up his hands—"I think you have to give this another try."

"How did you even know about her? How did you even know about her office here?" I looked up at the town house that I'd run out of just a few days ago.

"I found the card in your purse yesterday, when I was getting your pain medication, and I decided to make the call." When I huffed, he said, "Listen, Heiress, I really think talking to this therapist will help you grieve. You've been through so much that I'm afraid if it's not handled, you might crack. And I don't want that to happen to you."

My arms were still crossed and my lips were still poked out, but I had to admit that Donovan was probably right.

"Please," Donovan said. "Go in and give her another try. I'll be sitting right here when you come out. Even if you want to leave in ten minutes, I'll be right here." He grabbed my hand and kissed the top of it.

It took me a few more minutes, but finally, I got out of the car. I gave Donovan a hard glare before I made my way to Leslie's door. I looked back at the car to see Donovan motioning for me to knock on the door. I took a deep breath and rang the doorbell. Within a couple of moments, she answered the door.

With a smile, she invited me in. "I'm glad you came back," she said.

"Listen, I'm sorry about running out the other day."

"Oh, don't apologize. Sometimes therapy just takes time with some people. And who's to say that's not part of therapy."

I frowned.

"Whatever your process, Heiress, I'm just here to help you. So I'm glad you're back."

Once again, I followed her down the hall to her office. I sat in the exact same spot, and when she took her seat, the same uncomfortable feelings began rising up in me again.

"Like I said a couple of days ago, let's take this slow. So where are you from, Heiress?"

"Ohio, a small town in Ohio."

"So how did you end up here in California?"

"I came out here for college, and then I stayed to start my career."

"And what do you do?" She put her hand under her chin, as if she was focusing on my answers and was really interested.

"I had planned on becoming a journalist."

Leslie jotted a note on her pad, but still she spoke. "Planned?"

"Yeah."

"Did you do something else?"

It was her calmness and her sincerity that made me open up. "I met a man, and he didn't want me to work anymore."

Her eyebrows rose just a little. "You want to tell me more about that?"

I didn't know what came over me, but I was like a running faucet. I began to tell her all about King and how we met and the happy times that we had.

"Sounds like you really love him."

"I do, but our relationship hasn't turned out like the fairy tale I imagined it would be."

Flashes of the past few weeks popped into my head, and sadness once again washed over me.

"What did it turn out to be?"

"A bad dream, especially recently." I looked down at my feet, debating how much I wanted to tell her today. "I'm at a point now where I'm really trying to figure out if my life is completely screwed up."

"I doubt that. No matter what a person is going through, there is redemption."

I shrugged.

"Do you have a support system? Family or friends here in California? Besides King?"

The first image that popped into my mind was of the man sitting outside right now. The reason that I was even here.

"Yes, I have a friend, Donovan."

"That's right. The young man who called me."

I nodded again.

"He told me that you guys have been friends for a long time."

"Yeah, we grew up together."

"Does he know what's going on with you?"

"He does."

"And how does he feel about the situation?" She was still jotting notes on her pad.

"He thinks I need to leave California and go spend some time with my parents. He thinks that will help me regroup."

"Are you close with your parents?"

"Yes." I paused for a second to think about the last time I'd talked to them. "At least I used to be, but not so much lately. But we really are close."

She was quiet as she wrote more notes, and I wanted to ask her what was she writing. Finally, she put her pad and pen down. Looking at me, she said, "I think you should go."

I tilted my head, wondering why she thought that.

She explained, "It would be good for you to go home and reconnect with your family. It may help you answer some of the questions you've been asking yourself."

It was interesting to me that two people now were telling me to go home.

"Why don't we stop right here, Heiress? I think that's enough for today."

"Really?"

She smiled. "Uh-huh. See, that wasn't so bad, now was it?"

I shook my head.

"Plus, I want to make sure that you come back."

I wasn't sure if she was kidding about that or not, but I told her that I would call her.

When I left Leslie's office and bounced to Donovan's car, he gave me a look as if he wasn't sure if I was going to scream at him or not. But I reached over and hugged him.

"Thank you," I said.

"So it was good?"

"Very."

"Great. So let's go celebrate."

Over lunch I told Donovan about Leslie's remark that I should go back to Ohio.

"What do you think about that?"

"Well, that's what you said. And now Leslie." I nodded. "I'm going to do it. I'm going to go back to Ohio."

Just saying those words made me excited. Planning on leaving made me feel like I had room to breathe again.

Maybe that was what going home was all about—breathing.

Chapter 28

It was time for me to go back to Malibu and pack my stuff. I had been at Donovan's for almost a week, and I had only the outfit I showed up in and a few pairs of jeans he bought me when he went out to handle business at his store.

I decided not to have Donovan drive me back, because the last thing I needed in my life was a scene. So I didn't tell him what I was going to do. I waited until he went to the store, called a cab, and then tried to calm my nerves. The ride back home gave me an opportunity to categorize in my head everything I needed to pack so that I could move quickly and avoid King.

When we pulled up to the house and I saw King's car in the driveway, I almost asked the driver to take me back. But I couldn't avoid this. I paid the cabby, then made a beeline for the door and hurried up the stairs to our bedroom. I breathed. King was nowhere in sight. Would it be possible for me to get in and out without him even knowing that I'd been here?

I dragged my suitcases out of the back of my closet, then began pulling out clothes. But I was there for only about five minutes before King barged into the bedroom.

"Baby, you're back." He hugged me tight, like I had just come back from war.

I pushed him away from me and, without a word, went right back to packing.

"Baby, I am sorry about everything. I don't know what came over me."

For a moment, I stopped moving and debated in my mind if I should say something. But I decided against it. I needed to be in and out of here quickly, and a conversation would only slow me down. Especially a conversation that wouldn't matter.

"Baby, I know I messed up, and I know that lately I haven't been the man that I promised you I would be, but I love you."

I couldn't help it. I had to answer now. "Do you really, King?"

"Yes, of course I do. You mean everything to me, and not having you by my side . . . it's torture for me."

His words delighted me and pissed me off at the same time. King had tortured me, and so just thinking that he was experiencing even half of what I'd gone through pleased me.

"I guess you know how it feels now." By the look on his face, I could tell that my statement had hit him. I pushed past him to go into the bathroom to grab my toiletries.

"Baby, not knowing where you were and not being able to talk to you scared me, and I'm sorry. I'm sorry for everything," he said, following me.

I walked past him again, back into the bedroom, tossing the toiletries into one of the suitcases.

"Heiress, please talk to me."

I had never heard such desperation in his voice. I gathered my thoughts and prepared what I had to say. If he wanted me to talk, I hoped he was ready to listen.

"I don't think you get it, King," I said softly. "You think the last couple of days were hard for you? For almost two years I have sacrificed everything for you, and you walked—no, you stomped—over me. And now

I'm just tired, King." I searched his face to see if he understood where I was coming from. When he didn't respond, I continued packing.

"Where are you going?"

"I'm going back to Ohio. I need to spend some time at home for a while." I closed my suitcases and zipped them up.

"Baby, wait." King stopped me in my tracks and got down on one knee. I couldn't believe my eyes. Was he really about to do this?

"What are you doing?" I asked, half out of shock, and half out of annoyance.

"Heiress, I know this relationship has been a roller coaster." He grabbed my hand. "It hasn't been easy putting up with me, and you have stuck by my side through it all." From his pants pocket, he pulled out a ring, and my heart dropped to my stomach. "These past few days I've realized that living without you is nothing I ever want to experience again." He held the ring up for me to really see it. It was a two-and-a-half-carat cushion-cut diamond ring. So beautiful.

He slipped the ring on my finger. "I'm asking you to do me the honor and stick around a little longer. I'm promising you that I'll make up for everything that I've done to you. I'll be the man you fell in love with, and I'll give you the fairy-tale ending you deserve."

A tear fell down the right side of his face, and it sent a chill through my body. With the tip of my finger, I wiped the tear from his face and held my hand to his cheek. I looked deep into his eyes. Right then I saw the man I'd fallen in love with such a long time ago.

"What do you say, Heiress? Will you marry me?"

I had no words. This was what I'd wanted. For the last year and a half this was all I'd wanted from King. I'd wanted him to love the life he had with me. I'd wanted him to cherish me the way I cherished him.

"We have a lot of issues we need to work out, King," I finally said.

"I know," he said. His voice was full of hope. "And I promise that we will. We'll work on everything."

I looked down at the gorgeous ring that he had slipped on my finger. I was mesmerized by its size, by its beauty.

My eyes darted back and forth between the ring and King. The ring and King.

Could I trust him? Should I trust him? Was King sincere? Was he going to be true to his word?

I wondered if I really did love him or if I even wanted this to work.

"I'm not sure if I'm prepared to give you an answer," I finally said.

He stood up with shock on his face. "What was that?"

I glanced at the ring one more time. "I really need time to think about what I want out of life."

I slipped the ring off my finger and handed it back to him. He stood there, looking at me like he couldn't comprehend what I was saying. It was the first time that I truly considered whether he was what I wanted. I wasn't sure about this life anymore, and I could tell it was throwing him.

"But I love you, Heiress," he said as he tried to hold me in his arms. I moved back, not really wanting this contact. "I love you. I love you. I love you!"

"I hear it, and I understand it. I just wish I could believe it."

"You don't believe that I love you?" He sounded hurt that I would even insinuate that.

"At this point, King, no, I don't." I shocked myself with that statement. "Listen, we obviously need some time apart. I'm going to be with my family, and you can do whatever it is you want." I walked past him and grabbed my suitcases. I didn't look back to see the man that I had given my life to for the past year and a half. At that point all that mattered was me. As I walked out of the room and down the stairs, I could feel his eyes on me the whole time. I took a deep breath and said a small prayer that I had just made the right decision.

Chapter 29

The flight back to Ohio seemed extremely long. I was excited that I was going to see my parents, but nervous that they were going to grill me about King. I had no idea how it was going to go.

My parents were so traditional, and everything I'd done with King was just the opposite. I knew I was in for a long lecture, but at least I was going home with a little peace of mind. I had given King all of me, and I was exhausted. Being away from him felt good, but a piece of me sort of missed him.

When I finally landed, I held my breath, as if this moment was the most important one of my life. I didn't know why I was so anxious to see my folks. My parents were waiting in the baggage claim, and when I first saw them, I forgot all about my fears. My father, the first man that I'd ever loved, looked just like I remembered. His salt-and-pepper hair complimented his mocha skin, and since he was over six feet tall, he always stood out. My mother had her hair back in a neat bun, her khakis and sweater shirt fitted her petite frame to a tee, and the little bit of makeup she wore was applied perfectly.

"Oh, my baby is home," my mother gasped as I ran up to them and leaped into both of their arms. They held me like they never planned to let me go, and the feeling was mutual, because I wanted to stay in their arms.

"Welcome home, princess. We missed you," my father whispered in my ear.

"I missed you too, Daddy." I kissed both of them on
the cheek and finally released them from my grasp. I
stepped back to take a good look at them. I really had
missed being with my parents, and I cherished every
bit of this reunion.

I took my father's hand. "You guys have no idea how
good it is to be home."

My father smiled and kissed the back of my hand.
"You have no idea how good it is to have you back."

"We would've rather had you sooner than later, but
I guess something is better than nothing," my mother
interjected with all her sarcasm. All I could do was
smile. It had been way too long since I'd seen them, so
I guessed I deserved that.

We got my bags and made our way to the car. The car
ride was a little awkward. My parents wasted no time
in grilling me about my relationship, or lack thereof,
with King. It felt like they were trying to ask me every
question imaginable. I knew I hadn't given them much
information about him or our relationship the whole
time I was with him, but I wished they could've at least
waited until we got home. *Better to get it out of the
way, I guess.*

My mom started the conversation. "We're surprised
you didn't bring your boyfriend with you. What's his
name again?" I smirked at that question. My mother
really thought she was slick.

"You know his name, Mother. And like I told you
over the phone, we are no longer together."

"Oh, I do remember you saying something to that
effect."

"Uh-huh, I'm sure you do." I chuckled a little. Where
did this cruel sense of humor of hers come from?

"Who made the decision to walk away?" my father interjected before my mother could make another sarcastic remark.

"I did. Things weren't working, so we needed to go our separate ways." Those were all the details I was giving them. I didn't want to have to relive the last couple of months, especially not with my parents.

"You've always been a smart girl, princess."

"Thank you, Daddy." I wondered how smart I really was. I had nothing at the moment. No man, no child, no career, and at this point I didn't even know if I had myself. I just wanted to feel normal again.

We rode the rest of the way in silence, with only the sound of the car radio playing soft jazz from my father's favorite station.

I was grateful for the silence. It gave me a chance to reminisce as I looked out the window at all my old neighborhood spots. I broke into a smile when my father turned onto Washington Boulevard. "Aw, there's my elementary school," I blurted out. Then I recognized all the places where my friends and I had hung out after school. Just this ride made me feel better. It made me glad to be home.

When we finally pulled into the driveway, I couldn't believe how different my childhood home looked. "Daddy, you've been busy," I said, noting all the improvements he'd made, from the fresh coat of blue paint to the shingles on the roof.

"Oh, just a few tweaks here and there," my father said, waving my words away like none of it was a big deal.

While my father got my bags from the trunk, I rushed behind my mom, eager to see what they'd done with the inside of our house. Like I suspected, the inside looked as new as the outside. My parents had remodeled just about everything: the kitchen had all new stainless-steel appliances, the living room had a brand-new micro-suede couch, and I was stunned to see the forty-two-inch TV hanging on the wall. I couldn't wait to see what they'd done in the bedrooms. When I followed my mother upstairs to my bedroom, I was delighted to see that they had painted the walls a bright peach, they'd bought me a new television—though it wasn't as nice as the one in the living room—and they'd traded my twin bed up for a queen size.

"Mom, it's gorgeous," I said as I sat and bounced on the bed.

"You know your father. Once he started redoing the outside of the house, he had to come inside. And then he had to do every room." She shook her head like she was exasperated, but I knew she was as happy as I was. This felt like a brand-new home.

"So this is your room."

I looked up when I heard my dad's voice, and smiled. He dropped my bags by the door and then took a look around the room, admiring his work.

"How you like the room, baby girl?"

"It's perfect, Daddy."

I took a little tour around the room, studying all my awards, which my parents had left hanging on the walls. I stopped when I got to the scholarship letter I received from college, which my parents had been adamant about framing when it came in the mail. Besides my birth and my graduations, receiving that letter was one of the proudest moments for them as parents.

"I remember the day you came running in the house, screaming about that letter," my father said as I continued to stare at it. "Your mother and I were so proud."

I did my best to hold back tears. "I was proud of myself."

"Well, I leave you two ladies to it. I know I have some project around here I can start on."

"Or finish," my mother said, again in her sarcastic tone. "I do believe there is a leaky faucet that has yet to be completed."

That was my father's cue. He disappeared down the hall, and I gathered myself before a tear fell from my eyes.

"Well, I guess, I'll unpack."

While I rolled one of my suitcases to the bed, my mother sat on the other side. As I unzipped the suitcase and began unpacking clothes, my mother sat silently, staring. I couldn't tell if her expression was one of love or concern. It was probably both.

I tried not to make eye contact, because I didn't want to have this conversation yet. But I knew my mother. She wasn't the type who would avoid anything.

"Baby, you can do that later. Sit down right here," she said, patting a space on the bed next to her. "Sit here and talk to your mama."

I had no choice. I did what she asked me to do.

"What's up, Mom?" I tried to sound nonchalant, like I didn't know what this conversation was going to be about.

"Your father and I are really glad you decided to come home for a while. We've really missed you." She hugged me again.

"I've missed you guys too. Life in L.A. has just been really hectic, so I wasn't able to come back like I used to, but I'm glad to be here now." I pretended that that was all my mother wanted to talk about. I jumped up, acting like unpacking was the most important thing in the world that I had to do.

"About that . . . ," my mother said, shutting down my hopes not to have this conversation. "What exactly happened with you and King?"

I took a deep breath. I knew her thoughts, and I understood her concerns. I really just wanted to forget this whole subject altogether. It was hard enough reminiscing about the past in my head, but talking about it out loud seemed to be too much to bear right now.

She said, "I mean, you moved in with him after a short period of time, we've heard from you less and less since you met him, you completely abandoned your dreams of being a journalist, he got you pregnant without marriage, and then, all of a sudden, he's gone." She shook her head, as if she couldn't believe her own words. "Your father and I are very . . . uncomfortable about all of this. About him."

I was absolutely fine . . . until my mother mentioned my pregnancy. Though it had been weeks, losing my baby had left a hole in my heart, and I wasn't yet sure how exactly to tell my parents what had happened.

I looked down at my stomach, and I realized that telling my mother wouldn't hurt a thing. In fact, it might help. That would be one thing that she and my dad could take off the "We hate King" list.

Taking her hand, I said, "About the baby, Mom . . ." I held my breath and closed my eyes. "I'm not pregnant anymore. I had a miscarriage."

When I opened my eyes, the look of shock on my mother's face brought fresh tears to my eyes.

She might have reservations about the way I went about my relationship with King, but she could feel my loss, and she could feel my pain. She was a mother, so she knew what this had done to me.

"Oh, baby, I am so sorry." She squeezed my hands. "What happened?"

I shrugged, as if it had all been natural. "Just didn't go to full term, that's all." I definitely wasn't going to get into the details. Not if I wanted my parents to someday forget about this whole thing. They would never understand. They would never be able to move on the way I was planning to.

"How are you feeling?"

"I'm doing okay. It's been hard, but King was there for me." I paused as I thought back to those days and how Donovan had been the one who really took care of me.

My mother smirked, as if she didn't believe my words. Or maybe she just didn't want to hear them. "So why did you leave the man?"

"Look, Mom, King isn't perfect. I understand that, but he's a good man. We just had our differences."

I guess my mother didn't want to hear my defense of King anymore. She sighed and stood. "If that's what it was, then we'll leave it at that. You know we only want what's best for you. To be happy. To have a fulfilled life."

"I know, Mom, and I want the same thing."

We stared at each other in a moment of silence.

Then my mother acquiesced, a little. "I'm not saying I like him, but if you're happy, then I'm happy."

"Thank you, Mom."

She gave me a quick hug before she moved toward the door. Turning around, she added, "Just know that if it doesn't work out, we'll always be here." And with that, she was gone.

Actually, that turned out to be a good talk for me. Even though I knew it, I needed to hear that my parents still loved me in spite of how I'd handled my life over the past year and a half. I was feeling better about this trip already. Donovan and Leslie had been right. The support and care of my family were exactly what I needed.

I walked to my window and stared out into the backyard, where I'd had thousands of hours of wonderful playtime. The memories made me smile.

I was home. Home sweet home.

Chapter 30

I felt so much love from my family while I was back at home. I should have known the moment I told my mother I was coming home that she would call everyone who had ever known me. Aunts and uncles came by to see how the California girl was making it back in little ole Ohio. Cousins who I grew up with took me out on the town to show me the new things that had been built and the hot spots they kicked it at now. My first cousin Tamara introduced me to her husband, Matt, and their little girl, Hazel.

"I'm so sorry I missed the wedding." I told her, admiring her beautiful one-year-old.

"Girl, please. We did a courthouse wedding. I didn't want that added stress," Tamara replied.

It was surreal that my cousin who had sworn she would never get married was a wife and a mother. In that moment my heart fell to the pit of my stomach. I knew that at least half of what she had would never come true for me.

As good as it was seeing family, I was so glad that it was just my parents and me today. Saturdays were usually our days for the three of us. My father cooked his famous chocolate chip and pecan waffles, which he served with eggs and Canadian bacon. It had absolutely been my favorite meal since I was three. My dad was the king of breakfast, and I felt like a kid again as I stuffed my face.

Afterward, my mother and I broke out a thousand-piece puzzle and played oldies on the stereo. Marvin Gaye's sultry voice rang out, and it put me in such a great mood. I had always had a real connection with his music. I really thought Marvin and I had had a love affair in a past life.

My mother and I were sitting at the dining room table, singing along to "Ain't No Mountain High Enough," putting puzzle pieces together, when the doorbell rang. I popped up and then sang and bopped to Marvin and Tammi all the way to the door. I opened the door, and immediately I felt the blood drain from my face.

"Hello, beautiful."

I couldn't move. I couldn't breathe. I couldn't form words to come out of my mouth. All I was able to do was stand there. Surely, this wasn't real. Surely, I was dreaming, because I thought I had left my past back in Malibu.

"What are you doing here, King?" I managed to finally get out.

"I missed you."

"How did you even know where my parents live?"

He didn't answer at first. He just smiled slightly, as if to say, "That's for me to know and you to find out." Finally he said, "I was hoping maybe we could talk."

"Why? Didn't we talk enough in California?" I finally got some movement back in my body and crossed my arms.

"No, we argued in California. I don't want to do that anymore." When I didn't respond, he continued. "I know that there is absolutely no reason for you to talk to me ever again, but I was hoping that you would."

I took a moment to weigh my options. I couldn't imagine what else King had to say to me. Everything he said to me was starting to sound the same as I looked

back on it. What was going to be so different this time?
I looked at him, and I could tell he had been crying.
His hair looked like it hadn't been cut in weeks, and his
clothes were wrinkled. It was the first time I had seen
King looking like a bum. I sighed and then went to go
put on some shoes. I figured if anything went wrong,
I had my father here. I came out and closed the door
behind me, and we began to walk down the street.

"So how you been?" I could hear the nervousness in
his voice.

"Better, actually."

"I'm glad."

"I'm really not interested in small talk, King. What
did you come here for?"

"You." He stopped dead in his tracks and turned toward me, gently grabbing both of my hands. "I came
because I can't live without you."

"King, we have been through this before."

"This is different, Heiress." I rolled my eyes. "I'm serious. I've realized how bad I've treated you, and I don't
blame you for leaving, but I need you."

I had to admit this was the first time I had heard this.

"You are the only thing in my life that actually makes
sense," he continued.

"King, there are a lot of things that are seriously wrong
with our relationship."

"I know, and I'm willing to fix all of them. I want to
be, again, the man that you fell in love with."

I actually wanted to believe that. I missed those days
when we first started dating and he was everything
dreams were made of. I would love to see that man
again. I just didn't know if he would ever show back up.

"I do miss that guy," I said, toning down some of my
attitude. I didn't know why I was letting my guard down,
but it was becoming extremely hard to keep it up.

"I can be him. I am him. I admit, I let some things go to my head, but I've changed."

That statement made me laugh out loud. "In a week?"

"Okay, I'm changing, but it is for the better. Heiress, you are the best thing that has happened to me. Please reconsider my proposal. Come home."

I didn't know if it was the sincerity in his voice or the fact that he had actually come after me, but I was starting to rethink it all. I did still love him. I started shifting my weight from one foot to the other. I looked deep in his eyes, and I began to crumble.

"So what happens if I do give you another chance?"

"We can start over."

"There need to be changes, King." The stern tone in my voice really had his attention.

"I promise. Is that a yes?"

"I'm willing to start over."

He flashed me a big smile, like I had just told him he'd won the lottery. He reached down in his pocket and pulled out the ring he had offered to me back in California.

"King, I said I'd start over. I don't think we're ready to get engaged."

"I want to marry you. We can start over, but I need you to be my wife."

He slipped the ring on my finger, and I just stared at it. Was I really ready for this? I felt like King had realized how awful he could be to me sometimes and wanted to change. I shook my head to reassure him that I was on board, and he kissed me passionately.

Going back to the house for formal introductions was tough. My parents weren't too happy to meet King and less happy that in ten minutes I'd gone from being single to getting engaged.

My father asked, "Have you really thought about this? Marriage is a big commitment."

"Of course we've thought about this," I said. It was sort of a lie, because it had all happened so quickly for me. "We still have things we have to talk about and work out, but—"

My mother interrupted me. "I can't believe you would just rush into something like this without talking to us."

The words were barely out of my mother's mouth when my father jumped in. "Baby, this is a big step. Are you sure this is what you really want?"

The questions were coming from the left, then the right. They were being thrown at me like I was in a batting cage with a gone-haywire ball machine. I couldn't possible hit every one, and it was becoming overwhelming.

"Okay, both of you, please stop," I told them. I took a breath and looked around. The expressions on the faces that looked back at me were a mixture of confusion, shock, and disappointment. "Guys, I love you and I respect your opinions, but at the end of the day, this is my life."

I grabbed King's hand to make a statement to my parents. "I am an adult, and I have to make my own decisions. King has offered me the world, and I plan on taking it. So, yes, we are getting married, and that is that. I hope you can be happy for me, but if not, this is still something that I'm going to do."

I stepped away from them and ran to my room. Closing the door behind me, I fell across my bed. I didn't cry, but the pressure that I felt on me at this moment made it hard for me to breathe.

Life and love shouldn't be this difficult.

There was a light tap on my door, and then my father called, "Baby girl, are you okay?"

I didn't look up, but I heard my door open, then close. This was a familiar scene. As a little girl, whenever I ran to my room, my father was the one who was always right behind me, checking to make sure that I was fine.

I stayed in the same position, facedown on the bed; I didn't move at all.

"Baby, come on. Sit up and talk to me." He sat on the bed, pulled me up, and held me in his arms. "You know what the best day of my life was?"

"My birth," I answered, unenthused. This lecture always started out the same way, with that question.

"Absolutely. The day you were born was the happiest day of my life. You were so little and innocent, and I knew that for the rest of my life I had to make good decisions, because I had this beautiful little girl who would depend on me for the rest of her life. Sometimes, while your mother slept, I would take you in my arms and have deep conversations with you."

"Really?" I said, now a little more interested, since I'd never heard this version before.

"Absolutely. I promised you that no matter what, nothing and no one would ever hurt you because I would always be there to protect you. And up until now I've done a pretty good job."

I would agree with that. My father had always been there to protect me. The first time I could remember was when I was six years old and Edward Taylor pushed me off the swing set at the park. My father ended up in a scuffle with his father over the whole thing. That day I was sure he was Superman.

"You remember that Taylor kid?"

It was as if he'd just read my mind, and all I could do was laugh.

He continued with, "I understand that you're an adult and that you can make your own decisions. But I will always be the man who made that promise to always protect you. So all I'm here to do at this point is make sure that you're okay and happy." He paused, as if he wanted to really think about his next words. "And I'm sorry, baby girl, but I don't get that feeling from you with King."

Why were people always saying that? "I am happy, Daddy," I insisted. "King loves me." I looked him dead in his eyes so he could see the truth for himself. "And I love him."

"I hope so, baby girl. You know your mother and I will support whatever decision you make, but understand you have a man here who will always love you more than anyone ever could. I loved you before you were even born."

"I know, Daddy." I laid my head back on his shoulder, and he rubbed my back, giving me comfort.

"Just be careful with this man. You have already sacrificed so much of your life. Don't lose all of who you are." He kissed me softly on my forehead and then left me alone with his words and those thoughts still hanging in air.

There was one point that my dad had just made that I couldn't ignore. I had sacrificed a lot for King. I'd traded in my dreams for this glamorous life.

Standing, I grabbed my purse and pulled out my engagement ring, which I'd tucked away in the side pocket. I twisted the ring in the air, letting the light hit the diamond so that it glittered. This ring was proof that King was ready wholeheartedly for this relationship.

My parents were wrong, and I was right. I lay across my bed and admired the ring until I fell asleep.

Chapter 31

As much as I loved my parents, a few weeks with them under these circumstances was long enough. I wanted to get King back home, in his own environment, before my father took him out hunting and then returned without him.

I decided to call a cab to take us to the airport, sparing my parents—and us—that thirty-minute ride in uncomfortable silence. When the cab arrived, King said good-bye to my parents, then rushed outside, as if he couldn't get away fast enough. At least it gave me a few moments alone with my parents.

"I promise I'll do a lot better with calling . . . and visiting," I told them as I hugged my mother first. I felt like she was trying to squeeze the life out of me, and when she pulled back, there were tears in her eyes already.

"I love you so much, little girl."

"I love you too, Mom."

When she stepped aside, my father stepped up. He studied me like he was taking his last look. This was the way he looked at me on the day that I got on the plane to go to college. It was like he was taking mental notes, or trying to take a mental picture that he could keep. Then he grabbed me and held me tight.

I loved my father's hugs; he always made me feel five years old again. His arms were my safe place, my protection.

"Just remember what I told you, baby girl," he whispered in my ear. "Don't lose yourself."

We gave each other a kiss on the cheek and then stepped away from our grasp. I left my parents standing on their porch, and when the cabdriver pulled off, I couldn't hold back my tears.

But King was right there, comforting me, wiping the tears from my cheeks. Then he held my hand, not letting go until we got to the airport.

We were both completely exhausted when we finally stepped into our home in L.A., but even though he was tired, King came alive. It was like he'd been holding back in front of my parents, but the moment we hit our door, he grabbed me in a hug, kissed me, and then carried me up the stairs to our bedroom.

That night was one of the most beautiful I'd ever had with him, and the days that followed were exactly the same. King as a fiancé was way better than King as a boyfriend, and I was beginning to think that we should've done this a long time ago. For the next few weeks, we had romantic dinners by candlelight, he came home with "just because" gifts, and—the best one—he bought me a new car. It was a shocking thrill when he pulled me outside the house and showed me the parked Maserati.

"Oh my God, you got the new car." Earlier that day I had pointed it out in a magazine, thinking that King would love it.

"I got the car," he said. "But I got it for you."

Right there I kissed him with so much passion that I was sure someone would yell out for us to take it inside. We were back to being the couple we were when we started dating.

The next morning he woke me up with kisses, and then we showered together. I watched him get dressed and admired every inch of that man. He still had all the muscles that he'd worked so hard to get with his last project, and that made him even more attractive.

"Babe, you know I have that photo shoot today," he announced.

"Oh, I forgot about that," I said. "How long do you think it'll be?"

"It might run late, so why don't you come with me? You can hang out on set and watch me work."

"Oh, baby, that is so sweet, but I think I'd rather stay at home," I said as I walked over to him and helped him adjust his tie.

"You sure? I don't want you to be cooped up in the house all day."

"I'm sure. I'll be fine."

"No, you won't be fine. You are already so fine." He grabbed me, and I giggled. Then he kissed me like we were in high school, and when we broke away, I sighed. There was absolutely nothing better than being in love this way.

After he left, I hung out in our den for a little while, trying to decide how I was going to spend my day. I didn't feel like going shopping, and I wasn't up for a lunch date with anyone, though for a second, I did think about calling Blair. But we were so disconnected from one another. I hadn't talked to her in months, and with all that I'd been through, it didn't even feel like she was part of my life anymore.

I picked up my phone and dialed the only person I knew I could depend on.

"Heiress, my God, are you all right?" Donovan shouted into the phone. "I've been so worried about you."

"I'm fine, Donny." I tried calming him down with the tone of my voice.

"You just up and left me. No note, no nothing, and I couldn't reach you. I was so worried something bad had happened."

The concern in his voice made me feel bad for not calling him, but everything had happened so fast. I'd gone from leaving King to making love to him all in a matter of minutes. It just didn't seem right to call Donovan then.

"Donny, I'm fine. I took your advice and went home to be with my folks for a little while."

"Good," he sighed. "How was it?"

"Nice. You were right. Hanging out with my parents for a week did a girl good."

"See? That's great. So where are you now?"

I paused for a second and really thought about what I was going to say next. I hadn't mentioned King's name, and there was so much to tell Donovan. But I knew he would never be able to see the good part of King and me getting married. Still, I had to be honest with my friend, who had been there for me.

"Donny, you know I love you and appreciate everything you have done for me. You have been there for me through the hardest times of my life, and I am so grateful for that." I tried to butter him up with praise and appreciation to let him know that everything he had done wasn't in vain.

"Heiress?" Judging by the tone of his voice, he had gone back to being concerned.

"Donny"—I took a breath—"King and I are working everything out."

"Oh, no . . ."

"And we've decided to get married."

There was a long silence over the phone, and I was afraid of what was to come. Whenever Donovan was angry or disappointed, I couldn't tell, because he would shut down and become quiet. He had always done that when we were children, and at times it had scared me, because you never knew what he was thinking.

"I can't believe you, Heiress," he finally whispered.

"I know what has happened but—"

"I'm really not interested in the excuses you have for him," he interrupted me. "I'm thinking about you. How stupid can you be?"

"Excuse me?" His statement took me aback. He had never spoken to me in that manner.

"This man demands that you leave your dreams behind, he repeatedly disrespects you and loses his temper, to the point where you lose not only a baby, but all hope of having any more children. And you're telling me that all he has to do is say 'I'm sorry' and you're running back to him?"

"It's not like that. It's—"

"Or maybe it was the ring," Donovan said, interrupting me again. "I get it. How big is the ring, Heiress? Is that what he did? Buy you some huge diamond ring and now all is forgiven?"

I couldn't believe what Donovan was saying. Each word that came through the receiver hurt more than the last. I knew that King wasn't Donovan's favorite person, but I at least thought he would be happy that I had worked out my problems.

"I have been through a lot with this man, and I think I owe it to him to stick it out," I tried to explain.

"That's the thing, Heiress. You've been through a lot. King hasn't been through anything. He's been doing what he wants this whole time, and it doesn't matter, because apparently you keep going back. Talk about being a doormat."

I couldn't take this conversation anymore. The insults were unbearable. I didn't want to lose Donovan's friendship, but I wanted King more. We were happy, and I knew that he would give me everything he'd promised.

"Donny, please."

"Heiress. Open your eyes, and stop being some stupid, lovesick groupie."

With that, he hung the phone up, leaving me with words that had cut me deep, especially since the words came from Donovan's mouth.

I put the phone down, and the tears burst from my eyes. I didn't want to lose Donovan after everything he had done for me, but I was in love with King. I never wanted to disappoint anyone, but I needed people to be happy for me.

Didn't my parents understand? Didn't Donovan understand? Nobody in this world was perfect, and people changed. King was a good man, with good intentions. I just needed the people who said they loved me to understand that.

Well, if no one wanted to support me, that was fine. I guess it was just going to be King and me.

Glancing at the clock, I wiped my eyes. I decided that I'd go join King on his photo shoot, after all.

Chapter 32

I still couldn't say that I felt completely comfortable in this seat. I was always happy once I arrived here, but before we started, I wanted to run for the hills. Maybe it was just always going to be weird, sitting in front of a stranger, telling all my secrets. But every time I sat with Leslie, I felt better. So I just kept pushing myself to do it.

"All right, here we go." Leslie came into the room and handed me a cup of coffee. Then, when she sat down, she added, "I was really surprised to get your call this morning."

After my conversation with Donovan yesterday, I decided I needed someone to talk to. I certainly couldn't mention him to King, so I'd called Leslie.

"Don't get me wrong," she said. "I was glad to hear from you. So tell me, how was the trip back to Ohio?"

"It was interesting, to say the least." I sipped my coffee.

"Are you interested in saying the most and telling me about it?" She giggled, as if her words were funny.

"Well," I began, "it was the first time my parents met King, and it was a bit uncomfortable at times."

Leslie squinted, like she was confused. "I thought you were going home to get away from your issues with King. I didn't realize he was going with you." She jotted something on her notepad, and I realized that was beginning to get on my nerves.

"My plan at first was to go alone, but then King proposed and I thought it was time for him to meet my parents."

Leslie stopped writing. "So you're engaged?" she asked slowly, as if she wanted to make sure she'd heard me correctly.

I nodded and took another sip of my coffee.

She put her notepad down. "Are you happy with that decision?"

Everyone kept asking me that, but I didn't let a beat go by. "I am, actually," I said strongly. "I am, even if my parents and Donovan are not happy about my decision."

She started writing on her pad again, and I tried to discreetly sit up so that I could peek at what she was writing.

"None of the people in your life support your decision to marry King? Why is that?"

I began to tell her all about the conversations I'd had with each one of them and all their concerns. I spent quite a bit of time telling her how hurt I was by Donovan and how I wasn't so sure I wanted to repair that friendship.

"Can you catch me up on why everybody feels the same way?"

"King hasn't always been the Prince Charming everybody wants me to have."

I elaborated on some of the things I'd gone through with King. I gave her a little insight into his temper, and today I even told her a little bit about the fight we'd had when I'd miscarried.

As I heard my own words, I could understand how people saw King as a monster. But I didn't want Leslie to see him that way, so I explained that the pressures of his job had a direct effect on his moods. He came from Hollywood royalty, and he had a lot to live up to.

"I know that can be so hard on a man, having to live up to other people's standards. So I just want to be the woman who's in his corner, who stands by him," I revealed.

Leslie listened as I talked. And I talked as she wrote. She had no reaction, at least judging by her expressions.

When I finally stopped, she said, "Heiress, let me ask you a question. Do you feel like you have an addictive personality?"

"What?" I was completely puzzled by her question. "I'm not sure I understand your question."

"It sounds like to me you have a slight addiction to King. He built you up in the beginning of your relationship, only to tear you down, and now you're consistently chasing behind him to get that high you had in the beginning."

I wanted to laugh in her face. Was this lady serious? An addiction to a person? To King? It wasn't an addiction; it was a relationship. It was love.

And it was time. The time that I'd put in. I'd been through so much with King, trying to make things right, that I wasn't going to leave and make it easy for the next woman to swoop in and take my place. I was going to fight for my man and the family that I wanted.

So, no, it wasn't an addiction, and I was quite offended that she had even suggested that.

"I can tell by your face that that question struck a nerve." Maybe she should be a psychic, because she sure read my mind. "Listen, why don't I give you a homework assignment? Do you keep a journal?"

"No," I said, with my arms folded. I wasn't sure that I wanted to come back after what she'd just said, let alone do anything that she asked me to do.

"I think now is a perfect time to start. Go to a bookstore, pick up a journal, and start writing down your thoughts and feelings. This will help you verbalize things, and then later, when you go back to read what you've written, you may have a different perspective."

I wasn't happy with the way the session had gone, but I decided to do exactly what she told me to do. What did I have to lose? I used to have a diary when I was younger, but I was never consistent with writing in it.

On the way home I stopped by the Barnes & Noble in Marina Del Rey and chose a purple-flowered journal. As soon as I got home, I went out by the pool and sat down with the blank pages in front of me. But where was I supposed to start? Was I supposed to go back to the beginning or talk about how I was feeling now?

But then events began to pop into my head, and I finally put the pen to paper. I was ready to write my first entry.

Chapter 33

When King's mother called and said that she had set up an appointment with a wedding coordinator, I was shocked.

"But we haven't even set a date yet," I told her.

"That's okay, sweetheart," she said. "It's never too early to begin planning. Especially what's going to be such a fabulous affair."

"Okay," I told her, still so unsure.

"Don't worry, Heiress. This is how it's done in Hollywood. It's going to take a lot of planning."

"Well, I haven't even really thought of what I want the wedding to look like."

"That's why we need to sit down with the coordinator," Mrs. Stevens said. "I am so excited."

Well, I guess she was. She was more excited than me if she was ready to get started now.

"This is going to be fabulous," she continued. "I have been looking forward to the day when King would settle down with a nice girl. I'm glad he found you, Heiress. I've been waiting a long time for this."

I didn't know why the conversation was making me so uncomfortable. But then it got worse when Mrs. Stevens added, "And when you have children . . ." She stopped, as if she suddenly realized what she was saying. But it was too late. "Heiress, I'm so sorry."

"Mrs. Stevens, I have to go."

"Heiress . . ."

I hung up on her, but only because I needed to make it to the bathroom in time. The thought of what had happened to me literally made me sick to my stomach for lots of reasons.

Glancing down at my stomach, I tried to remember when it had protruded just a little. And I knew that it would probably never look that way again. I wanted to cry but was tired of doing that. I needed to look at the bright side of this. King knew that I couldn't have children, and he still wanted to marry me. That was the bright side. That was what I needed to keep focused on.

Still, the next day I met with King's mother and the wedding coordinator. We spent the day talking about possible venues, looking at photos of table settings, thinking about what kind of flowers I'd want and a whole bunch of other things, which at this point, I was willing to let Mrs. Stevens handle.

It was after six by the time I got home, totally exhausted. If that was what one day of wedding planning was going to be like, how would I survive months of it? All I wanted to do was get in the house, crawl onto the couch, watch TV, and wait for King to come home.

I noticed the envelope on the front door the moment I drove up, and wondered who would tape something to a door like that. My first thought was it might be something from the wedding coordinator. There was no name on the envelope, no kind of identification. It was just a plain yellow envelope.

While I never opened King's mail, I didn't know if it was for him or for me, so I went through the rest of the mail and then ripped open the envelope. I frowned when I pulled out the pictures. They were black-and-white eight-by-ten photos of King and some woman.

As I went through them, my mouth dropped open. The first picture was of the two of them entering a hotel, then checking in at the front desk. The next was a photo of them kissing in front of an elevator. But I almost collapsed from shock when the next picture showed the woman completely naked, riding King. Then there was a picture of King with his head buried between her legs.

I fell onto the floor right there with the pictures still in my hand. Sitting there, I went through each one over and over again. Who had taken these? I brought the photos closer to my eyes, but the thing was, none of them were a good shot of the woman. I couldn't see her face in any of them.

Finally I stood up. Inside the den I put each picture through the shredder. These couldn't be real. First of all, King would never let someone take pictures of him. Secondly, why wasn't the woman's face ever shown?

I had just gotten my happiness back in this relationship, and I wasn't about to let it go that easily. No, these had been Photoshopped, just like the photos in magazines. They weren't going to get me that easily this time.

As soon as I shredded the last picture, the phone rang and I froze as I looked at the caller ID screen. Was this a sign?

I had to take a long, deep breath before I answered. "Hey, babe," I said, as if I hadn't just seen pictures of him naked.

"You are not going to believe this!"

He was so excited, I forgot for a moment what I'd just seen. "What is it? What happened?"

"I was just nominated for an Academy Award!"

"What!"

"Yeah, baby! Can you believe it?"

"No! I mean, yes. Of course. Oh, King, I'm so happy for you."

"Thanks, baby. That means when I get home tonight, we have to celebrate."

"Oh, we'll celebrate, all right."

When King came home, I was ready for him. I met him at the door, dressed in nothing but Versace pumps. He didn't say a word to me. Just lifted me up and carried me up the stairs.

And I didn't say a word to him. Nothing except "Congratulations!"

There was no need for me to think about the pictures now. I knew for sure they were a lie designed to take all of this wonderfulness away from me.

And I was not going to let it happen. Ever.

Chapter 34

King and I had a couple of really good weeks. With the Academy Award nomination, our schedules were so busy, with interviews here, parties there. I fell into the excitement with King, with only one thing holding me back—those pictures.

I had tried to put the pictures out of my mind, but they were still there. They were there in my mind when I went to sleep, and they were there in my mind when I woke up, as well. Every time King kissed me or we made love, I wondered if those pictures had been real. Was he having an affair?

There was no way I was going to ask him. No way that I was going to ruin this wonderful time for him. But still, I needed to talk to someone about them.

But who?

Donovan was out of the picture, so all I had was Leslie.

So here I was again, feeling uncomfortable, the way I always did when I first arrived at therapy.

"So how are things?" Leslie asked me.

I shrugged. "Fine."

Leslie frowned. "That's all you have to say?"

All I did was shrug again.

"I would've thought that you would have told me about King's Academy Award nomination."

"Oh, you know about that?"

She chuckled. "Who doesn't? That's all that's been on the news. The son of Hollywood royalty finally stepping into his own."

"Yeah, I'm happy about that."

She frowned a little before she asked, "Is there anything in particular that you wanted to talk about today?"

The pictures! "Yes," I said. "I want to talk about . . . Donovan."

"What about him?"

"His being mad at me is really bothering me. I miss his company."

"Why don't you expound on your relationship with Donovan?"

I shrugged. "What about it?"

"How did you two meet?"

"I told you. We were friends from the time we were kids. We grew up in Ohio together. We met in the first grade and have been best friends ever since. Our parents are good friends too."

"So you go way back."

I nodded. "I can't remember a time when he wasn't in my life. He's always been my friend, my rescuer. When kids would pick on me at school, Donovan was always there. One time I slipped into the deep end of the pool at the community center and almost drowned. But Donovan was right there. He didn't even really know how to swim, but he got me out of there before the lifeguards could do a thing."

"So let me ask you something. Did you ever see yourself with Donovan?"

"You mean like a couple?"

Leslie nodded.

I shook my head. "I think there were a lot of people who thought we would be together, including our parents. But I don't see him like that."

Leslie nodded, but something made me think that she didn't really believe me. "Okay, so have you written in your journal?"

I was surprised that she changed the subject. I wanted to talk about Donovan just a little more. I wanted to know how I could fix things with him.

"No," I lied. I had written in my journal. From the first day. But I was afraid that she might ask to read it or something, and I definitely wasn't ready for that.

I'd written too much in my journal, including about how it was King's fault that I lost my baby and about those pictures. I wanted to keep that journal to myself . . . at least for now.

"I'm telling you, Heiress, writing your thoughts and feelings down is really a great exercise."

I nodded.

She said, "Why don't you go home and start with this? Start with writing your feelings about what's happened between you and Donovan."

"Okay."

"Writing it down just might help you find the answers you're looking for."

Those words actually made me feel a little better. Maybe I was like Dorothy in *The Wizard of Oz*. Maybe I did have the key to how I could fix this thing with Donovan already inside of me.

I left the session with Leslie feeling better than when I went in, as always. And just like before, I did what she told me.

I went home and wrote in my journal.

Chapter 35

Our house was aflutter with excitement, and it was only noon. That was because we had to be ready when the limousine came at four to take us to the Kodak Theatre for the six o'clock taping of the Academy Awards.

So there were hairstylists and makeup artists and even a seamstress here to make sure that my gown was perfect, even though I'd had about five fittings. King wanted me to look fabulous, and he'd hired all these people to take care of me. While I sat in the chair in front of the vanity in our bedroom, King stood in the doorway.

"Which would you prefer?" Drake, the hairstylist, asked me. "An updo or letting curls fall on your shoulders?"

King and I spoke at the same time. I said, "An updo."

King wanted just the opposite. "I always like your hair down, baby," he said. Then he motioned to Drake to do exactly what he'd said.

When the seamstress came in our bedroom with the two dresses I'd chosen, King made the decision for me again. "She's going to wear the gold one," he said. "She's going to match the Oscar when I win tonight."

Everyone in the room laughed, and I did too. After that, I just sat back and enjoyed the way King took care of me.

Four hours later I was ready. King's choices had been right. My hair looked fabulous the way it draped my bare shoulders. And the Yves Saint Laurent gown . . . Even I had to say, "Wow!"

No matter what, I didn't look as good as my King! He wore a classic tuxedo, but there was nothing ordinary about him. It had to be his air; he exuded confidence.

"I'm going to win this, baby. I can just feel it."

He tried to kiss me, but I turned so that his lips would touch my cheek. I didn't want to mess up the fabulous, flawless job that the makeup artist had done.

The moment we slid into the limousine, King's cell phone rang.

"What's up, Marty?" he said to his manager.

From the rest of the conversation, I could tell that King was on a three-way call with his manager and publicist, going over the logistics of the night and his acceptance speech if he won.

"I'm going to win this thing," he told them, just like he told me.

I was disappointed that King and I didn't have this time alone. I'd wanted to bask in these moments, holding King's hand, giving him encouragement, and letting him know that I loved him no matter which way tonight turned out. But I didn't want to say anything, stress King out in any way. So I just sat back and enjoyed it all, taking in the moments.

It was nothing but madness when we pulled into the long line of limos leading to the Kodak Theatre. The streets were lined with fans trying to get a peek through the tinted windows. Once our car finally pulled up and we stepped out, the fans screamed. King slid out first, then turned to help me out, and for the first time since we'd been together, I felt like a star. Cameras were flashing, including those belonging to the media who'd been approved for the event and to the fans who stood far away but were still trying to get a picture.

Sherri, King's publicist, met us at the limo and led us down the red carpet. The media called out to King, but Sherri chose who he stopped to speak with. Even though it was February, I was hot with all the excitement going on around me. All I did was stand by King's side and smile as he spoke to one journalist after another. And for just a moment, I wondered what it would be like if I were on the other side, if I were a journalist covering this event. But I pushed that thought aside. It was much, much better being on this side.

I'd been to lots of Hollywood affairs with King, but truly, this was overwhelming. Inside, we were seated just two rows from the front, with King on the aisle.

"That's what they do in case he wins," Sherri explained. "Then he won't have to step over anyone."

"Great, 'cause I'm gonna win this thing," King said.

I just smiled.

I'd watched the Academy Awards on TV for as long as I could remember, but nothing had prepared me for sitting here live. All around me were stars who knew my name . . . because of King. And who spoke to me . . . because of King.

And the show . . . it was like being at an elegant comedy event with Billy Crystal as the host. I laughed and clapped, but I noticed that King didn't. I guess it was hard sitting there. Especially if you were waiting for the winner of the award for best actor to be announced. It was one of the last categories.

As the time passed, I could feel King's tension. But I tried to ignore it and focus on the show. I didn't know how many times King and I would ever be at the Academy Awards, and I wanted to enjoy this as if it was our last time. Finally, Meryl Streep came out to announce the nominees for best actor.

"And the nominees are . . ."

To me, time slowed down. Meryl seemed to drag out all the names. And then she took her time opening the envelope. And finally, she called out the winner.

Only, it wasn't King Stevens.

Around us, people applauded, and I did too. King didn't. I could feel it as if it was my own spirit; I knew that King's spirit had been crushed.

I was glad that best actor was one of the last categories, because I wasn't sure how much longer he was going to sit there. Not very long after the show ended, King took my hand.

"Come on," he said, kind of jerking me a bit.

I kept the smile on my face, hoping that King would be in a better mood once we got to the *Vanity Fair* party. But the moment we stepped outside of the theater, he told me that we were going home.

"Really?" was all I said. I wanted to ask him why, I wanted to encourage him to go to the party, and I wanted to tell him that he didn't want to look like a sore loser. But I said none of those things. I just followed him to the curb to wait for our limousine.

Inside the limo, I put my hand over King's, but he snatched his away. Leaning forward, he pulled out a bottle of scotch from the bar on the side panel, and without using a glass, he swallowed a swig.

"King . . ."

"What?" he snapped.

"I just wanted to say—"

"Save it, Heiress. Just save it." And then he took another swallow.

I scooted away from him to the other side of the leather seat, trying my best to stay out of his line of fire. But I kept my eyes on him, watched him wallow in his emotions.

I wanted to tell him to snap out of it. He was a grown man, and at least he'd been nominated. How many actors—especially black actors—could say that? But I was smart enough to keep my mouth shut.

I'd hoped that things would be better once we got home, but King stomped into the house, then marched to the den and slammed the door.

I knew not to follow him.

All I did was stand outside the door to the den and sigh.

Chapter 36

Talk about a loser's funk. The next day King was still acting the same way. Drinking, snapping at me, moping around the house. He was like a kid throwing an extended temper tantrum.

I tried everything I could think of. I had our chef make King's favorite breakfast, but King wouldn't eat a thing. I put his favorite Sade CD into the stereo, letting it play through the house, but he took it out and broke it in half.

There was nothing I could do. And there was nothing anyone else could do. King wouldn't answer calls, and I kept hearing the text alert on his phone go off. But he didn't respond to anything or anyone.

After breakfast I turned on the television, not wanting to leave the house, not wanting to leave him alone. But then King came into the living room, where I was watching *The View*. They were talking about the Academy Award winners.

King screamed, "Turn that damn TV off!"

I grabbed the remote and turned the power off. I was surprised when King stayed standing in the doorway.

Finally, I said to him, "Baby, do you want to talk?"

"Talk about what?"

The way he responded should've been my clue to leave him alone. But I loved him and wanted to help him through this. So I said, "About what happened last night."

He stood still for a moment, as if he was pondering my words. As if he might want to talk. And then he said, "You want to talk about last night?"

I nodded.

"You want to talk about the way I lost?"

"You didn't lose, baby. Not really. You were nominated."

"You want to talk about the way I lost because of you!"

My head snapped back. "Because of me? King, I . . ."

"Yeah. Because you're a fat cow and because you're a loser."

"What?" Where were these words coming from?

"You lose everything. You lost our baby, didn't you?"

Oh my God! I couldn't believe he'd said that to me.

"I lost because I'm with a loser. No one gives awards to losers."

"King!" I cried.

He shook his head. "I don't even know why I'm with you. If I'd married Marlaina, I would've won last night."

I had never been so grateful to see him stomp away. I tried to breathe and to remember that he was drunk and he was hurt. And hurt people hurt people.

But I couldn't find any words to justify what he'd just said to me.

Our baby? He'd really gone there, when it was his fault?

When the front door slammed, I turned the television back on. I watched every single show that talked about last night's winners and losers.

And I cried the entire time.

Chapter 37

It was time. After what King had said to me last week, I needed to talk about it. I needed to talk about my miscarriage and the way I'd lost my baby.

So here I was, back in Leslie's office, and ready to talk this time . . . for real.

"It started when King left for his trip," I said. "We didn't talk much while he was away, but then when he came back . . ."

I kept talking, laying it all out for Leslie: how King returned after being away for three weeks and treated me like he'd just come back from the store. I told her about the fight, about how I left and planned to leave for good.

And then the hard part. How he'd tossed me down the stairs. To this day King said it was an accident. And I didn't really think that he pushed me on purpose. But in my mind, I saw it as being tossed.

As I told Leslie about it, I could actually feel the way I rolled down those stairs, hitting every single step. I was crying, once again, when I got to the part about being in the hospital and hearing my new truth. I sat silently, just sobbing, when I finished; and Leslie stayed quiet for a while too.

Finally, she said, "You know, what you just did was really important."

I didn't know what she was talking about.

"You just had a breakthrough moment. That's a good thing."

If it was so good, why did I feel so bad? It was the first time I'd ever said all those words out loud. The first time that I'd ever put this whole situation together.

"So how are you feeling about this now?" Leslie asked me.

I wondered what she wanted to know. Here I was, sitting here, crying, even though this had happened months ago.

"I mean," Leslie explained, "how do you feel about King?"

"I love him."

"Do you realize that's what you say all the time?"

Wasn't that what someone was supposed to say when they were in love?

Leslie clarified her question. "How do you feel about King as he relates to this situation? Your miscarriage?"

"I still hold a lot of anger toward him. And, really, I thought about leaving him because of it."

"But . . . ," Leslie said, then stopped, as if she wanted me to finish her sentence.

"But . . ." I didn't want to say it, but it was the truth. "But my love for him is greater than wanting to leave him."

"Why do you think you love him so much? Even after all that the two of you have gone through?"

"Because he loves me. Even though I may not be able to have children, it doesn't matter to King."

"But he caused that."

"Not on purpose. And, anyway, is there another man out there who would want to be with a twenty-six-year-old woman who can't have children?"

"Definitely. There are plenty of men who would accept that *and* who would love you. Plus, you have so many other options. You could adopt. . . ."

"What?"

"Or use a surrogate."

"You mean, have someone else give birth to *my* baby?"

"Yes." Leslie nodded. "It's a perfectly legitimate way to have a baby and—"

"No!" I screamed. "No!"

"Why?" I might have been screaming, but Leslie was as calm as she always was. "Millions of women do this. Millions of women are happy with these other options."

"I want children of my own."

"Heiress, these children would be yours."

I didn't understand why Leslie was saying this to me. Wasn't she hearing me? Didn't she understand?

I shook my head. "They wouldn't really be mine. They'd belong to someone else. And if I married anyone else, he might cheat on me just so he could have children," I cried. "He might cheat on me the way King is cheating. That's why I think King cheats. Because he wants children and . . ." I stopped, wishing I could take back my words. Had I really just said that out loud?

After a moment of silence, Leslie said, "King's cheating on you?"

I folded my arms. "I don't want to talk about this."

"But you should, Heiress. A lot of your issues might be wrapped up in this."

I shook my head.

"Heiress . . ."

"No!"

"All right, all right. We'll stop here," Leslie said. "That was a lot for today." She paused. "You did good, Heiress." She smiled.

I guess her smile was supposed to make me feel better. It didn't.

"So I'll see you next week."

I half nodded, half shook my head as I pushed myself up from the couch. Leslie didn't know it, but I was never coming back to this place. Not after today. Not after the way I felt.

"Heiress, I want you to know that you did good today," she said again, as if she had to reassure me.

Whatever! I turned away from her and barely said good-bye before I ran out of there.

Chapter 38

Time had passed. Really, enough time for King to have gotten over his tantrum. But even though it had been weeks, the house was still tense. King just had not recuperated from his loss, and it was like he was consumed by his own sorrow.

I did my best to tiptoe around him, treating him like he was some kind of fragile puppy. But whenever I talked to him, he snapped. Whenever I suggested we do something, he told me how dumb it was.

He treated me like I was the enemy.

He treated me like he really thought I was the reason for his loss.

Just when I wasn't sure what else to do, his parents showed up. Literally. I was in the backyard, and when I heard the doorbell ring, I frowned.

No one ever came to visit, but when I went to the door, there were his parents . . . Mr. and Mrs. Stevens, in all of their wonderful Hollywood glory.

"How are you, dear?" Mrs. Stevens asked me as she stepped inside before I could give her and her husband an invitation. She gave me a hug.

"I'm doing good," I said, hugging her back.

Mr. Stevens stood behind her, as if he wasn't very happy to be here.

"I didn't know you were coming by," I said, closing the door behind them. "Did King?"

"No." She shook her head. "No, he didn't know we were coming by, but after speaking to him this morning, I just knew I had to." She lowered her voice. "He's still upset, isn't he?"

I nodded but didn't say a word. I wasn't going to get in the middle of anything.

"Well, after I spoke to him this morning, I decided that we needed to come to help both of you. So"—she moved toward the kitchen, and I followed her—"we're going to have dinner."

"Oh, well, I didn't cook anything, and our chef . . ."

"Is off today," she said, finishing my sentence for me. "I know." Then she added, "I don't know how you and King do it without a chef on the weekend. But not to worry. I brought my favorite caterer. He's bringing dinner in around the back."

I was stunned. Who traveled with their own caterer? However, Mrs. Stevens was like a force of nature, and I watched her as she let the caterer in, then as she directed him as if this was her kitchen. When I sat in the nook, Mr. Stevens joined me.

"So how are you really doing, Heiress?"

"I'm good." That was all he too, was going to get out of me.

"I know my son has been in a funk." He shook his head. "I told him not to make that movie."

I frowned. What was wrong with that movie? King had been nominated for an Academy Award. Wasn't anyone in the Stevens family going to acknowledge that? I said nothing, breaking my silence only when he asked me where was King. I pointed him to the den.

By the time King and his father came out of the den, Mrs. Stevens had the dining room table set and we all sat down to dinner. But right away I could feel this was going to be a disaster. It was because of King's parents, especially his father, who didn't even seem to understand the word *supportive*.

"You know, I won *my* first nomination," Mr. Stevens told all of us, although everyone sitting at the table already knew that.

For the first time, King spoke. "I'm sorry, Dad. I'm sorry if I disappoint you."

Mr. Stevens nodded, as if he was accepting King's apology. "But you know, I told you not to make that movie."

"Sweetheart," Mrs. Stevens said to her husband, as if she was trying to warn him.

But he shook his head. "No, I told him not to make that B movie. But did he listen to me?"

"But, Mr. Stevens, King was nominated," I asserted.

He waved his hands. "Heiress, you need to be quiet, because you don't know anything about such things. You're not an actor."

I couldn't believe he'd spoken to me that way, and I waited for King to defend me. But all he did was stuff a piece of roast turkey into his mouth.

But then why did I think that King was going to defend me when he spoke to me the same way?

Mr. Stevens continued, "Son, you need to be more selective in your roles. You have to be discerning, because if you're not, if you don't fix this soon, you will never reach the ranks of me or your uncle Herman."

I could not believe what I was hearing. As Mr. Stevens spoke, King sank deeper and deeper into his chair.

"Sweetheart!" Mrs. Stevens said again.

"Don't sweetheart me," Mr. Stevens responded. He was on a roll, and I guess he wasn't about to stop. "King needs to hear the truth. He's wasting his time and his talent, and he will never be an A-list actor if he doesn't get it together. He will always be a disappointment."

"You know what, Dad? I'm sorry if I'm a disappointment, but maybe it would help if you would be a bit more supportive," King snapped.

"Don't get mad at me! I'm not the one who's a loser."

"Oh, God," I whispered.

And Mrs. Stevens sighed.

"Well, I might have lost the Oscar this time, but at least I'm not a loser as a father," King grumbled.

Mr. Stevens raised one eyebrow.

"Maybe it was good that I lost, because that means I'm nothing like you."

His father chuckled. "You got that right."

King went on. "And I don't want to be like you. I don't want to be a man who puts down everyone around him. I don't want to be a man who builds himself up by breaking everyone else down."

"So is that what you think?" Mr. Stevens asked, though from his tone, it didn't sound as if he was very affected by his son's comments.

"Yeah, Dad. You've never supported me. I was never good enough, could never learn lines fast enough, nothing. Nothing was good enough for you."

"That's because I always wanted you to be the best."

"And I tried."

"I was trying to teach you how to be a man. But it looks like I failed."

King glared at his father, then shook his head and stomped out of the room.

I sat in place as I heard the door to the den slam. I sat in place as Mrs. Stevens apologized, but Mr. Stevens said nothing. I sat in place as she cleaned off the table, then kissed me good-bye before the two of them finally left our home.

It was only after I heard the front door close that I pushed away from the table and walked past the living room to the den.

I knocked on the door, but King didn't respond. I tried again before I pushed the door open. But before I could step inside, King yelled, "Get out of here, Heiress. Leave me alone!"

I jumped back and closed the door. Leaning against it for a moment, I caught my breath. I wanted to be angry, but how could I? After what I had just witnessed, I understood King a whole lot better.

This wasn't his fault. The way he acted just wasn't his fault. It was clearly in his DNA.

So I backed away from King. I backed away from the door and did what I'd been doing for weeks now. I went up to bed . . . alone.

Chapter 39

It was hard to live without having someone to talk to, and since I wasn't going back to Leslie, I felt like I was all alone.

With the distance between me and King, I couldn't take it. I had to reach out to Donovan.

I was determined to reach him today, but he was making it impossible. I couldn't reach him on the phone, so I drove all the way to Beverly Hills. But after paying twenty-five dollars for parking, Donovan wasn't even at his store.

"Do you know where I can find him?" I asked the same blond woman who had brushed me off before.

And just like last time, she was no help.

Desperation made you do desperate things, and I drove to his home. Again, no matter how much I pounded, he was not there.

"Where are you, Donovan?"

And as fast as I asked the question, I had another answer. The warehouse in Pasadena.

Forty-five minutes later I found out that I was right. I breathed, relieved when I saw his car parked in front of the building, but at the same time my heart pounded. We were going to have a showdown, and I didn't know how this was going to turn out.

Still, I got out of my car, because I wanted my friend. Taking the same path that I did last time, I knocked on the huge door. After a couple of knocks, it was opened, but not by Donovan.

"Can I help you?" the guy asked over the sound of several machines going at once.

"I'm here to see Donovan."

The guy pointed. "He's over there."

There were several people in the warehouse this time, working, and I remembered that Donovan told me that he hardly had to come up here. But I spotted him at the same machine he used to make me the glass when I was here. I got closer, but still he didn't notice me. Even though he was dressed in overalls and was covered in sweat and soot, he looked so wonderful to me.

I yelled out to him. And waved. I could tell that he saw me, but he continued spinning the wheel of the machine. I took a breath and told myself that he wasn't ignoring me. He just had to finish what he was doing.

And I was right. Finally, he stopped, took off his gloves, and took slow steps in my direction.

"What are you doing here?" he asked without even a hello.

I inhaled. I deserved this. But I wasn't going to give up. I said, "I hated the way we ended things. I hate not talking to you, not being able to call you."

He shrugged and looked around like he didn't care about my words.

"I'm here to make up," I continued. "I want us to be friends."

He shook his head. "No, I can't do it anymore, Heiress. I can't keep going back and forth with you."

"But . . ."

He held up his hands. "One minute you want to be with King, and the next minute you're crying on my shoulder, right before you go back to him. It's too much."

"I know, and I'm sorry. But I go back to King only because I love him."

He chuckled, though there was no humor in the sound. "You need to check that out, because it's got to be an illness."

"What do you mean?" I frowned.

"Anybody who keeps going back to someone who hurts them more than makes them happy has got to be sick."

I swallowed the lump in my throat. In a way, he was right. But he just didn't understand.

He kept on. "And you know the worst part . . ." Now he stepped closer to me. "What's worse is that you're too blind to see a man who loves you unconditionally. You're so blind that you can't see the truth."

"But there's so much you don't know," I said, needing to defend myself. "You weren't there when King treated me like a queen."

He shook his head again. "Why do you keep holding on to the good things in the past, instead of opening up your eyes to what's going on in the present?"

I blinked my eyes, because I refused to cry. No matter how much he was hurting me.

Donovan said, "These kinds of situations never turn out good, Heiress. For the life of me, I can't figure out why you don't see this." He paused. "But it's your life, your decisions, totally up to you. Just don't expect me to stick around and wait for you to go through it anymore."

I wasn't doing a good job of hiding my emotions. Really, all I wanted to do was turn around and run out of there. But I had to give it one more try.

I said, "You said you would always be here for me. You said that if I ever needed you, I never had to turn to anyone else. What happened to all of that? What happened to that promise?"

"You don't need me. You just need yourself. You need to find the old Heiress, the strong, independent Heiress who wouldn't put up with half the stuff this new Heiress has lived with. When that girl shows up, I'll be there for her. But until then . . ." He stopped, turned around, and went right back to the machine. He didn't look over his shoulder, didn't look at me in any way. It was as if I wasn't even there.

I stood there for a few more seconds, completely humiliated. I'd come here to find my friend, but that guy was gone. And it looked like he would never be back.

I turned around and headed toward the door, holding my tears until I got to my car.

Chapter 40

The text alert button flashed on my cell, and I hesitated before I reached for the phone. I read the text.

King never loved you.

I fell down onto the sofa. I closed my eyes and wondered why someone was trying to push me to the brink of insanity.

This was at least the fiftieth text I've received, not to mention the phone calls. And the pictures, of course.

The pictures had come only once. Weeks ago. But the day after I went to Donovan's warehouse, I received the first text. Did you get my pictures?

Then, that night, came the first phone call. "You better leave my man alone," a voice warned.

All the calls were from a blocked number.

The text alert buzzed again, and I grabbed the cell. I read the text.

Soon u will find out the truth.

The truth about what? About King?

I wished to God that I could talk to King about this. But I had never once mentioned it to him. How could I? I didn't know what was real and what was fake. And as distant as King had been since the Oscars, I was doing everything I could to hold us together. I didn't need to bring the stress of these accusations to him.

But it was becoming harder and harder not to say anything. Especially since I didn't have anyone to talk to about this. Blair had fallen off the face of the earth, and Donovan had completely written me off. There were my parents, of course, but I could imagine that call. After I told them what was going on, they would tell me to get on a plane and never look back.

So I had to keep this all inside, until I could find a way to talk to King about it.

My text alert buzzed again, but this time I didn't read the text. I just turned off my phone. My headache was instant, and all I wanted to do was get away.

Sleep was my refuge, my greatest friend now. Sleep never deprived me, never turned me away. And so I did what I'd been doing a lot. I crawled back into bed, even though it was two o'clock in the afternoon.

But sleep wasn't a good escape. Not really. Not when dreams met me there. The dream about shooting King on our wedding day played over and over. Almost every day now. It started the same way and always ended the same, with me waking up, shivering, cold, yet dripping in sweat.

But this time in my dream, when I was flat on my face and staring into King's dead eyes, he spoke to me.

"Why, Heiress? Why?" he cried over and over.

This time when I awakened, I was more than shivering, more than cold, more than dripping with sweat. This time I was terrified.

Grabbing my cell, I powered it back on. I scrolled through until I found the number.

"Leslie!" I said frantically when she answered the phone. "I have to see you."

"Heiress?"

"Yes! Please! Can I see you now? Are you with someone?"

"No, my appointment just canceled. Are you all right?"

"I just need to see you."

"All right. Come right over. I'll be waiting for you."

I didn't even bother to change out of my sweats. I jumped into my car and tore over to Santa Monica. Within thirty minutes I was sitting on Leslie's couch.

"What's wrong, Heiress? What has you so upset?"

"I keep dreaming."

"Okay, but dreams are normal."

I shook my head. "Not this one." I told her about the dream about my wedding, about walking in with my father, about seeing King and then shooting him. "I have this dream over and over and over. Only today, even though King was dead, he spoke to me. What does this mean, Leslie?"

My heart was pounding as I spoke, and I was sure that in the silence that followed, Leslie could hear my heart pumping.

"I don't analyze dreams, but let's look at this together. It sounds to me like it may be a warning. It sounds to me like your mind might be telling you to get away from King before something like this happens. Maybe that's why you dream it over and over again."

I nodded.

"Heiress, I like for my clients to come to their own conclusions about their situations, but in this case, I think it's time for you to get out. Get away from King."

I shook my head. "I don't know if I can."

She took my hand. "Yes. You can. This relationship is not healthy, and I think you've known that for a long, long time."

I nodded . . . a little.

"Maybe all you need is a little time away from King. I'm not saying it has to be permanent, but I am saying that you must go."

I took a few more breaths and then nodded.

"What about going home to Ohio, without King? Just for a little while. Just so you can get clarity."

I nodded, though I wasn't sure that was what I wanted to do. But Leslie was right. If I was honest with myself, there was nothing left of me and King. Like Donovan said, I was holding on to the memories of the past and not the truth of the present.

"All right," I said. "All right." I stood and thanked Leslie.

She reached for my hand. "Let me ask you something. Do you have a gun?"

I shook my head but then nodded. "I don't have a gun, but King does."

"Is it in the house?"

"Yes, I think so. In the closet. King doesn't carry it. He got it a couple of years back, before he met me. He had a stalker or something. I don't know. But the gun's not mine."

She nodded. "Please, just get away. Like I said, it doesn't have to be permanent." And for the first time, Leslie did something that she'd never done before. She hugged me. "Be careful, Heiress. And have a good trip."

"Thank you," I said before I turned to the door and headed home.

Chapter 41

When I pulled into my driveway, I sighed. King was back home, and there was a car parked next to his. I didn't recognize the BMW, though I was sure it belonged to either King's publicist or his agent.

Good!

Maybe one of them could help him climb out of the never-ending depression that he'd fallen into.

After another minute I got out of my car. Even though I wanted to, I couldn't sit in it all day. And who knew? Maybe there was good news behind the front door. But the moment I stepped inside my home, I froze. There, at the bottom of the steps, stood King . . . and someone from my past. Blair!

They were just standing there shoulder to shoulder, but King's eyes were wide, as if he'd just been caught. Blair, though, was smiling.

"Hey, girl," I said tentatively, not sure what this was about. I had to admit, she looked good. She was dressed in True Religion jeans and a silk blouse that looked like it cost a million dollars. She looked glamorous, especially next to me and the sweats that I had on. I said to her, "I've been trying to call you."

She folded her arms. "Really?"

"Yeah, your number was disconnected, and I didn't have another way of getting in touch with you."

"Yeah, well, Blair was just leaving." King glared at Blair, but she rolled her eyes and turned back to me.

"Why?" I asked. "Didn't you come by to see me?"

Blair nodded. "As a matter of fact, I did."

"Blair!" King yelled, and that made my heart pound.

Blair shook her head. "No, King. I'm sick of this. She needs to know."

"Know what?" I asked, my eyes darting from King to Blair and back to King.

King grabbed Blair's arm and tried to drag her across the floor, but she held on to the banister.

"King! What are you doing?" I shouted.

Blair answered for him. "He's trying to stop me from telling you the truth. The truth about the two of us."

"Shut up, Blair!" King shouted.

"No, I'm tired of living this way." Turning to me, she said, "I've been with King for almost as long as you have. From before you two took that trip to Connecticut."

"Blair!" King yelled.

"He's been taking care of me and practically living with me."

"Blair!"

"Where do you think he has been when he comes home late at night? What do you think he's been doing, and who do you think he's been doing it with?"

This time King and I screamed her name together.

Blair went on. "It's time for you to know the truth, Heiress. So that you can move on, and King and I can be together the way we want to be."

The shaking started at my soles and moved up until every part of me was trembling.

"You can't handle a man like King," Blair said. "Just admit it. That's why you two have so many problems. He needs someone who's strong. Someone like me."

I guess because he couldn't get her to stop talking, King thought he might be able to stop me from listening.

"Let's go, Heiress. You don't need to be here with this madness," he said.

My eyes were already red, I was sure. This could not be happening. This could not be true.

"You've been sleeping with King?" I whispered.

She smirked. "It's been more than sleeping. We've been having sex, making love, and now we're in love."

"No, we're not, you crazy bitch," King screamed.

King's words didn't seem to faze Blair. "That's what he's saying now, because he didn't want you to find out. But I'm tired of sharing my man."

Her man? How could she call him that? But King stood there, not really denying any of it.

I couldn't believe that Blair had done this to me. That King had done this to me.

But it was what came next that pushed me to the edge.

"It's about time that you knew the truth," Blair said. "Because I'm pregnant."

Pregnant?

"And King's the father."

Oh my God!

"And since you can't have children . . ."

My head snapped up. "What?" I had never told her about that. I'd wanted to, but I couldn't find her to talk.

Blair nodded. "Oh, yeah, I know all about it. King tells me everything. So, since you can't have children, it's time for you to go so that King and I can raise our child together."

I didn't know how I did it, really. Didn't know how I stood there and listened. It was probably just a couple of minutes, maybe three. But it felt like a lifetime.

I had to get away from both of them.

Turning toward the kitchen, I ran. I didn't know why, didn't know what I was going to do, but I had to get away. But running gave me no relief. Blair followed me. And King followed Blair.

"That's right, Heiress. I'm pregnant," Blair repeated.

Why was she taunting me? Why did she hate me? We were friends. In an instant I replayed in my mind the years that we'd spent together, talking and laughing and sharing. Sharing! I guess we were sharing now.

"I'm having King's baby."

I had to lean on the counter for support. Or else I would fall and I might never get back up. I looked up and faced my tormentor . . . and Blair.

Looking into King's eyes, I asked, "Is this true?" My voice quivered.

"Heiress, I love you."

How many times had I heard that before? How many times had he said that while he was sleeping with Blair? While he was getting her pregnant?

"I really do!"

It was because of everything. It was because of the way King had grabbed me and pushed me around. It was because of the way he had spoken to me and disrespected me. It was because of the way he had treated me, when all I'd wanted to do was love him.

But it was really because of the fact that Blair was pregnant. And I was not.

"So what are you going to do, Heiress?" Blair asked.

It took me only a second to decide. I reached across the counter, grabbed a knife from the butcher block, and then I charged.

The only thing I heard after that were screams. Blair's screams. King's screams. And my screams.

Chapter 42

It wasn't a gun, but the result was the same. It was a knife, and it was still King.

I stared at him as he lay on the floor and Blair cried over him, even as she had the phone in her hand.

"Please," she cried. "Please hurry."

I just stood there and watched as the blood gushed from King's chest, soaking Blair. There was blood on me too, mostly on my hands. Not that I completely remembered how it got there.

I was still standing there, frozen, still holding the knife when the police arrived. One of the officers had to pry it from my fingers.

Not too much longer after that, though, one officer started reciting words that I'd heard on TV all the time.

"You have the right to remain silent. . . ."

Was I being arrested?

"Do you understand these rights as they've been explained to you?" asked the officer.

I nodded as the other police officer locked handcuffs around my wrists. Then they stuffed me into the back of a police cruiser.

But I didn't really know why this was happening. What had I done? I didn't really remember. The last thing in my memory was Blair asking me what I was going to do. The next thing I knew, King was on the floor.

This was bad. I knew that. I had to call someone.

Donovan!

I wondered what he was doing right now. Was he at work or at home? Or maybe he was at the warehouse, working on a machine. He sure looked good when he did that.

At the police station I was shocked to see the number of people standing outside. And then, when the officers helped me out of the back of the cruiser, I realized who these people were.

The cameras flashed as the officers, one on each side of me, escorted me into the building.

"What happened?" asked one of the onlookers.

"Was there a domestic dispute?" asked another.

The questions flew by me. But it was the last one that I heard before we ducked into the building that made me pause.

"Heiress, did you kill King Stevens?"

Kill King? Is he dead?

Oh, my God. I had to talk to Donovan.

"Heiress, you can wait for an attorney, but do you want to talk to us?" asked one of the officers.

I wasn't sure, so I just shrugged.

"Did you attack King Stevens?" the officer asked.

I shook my head a little. I wasn't saying yes. I wasn't saying no. I just didn't know.

"Did he attack you?"

"I'm . . . I'm . . ." I wasn't sure if I should say anything. I needed to ask someone. "Can I make a call?"

My question seemed to shock the officer, but he unlocked the cuffs that were around my wrists and pointed to the phone on his desk.

I dialed Donovan's number as fast as I could, closed my eyes, and prayed that he answered. I wasn't sure he would, because he'd told me he didn't want to have anything to do with me.

But then he answered.

"Hello!" He sounded frantic, and I wondered what was wrong.

"I'm so glad you answered."

"Heiress, where are you?"

"I've really missed you."

"Heiress, it's all on the news. Did you attack King? Did you stab him?"

"Our friendship has meant a lot to me."

"Heiress, please, please tell me what happened. Where are you?"

"The police came and got me."

"Oh, God," he moaned.

"Can you do me a favor?" I asked.

"Anything, Heiress. Anything."

"Can you go to my house and get my journal?"

"What?"

"My journal. It's in my nightstand drawer, and I really need it."

"Okay," he said slowly.

"Do you promise?"

"I don't think they'll let me in the house, but I'll see what I can do. And then I'll be right there, okay? I'm coming, Heiress."

"Thank you, Donny. Thank you so, so much." And then I hung up, so grateful.

I turned to the officer. "I'm ready to talk now."

Chapter 43

It had been months and months of just one thing . . . the death of King Stevens and the trial of Heiress Montgomery.

I still could not believe this was happening to me. I was on trial for murder. How had this become my life?

But here I was, with lawyers and judges and the media all up in my life. It was hard for me to handle, but even harder for my parents.

That was the thing that hurt my heart the most—my parents were hurting. Sometimes it felt like they were on trial. They had given up their life in Ohio, mortgaged their house for my bail, and moved to Los Angeles to be close to me while I was going through this. We'd all moved into a small two-bedroom apartment right outside of downtown Los Angeles, so we weren't too far from the courthouse.

But at least my parents were with me. And I needed them.

Actually, I had quite a team. In addition to my parents, there were Donovan and Leslie and my hotshot attorney, Chyanne Monroe. Chyanne was new to California, but she had built an incredible reputation and was one of the best defense attorneys in New York. Recently she'd brought her talents to California . . . just in time to help me.

I wasn't quite sure how my parents afforded Chyanne, but I suspected that it was a group effort: my parents, Donovan, and Leslie had invariably pitched in, and Chyanne had probably lowered her fee quite a bit.

Chyanne had never told me if what I suspected was true, but if it was, she was working hard for her money. She'd gotten me out on an enormous bail, but the trial was a different story. For the past few months, the media hadn't given me much of a chance of getting off. It was an uphill battle since all the evidence was against me. After all, Blair, the prosecution's key witness, was an eyewitness, and she had gotten on the stand and sung like a jailbird about how I had stabbed King over and over and over.

My ex–best friend was telling the truth. I *had* stabbed King over and over again. Seventeen times, according to the forensic pathologist.

Then it was the defense's turn to present our case, and Chyanne had quite a lineup. She'd already put a psychologist on the stand, who said that these kinds of attacks were usually done by someone who had been abused, emotionally or physically. And then Leslie had gotten on the stand and had said she had been concerned about something like this happening. She was convinced that I had been abused and broken down by King. Even Donovan had had a chance to testify on my behalf. He'd told the jury how King had mistreated me over and over again. He'd talked about how I had changed completely, trying to please a man who was never satisfied.

Today, though, was the biggest day of the trial. It was the day when Chyanne's final witness would take the stand—me! And she'd warned me that the courtroom would be packed.

"Isn't it packed every day?" I'd asked her. After all, this trial was as big as O.J.'s had been. King Stevens was a Hollywood star and had been murdered by his fiancée while his pregnant girlfriend stood by.

"Yes," she'd told me. "But today there will be standing room only." She had paused. "And today I expect that the prosecution will have King's parents there."

"Oh no," I'd cried.

She'd nodded. "Just in case you come off as a sympathetic victim—and you will—they want the jury to see King's parents. They want the jury to remember the people they consider the real victims."

After hearing that, I hadn't been able to sleep at all last night, knowing that I was going to have to face King's parents for the first time since that fateful day. So many times I'd wanted to call them and tell them just how sorry I was. I wanted to explain that I'd just lost it. I was sure that on some level, Mrs. Stevens would understand. But I never had the courage. I was angry at myself about that, but I just couldn't do it.

Now I sat on the stand, facing them. But I kept my eyes focused on Chyanne, which was exactly what she'd told me to do.

"So, Heiress, you loved King Stevens?" she asked.

That was an easy question. "With all my heart."

For a moment, I did what Chyanne had told me not to do. I sneaked a peek at King's parents. They sat close together, as if they were holding each other up. There were tears in Mrs. Stevens's eyes, but Mr. Stevens just sat there, stiff and strong, staring me down. I turned my glance quickly back to Chyanne.

"Can you tell us about the day of the incident?"

I nodded. "I don't remember a lot."

"Tell us what you do remember."

I closed my eyes and tried to recall those last moments. "I remember that Blair was shouting that she was pregnant and that I needed to leave."

This part had already been entered into evidence. Chyanne had broken Blair down when she was on the stand. She'd got Blair to admit that she'd been tormenting me, trying to get me so upset that I would just leave King so that she could have him to herself. According to Chyanne, that was good for my defense. Everyone would understand someone being driven to the edge by being tormented.

"How did that make you feel?" Chyanne asked.

"I don't even have the words. I was devastated. I'd just lost my child because of King."

"Objection!" the prosecutor said.

"Overruled," the judge countered.

That part had already been submitted as evidence too. Not only had the doctors already testified about my miscarriage, but in a brilliant move, Chyanne had also had my journal entered into evidence. For weeks and weeks I had confided in my journal, chronicling my abusive relationship with King—from the first time he abused me in Connecticut to everything that I'd gone through since the Oscars. I'd recounted a plethora of incidents where King behaved badly and I was the long-suffering girlfriend who stood by his side.

"So you lost your child because of King," Chyanne repeated, bringing me back to the moment.

"Yes, and I was . . . I'm still devastated about that."

"So when Blair told you she was pregnant by King Stevens, what were you thinking?"

I shook my head. "I don't even know. At first, I was confused, and then I thought she was lying. But then I asked King about it."

"You asked him, and what did he say?"

I had been over all these questions with Chyanne, but it didn't matter. It still hurt. "He didn't answer, but in a way, he did. I could tell by the look on his face, it was true. And I was just crushed."

"So"—Chyanne came closer to the stand—"tell us what happened next."

Again, I closed my eyes and really tried to remember. But there wasn't much there. "I was so hurt, just crushed. I just wanted my pain to go away. There had been so much pain. So much." I glanced again at the Stevenses. Mrs. Stevens still had tears in her eyes, but this time she was nodding. I was not even sure she realized she was doing it, but she was giving me courage. "All I kept thinking was that I wanted the pain to go away. And then . . . and then . . . and then . . ."

Chyanne nodded. "That's fine, Heiress. Thank you."

She sat down, and the prosecutor, a black man who looked a little like P. Diddy, stood up.

"I have just one question for you, Ms. Montgomery," he said. "Did you kill King Stevens?"

"I . . . I . . ."

"Did you stab him seventeen times?" he asked me, though he was looking at the jury.

"I don't remember."

"You don't remember?"

I shook my head. "No, no, I really don't."

"But King Stevens is dead, isn't he?" The prosecutor held up his hand, stopping Chyanne from objecting. "I have no more for this witness."

"You may step down," the judge told me.

I was so glad to get down from the stand, and my legs felt shaky as I wobbled back to the defense table.

When I sat down, Chyanne stood up. "The defense rests," she said.

"We'll recess for today," the judge said. "Closing arguments tomorrow." She banged her gavel, the courtroom stood, and the six-month ordeal that could send me away for the rest of my life was nearing the end.

Chapter 44

The guilty verdict wasn't something that anyone was prepared for. We all thought that Chyanne had done a wonderful job in establishing reasonable doubt, but it wasn't good enough. Honestly, I wasn't extremely shocked about the verdict. I kind of knew this was coming. The dreams I'd been having were my warning, and I should have stayed away from King in the first place.

Out of life, twenty years had gone by, and the moment I met King still played in my head. I tried to imagine scenarios in which I got out of that room at *Black Media Elite* before he ever walked in. I probably would still be working at *BME* if I hadn't met King. I probably would be editor in chief by now, running things. One of the correctional officers who sympathized with my story slipped me a newspaper article about myself.

She was a sweet girl with a bright future, until she let love walk through the door. That line in the article stuck with me for years. It was so true. Before I met King, I had had my life set up for greatness. I'd been heading in the direction I had always seen myself going in. When the women in here asked me if I would take it all back, do things differently if I could, I never gave them an answer. I didn't have one.

I kept in touch with Leslie and Donovan for a little while, until they slowly started to fade. In one of the many letters my mother sent, she told me Donovan's company had expanded tremendously and he'd sold it for millions. He'd married a pediatrician, and they had two children. I often thought about what my life would be like if I were with Donovan. I knew it wouldn't consist of jumpsuits and bars.

Leslie decided she wanted to go around the country and help battered women before their situation ended up like mine.

"I think I feel guilty about not helping you more," she told me during her last visit, before she left.

"Don't feel bad about me, Leslie. You did all you could do."

"How are you doing in here?"

"I've seen better days, but I'm making it." We sat in an uncomfortable silence for a moment, trying to figure out what to say next.

"How are you spending your time?"

I didn't answer. Just looked down at the table in sadness.

"Listen, I brought you something. Maybe you can make some good use of it." She slid me the little purple flower book that had become so familiar to me. With that, she got up and walked away.

The guard took me back to my cell, and I thumbed through my journal. I didn't know how Leslie was able to get it to me, but I was kind of thankful she had. I started with page one and began to read the thoughts I'd written down. Devouring page after page, I relived the events of the past in my mind. The sad life that I had lived was right in front of me all over again.

There was something about seeing my words again that made me want to write. I needed to get back to the thing that had started it all. I worked out a deal with the prison librarian whereby she allowed me to use the old typewriter they had. Every day I went into the library and typed. It was surprisingly therapeutic. I was releasing all the hurt, pain, and regret I felt about this whole situation with each stroke of a key. I began to forgive myself as I turned my journal into my memoirs. It took me years to complete my memoirs, and when I finished the last chapter, I read the final line over and over again. *As I close this book, I now understand my strange addiction. Sweet dreams.*

Notes

Notes

ORDER FORM
URBAN BOOKS, LLC
78 E. Industry Ct
Deer Park, NY 11729

Name:(please print):_____

Address: _____

City/State: _____

Zip: _____

QTY	TITLES	PRICE
	16 On The Block	$14.95
	A Girl From Flint	$14.95
	A Pimp's Life	$14.95
	Baltimore Chronicles	$14.95
	Baltimore Chronicles 2	$14.95
	Betrayal	$14.95
	Black Diamond	$14.95
	Black Diamond 2	$14.95
	Black Friday	$14.95
	Both Sides Of The Fence	$14.95
	Both Sides Of The Fence 2	$14.95
	California Connection	$14.95

Shipping and handling-add $3.50 for 1st book, then $1.75 for each additional book.

Please send a check payable to:

Urban Books, LLC

Please allow 4-6 weeks for delivery

ORDER FORM
URBAN BOOKS, LLC
78 E. Industry Ct
Deer Park, NY 11729

Name:(please print):_____

Address: _____

City/State: _____

Zip: _____

QTY	TITLES	PRICE
	California Connection 2	$14.95
	Cheesecake And Teardrops	$14.95
	Congratulations	$14.95
	Crazy In Love	$14.95
	Cyber Case	$14.95
	Denim Diaries	$14.95
	Diary Of A Mad First Lady	$14.95
	Diary Of A Stalker	$14.95
	Diary Of A Street Diva	$14.95
	Diary Of A Young Girl	$14.95
	Dirty Money	$14.95
	Dirty To The Grave	$14.95

Shipping and handling-add $3.50 for 1st book, then $1.75 for each additional book.
Please send a check payable to:
Urban Books, LLC
Please allow 4-6 weeks for delivery